STACY M. JONES

The Forever Curse

First published by Stacy M. Jones 2020

Copyright © 2020 by Stacy M. Jones

All rights reserved. No part of this publication may be reproduced, stored or transmitted in any form or by any means, electronic, mechanical, photocopying, recording, scanning, or otherwise without written permission from the publisher. It is illegal to copy this book, post it to a website, or distribute it by any other means without permission.

This novel is entirely a work of fiction. The names, characters and incidents portrayed in it are the work of the author's imagination. Any resemblance to actual persons, living or dead, events or localities is entirely coincidental.

Stacy M. Jones asserts the moral right to be identified as the author of this work.

Stacy M. Jones has no responsibility for the persistence or accuracy of URLs for external or third-party Internet Websites referred to in this publication and does not guarantee that any content on such Websites is, or will remain, accurate or appropriate.

Designations used by companies to distinguish their products are often claimed as trademarks. All brand names and product names used in this book and on its cover are trade names, service marks, trademarks and registered trademarks of their respective owners. The publishers and the book are not associated with any product or vendor mentioned in this book. None of the companies referenced within the book have endorsed the book.

First edition

This book was professionally typeset on Reedsy.
Find out more at reedsy.com

For Nichole who loves this series and who laughed with me as we figured out how authors sign books

Acknowledgement

The Forever Curse would not have been created without a wonderful creative team working with me. A special thanks to 17 Studio Book Design for the great cover, and Dj Hendrickson for her invaluable editing and suggestions. Thanks to Liza Wood for proofreading and revisions. A special thanks to all of the magical women who have shared their knowledge with me about crystals, ghosts, and spells.

Thanks to the people of New Orleans who shared stories with me, the city's history, and all things voodoo as I researched this book. In the story, I refer to burial sites as tombs, which some technically were. Others were larger mausoleums. For simplicity's sake, I used tomb or tombs, which is what most people I spoke to called them. This is one of those forks in the road writer's face - technical term vs local vernacular, and I went with local.

To all my readers and those who continue to support me on this journey – thank you.

Chapter One

Hattie's Cauldron: Potions & Pastries hummed with customers on a crisp October morning. The summer heat and humidity had finally broken and had given way to a fall chill in the air. Tables were full of people reading and relaxing, and the swath of older ladies who had become staples in the shop chatted loudly and happily with each other as they sipped their tea and nibbled on scones.

The owner of the shop, Hattie Beauregard-Ryan, hunched behind the pastry display case refilling the treats her customers couldn't get enough of. When Hattie first opened the shop, she sold a handful of cookies and maybe a brownie a day. Most of the treats ended up at home where Hattie would feed her now late husband, Beau, the kids in the neighborhood, and, to be perfectly honest, her own growing midsection.

Thankfully, these days, the shop buzzed with so many happy customers she had put a Starbucks out of business. They had tried unsuccessfully to compete with Hattie from a few shops down on Kavanaugh Boulevard in the Heights neighborhood of Little Rock. But nothing was a match for Hattie's teas, treats, psychic readings, and spells. She always had a little magic and a kind word for those who frequented her shop. Her regular customers became her family.

After she refilled the pastry display, Hattie went to work cleaning up the back counter. Sarah, who had been working with Hattie for nearly a year, was busy refilling some of the more metaphysical products the shop offered. There were Reiki charged candles, stones, and meditation items. Hattie found herself reordering more and more. The shop had seen great success in its years of operation but nothing like the last couple of years.

Hattie credited the success in part to her niece, Harper, who had lived with her for close to eighteen months now. She had made some great suggestions to make the shop cozier with the addition of couches, chairs, and a coffee table. There was also a shelf with a selection of books. Customers often donated books and grabbed others to read. It was a revolving library on the honor system.

The front bell chimed just as Hattie finished cleaning the counter and a familiar face walked through the door. Hattie knew he'd be back, but she hadn't known when. She took a deep breath and exhaled slowly still not sure how she felt about the man.

Dante La Croix waved to Hattie as he approached the counter. He looked much the same as the last time Hattie saw him in May. While Hattie believed Dante was in his late sixties like her, he appeared significantly younger. If Hattie hadn't known him in her youth, she would have guessed him to be no more than fifty, if that. Dante was tall, slender, and had angular features. His black hair had to be dyed because there wasn't a gray among them. Hattie wanted to know his secret. It was more than any anti-aging product on the market could offer.

Their relationship was complicated, to say the least. Dante had tried to recruit Hattie into his voodoo-practicing family when she was in her twenties. He claimed he loved her then, but Hattie didn't understand how love could produce the revenge he had sought on her for saying no.

Earlier this year, Dante showed up in town from New Orleans. She hadn't seen him in years, and that had been fine with her. It seemed Dante had been hired by a corrupt local prosecutor who, Hattie knew,

CHAPTER ONE

had murdered a man. Dante was supposed to use his voodoo to run Hattie out of town. Instead, he had helped Hattie take down a killer and ensure he went to prison. For that, she was forever grateful, but still, Hattie didn't have a lot of trust for Dante.

Last year, at the same time Dante reappeared in her life, someone had planted voodoo in her yard to block her and every gifted person in the city from talking to the dead. It had worked for a while, but Hattie had found the voodoo spells, dug them from her yard, and broke the curse.

Hattie had thought it was Dante, but after he examined the voodoo doll, the signature of the practitioner had been apparent to him. Sewn into the doll was an arrow with lines flowing from it. The end curved into a letter that Hattie still couldn't quite discern, and Dante had never explained.

The only problem was the practitioner had long since been declared dead – fifteen years ago. Celeste Laurier had been Dante's fiancée until she called off the relationship a few months before her death. All assumed she was dead until her spell work showed up in Hattie's yard.

Now Dante was back. Hattie assumed he was there to ask for help to find the woman. Hattie wanted to find Celeste too, but at what cost? Hattie wasn't sure dredging up the past would do anyone any good, but now, here he was standing in front of her.

"Dante, it's good to see you," Hattie said even though she wasn't sure that was the absolute truth. "Can I get you some coffee or a pastry?"

Dante's lips set in a firm line. "Anything will do. Please sit with me when you have the chance." Dante moved to an empty table against the back wall.

Hattie prepared some coffee, instead of tea, and grabbed one of the blueberry scones he had enjoyed the last time he was in the shop. She poured herself some chai and headed to his table. She set the items down for him.

As Hattie sat across from him, she asked, "It's been a few months since I've heard from you. Is everything okay?"

Dante took a sip of his coffee and set down the cup. He exhaled loudly. "It's not, Hattie. It's far from okay. I've been searching for Celeste for months now to no avail. I've gone to old friends of ours in New Orleans to see if anyone has heard from her. Of course, they all think I've lost my mind. She's dead, they tell me."

Hattie started to reach for him to comfort him like she would do for anyone but pulled her hand back. The last thing she wanted was to give Dante the wrong impression. "Maybe Celeste has reasons for not wanting to be found or maybe she really is dead. Could someone else be using her voodoo signature?"

"No one even knew the symbol Celeste used but me," Dante said sternly. "She's out there. I've never felt she was dead, Hattie. For years, I thought it was just because we had always been so connected that I didn't want to believe she was dead. Now, with proof, I'm sure she's not. I'm worried now Celeste might be in danger."

"If Celeste is alive, and that's a very big if, then she faked her death and has been hiding out all these years," Hattie responded. "Also, you're the one who said the voodoo used against me was created by Celeste. Why would she be in danger?"

Dante rubbed his brow, but he didn't say a word for several moments. Finally, he locked eyes with her. "Hattie, there's been a few murders in New Orleans. Each victim was found with a voodoo doll near the body. The police aren't sure what to think. Many in the city believe it's some kind of voodoo ritual. I don't know any kind of voodoo that includes human sacrifice, but someone is trying hard to make it look like that."

Confused, Hattie asked, "What does any of this have to do with Celeste?"

Dante looked down at the table. "They showed the dolls on the news. Each one had the same stitching as yours. I cannot believe that Celeste

CHAPTER ONE

is murdering people in New Orleans. I believe someone is trying to send me a message. I think that's what the voodoo in your yard was as well. I don't think Celeste did it at all, but rather, someone posing as her."

Hattie wasn't sure what to say. The entire situation seemed far-fetched for her, but that's how it always was with Dante. She toyed with her cup, wanting to get the words right. "I'm not sure I understand what you're saying. I had very specific information, and not just from you, that it was a woman named Celeste who put that voodoo in my yard. But I don't know what to believe. Do you think Celeste is alive or not?"

Dante shook his head sadly. "I don't know anymore. As I said, I've spent the last few months contacting everyone who knew Celeste. I searched old bank records, credit cards, and everything ever connected to her and found nothing. No one other than Celeste and myself knew her voodoo signature. Someone clearly wants to send me a message. I just don't know who or what that message would be."

Hattie didn't say anything. She grabbed Dante's cup and went behind the counter. She poured him another cup of coffee, and this time poured one for herself. Hattie was stalling, trying to gather her thoughts.

As she set Dante's cup of coffee down in front of him, Hattie got straight to the meat of it. Pointedly, she asked, "What is it you want from me, Dante? You're here telling me this. Is there some way you think that I can help you?"

"Yes," Dante said, his voice breaking with emotion. "You and Harper have solved other murders. From what I've seen, you're even better than the cops. With Harper's detective skills and our powers, I think we can get to the bottom of the murders and find out if Celeste is still alive."

Chapter Two

Harper Ryan wrapped her interview with Little Rock's Mayor about an upcoming fundraiser for a children's art program. She left City Hall and headed back to her car quickly. She glanced at her watch as she threw her bag in the passenger seat and cursed softly. Harper only had ten minutes to make the fifteen-minute drive to the restaurant to meet her boyfriend and Hattie's neighbor, Jackson Morris, for lunch. She was so busy with *Rock City Life* magazine she barely had time to see him.

A few months ago, Jackson, a retired Army Colonel, had taken some consulting work and had become just as busy as Harper. Finding time together had strained their relationship over the summer, but they made it through. Their promise heading into the holidays was to find more balance in their lives, each of them prone to overworking themselves.

Harper texted Jackson that she was on her way and to order her a sweet tea. She drove quickly out of the city back into the Heights neighborhood where they all lived and Hattie had her shop. The restaurant where she was meeting Jackson was just a few shops down from Hattie. Harper had hoped she'd have time to stop in and see her aunt before lunch, but now, it would need to be after.

Harper found a place to park across from Hattie's shop. She gathered up her things and crossed at the crosswalk. As she zipped directly in

CHAPTER TWO

front of the shop, Harper caught sight of a familiar face. It stopped her in her tracks. Harper stood outside of her aunt's shop and peered at Hattie sitting with Dante, talking with their heads together. Harper had hoped she'd never have to see Dante again. It wasn't that he had proven himself a bad guy when she recently met him. Harper knew her aunt's history with the man and she didn't trust him. There was also the intense energy surge she felt when she had touched his hand. It unnerved her.

Harper didn't know what Dante and Hattie were discussing, but it appeared serious. She'd have to talk to Hattie later, but right now, she had to get to Jackson. Harper rushed down a block and pulled open the door to Heights Taco & Tamale. Jackson had already ordered their drinks and was snacking on chips and salsa.

"No cheese dip?" Harper asked as she slid into her chair, offering apologies for her tardiness.

Jackson patted his belly. "I was attempting to be good, but we can order some if you'd like."

Harper peered over the table at his belly and smiled. It had grown a bit rounder in his retirement, but she liked every inch of him. Harper glanced over the menu even though she ordered the same thing every time they came – pickle-fried chicken tacos and a side of black beans. She just liked looking at the menu in case a creative mood struck.

Harper set the menu aside. "You don't have to be good if you don't want to. If you're just trying to eat healthier, please do, but if you're worried on my account, I like you just the way you are."

Jackson smiled at her. "I've been running more, too. I'm trying to get back to where I was when I retired. I don't think I'll ever have those abs again, but I can try."

Harper shrugged. "Whatever makes you happy."

The server came and they both ordered. When she left, Jackson asked, "Did you go by Hattie's shop on the way here?"

Harper knew why Jackson was asking. "You saw Dante, too?"

"Why is he back in town? I thought he left." Jackson took a sip of his drink.

"I don't know. I'm not a fan, but it seems Hattie trusts him so maybe we need to give her the benefit of the doubt at least for now."

Jackson's eyes roamed up over Harper's shoulder. She turned to see what he was looking at. It was her long-time friend from college, Maggie Delacroix. Harper jumped up out of her chair and embraced her friend. Maggie had moved to Little Rock from Nashville several months back. Although they had promised to keep in touch, work had gotten in the way for both of them.

With her arms still wrapped around Maggie's neck, Harper said, "I'm so glad to see you. We kept rescheduling lunch until we both just didn't bother. We have to do better."

"Agreed," Maggie said.

Harper introduced Maggie and Jackson and asked her to sit with them. Maggie explained she only had a few minutes before she met with a client whose house she was designing.

"We are focused on drapes and pillows today," Maggie explained with a laugh. "That can be an all-day adventure for some people." Even though she said she was in a hurry, Maggie still pulled out the chair next to Harper and sat down.

"You knew Harper in college?" Jackson asked.

"We were roommates for a while."

With a mischievous grin, Jackson said slyly, "That means you know all of Harper's secrets."

Maggie reached for Harper's hand. "I do and they are going to die with me."

"That's no fun." Jackson fake frowned.

"Did you hear what's been happening in New Orleans?" Maggie asked. She was originally from New Orleans. It's where Maggie was raised before heading to Massachusetts and going to Wellesley College with Harper.

"I hadn't heard anything," Harper said. "Should I have?"

"Well given your family roots I thought it might interest you. There have been a few murders in the city. Voodoo dolls have been left with each of the bodies. Creepy, right?"

Harper shook her head in disgust. "Very creepy. Do the police have any suspects?"

"None that I've heard. My parents are very concerned. There have been six bodies found in the French Quarter. I think the cops are trying to downplay it for tourism's sake."

Jackson raised his eyebrows. "Have any of the victims been tourists?"

"No, just locals." Maggie sat back in her chair and looked to Harper. "Do you have any ideas who could be doing it?"

"I'm not psychic. I don't even know if we asked Hattie that she'd be able to pick up something like that. If solving crimes were that easy for gifted people, there probably wouldn't be any crime." Harper shrugged. "Plus, our ancestors weren't into voodoo. It's not in our skillset. Hattie does have a friend, Dante, who is from New Orleans and is a voodoo practitioner. He might know more."

Jackson toyed with his fork. "I wonder if that's why Dante is over there talking to Hattie."

"Could be," Harper speculated. "I bet he's still looking for Celeste."

"Celeste?" Maggie asked, with a hesitation in her voice.

Harper explained to Maggie all about what had happened with Dante and Celeste and the voodoo left in Hattie's yard.

"It's funny. When you said Dante and Celeste, my mind went back to my family history. There's been an old family tale on my father's side going back to the 1700s that there was a relative named Dante who was cursed with immortality when he was forty-five. He'd never die and never age. He would stay the same age forever. At the time, his wife was named Celeste. She was cursed, too, but not in the same way. She was cursed to meet Dante and fall in love with him over and over again through all of her lifetimes. They'd lose each other over and over again. The pain each of them must have gone through."

Jackson raised his eyebrows. "To buy that tale you'd have to believe in both immortality and reincarnation. Does your family believe the story is true?"

Maggie put her hands up. "I don't know. I think some people do. My grandmother still has a portrait of Dante and Celeste when they were first married. It's a tale that's been told through the generations. That portrait has been handed down and always hung in the family home. A man and woman named Dante and Celeste were in my family at some point, that much is true."

"Aren't those fairly common names in New Orleans?" Jackson asked, taking a sip of his drink.

"They are definitely. I've been back and forth on my own belief. But that's New Orleans for you. There are always tales of strange happenings, voodoo, and such. Now it seems there's a killer who has taken it a step too far." Maggie looked at her watch. "I'm late. I need to run."

Harper stood and hugged her goodbye, both promising to call the other soon. She sat back down as the server dropped off their plates.

"What did you think of that?" Jackson asked, taking a bite of his taco.

"From what I've heard, New Orleans is a weird place. I've never visited so I don't know. I'd like to visit to see the history and such, but you know, even with my gifts, believing in vampires, immortality and all is a stretch."

"Same for me. I don't know how much stock you can put into family legend, but funny the names are still the same." Jackson laughed. "Let's not even mention that Dante doesn't look anywhere close to the age that Hattie thinks he is."

CHAPTER TWO

Harper finished chewing, mulling over that fact because Jackson was right. Dante didn't look much older than fifty. She had noticed it before but hadn't said anything. "I should tell Hattie the story. I bet she'd get a kick out of it."

Jackson nodded. "She loves a good story."

Chapter Three

Hattie knew Harper was going to be angry she had asked Dante to stay at the house. He was in a spare bedroom unpacking while Hattie sat at the kitchen table wringing her hands.

Beau, Hattie's deceased husband who often visited her in spirit, appeared in the kitchen next to the table. He looked as angry as Hattie assumed Harper would be. "Why is that man in my home?" Beau asked, pointing to the second floor. "This is probably one of the dumber things you've ever done, my love. I don't quite understand it."

"I knew you'd be angry. I'm worried about how Harper will react, too."

"Then why did you invite him here?" Beau stayed back from Hattie not allowing his energy to merge with hers. It was akin to holding back affection, and Hattie knew he was angry with her.

"I'm not even sure how it happened, Beau. Dante and I are trying to find the same person. It seems there have been murders in New Orleans that might be connected. Dante isn't going to be here long. I thought it would be easier for us to talk. It's just for a night or two."

"You shouldn't be around him at all."

"I know. I know," Hattie said quietly. She knew her husband was right, but she was pulled to find Celeste. Hattie had no idea why she wanted to find the woman so badly and couldn't let it go.

"I'm going to keep my eye on him while he's here. He won't get an

CHAPTER THREE

ounce of privacy from me," Beau said, folding his arms over his chest and peering down at Hattie.

"You do what you have to do, Beau. It's fine with me. I admit I'm flying by the seat of my pants here and not entirely sure what to believe."

"Harper's back. I'll leave you to explain everything to her. I'm sure she's not going to be happy about this." Beau disappeared without another word.

Hattie knew she had angered Beau. He had never treated her so coldly. The back door opened and then shut and Harper made her way into the kitchen. She pulled up short when she saw Hattie sitting at the table all alone, looking like she had lost her best friend in the whole world.

"You okay?" Harper asked, dropping her bag on the floor and coming over to her aunt.

Hattie patted the table next to her, and Harper sat. "I have to tell you something, and I don't want you to be upset with me."

"Dante's back, right? I saw him in your shop today."

Hattie nodded once. "He is back, and he's asked for our help. I'm letting him stay here in one of the spare bedrooms just for a night or two."

Harper pulled back. "I'm not comfortable with that. This is your house, and I respect that, but I'm not comfortable with him here."

Harper was less angry than Hattie had thought she'd be. "I know you're concerned."

"What does he want?"

Hattie described the murders happening in New Orleans. Harper nodded along, explaining that her friend Maggie had told her about the murders earlier that day. Harper still didn't understand. "What does that have to do with Dante?"

"Well," Hattie started slowly, "the markings on the voodoo dolls that we found here in the yard are the same as the markings found on the voodoo dolls at each of the murder scenes."

Harper rubbed her head. "That's incredibly concerning. Let me ask you this. How do you know Dante doesn't have anything to do with these murders? He was here in Little Rock when that voodoo was placed in your yard. He even said that the voodoo had the signature of his former fiancée. Now the same signature is being used in a serial homicide case."

Hattie patted Harper's hand. "I don't trust Dante fully, but I'm certain he is not a serial killer. When I showed him that voodoo doll months ago, he had an expression of genuine shock."

"What exactly does he expect us to be able to do? I'm not sure how we could help him." Harper reached for her phone and typed something on the keypad.

"What are you doing?" Hattie asked before answering her question.

"I asked Jackson to spend the night here. If we have to live with Dante under the roof with us, we shouldn't be alone."

Hattie was happy Harper did that but didn't want to show her concern. "Your uncle is here, too. He'd be more than enough protection for us."

Harper cocked her head to the side and sighed. "You're being impossible. Uncle Beau isn't going to be able to do much. Jackson is living and present and could protect us."

Hattie stood and paced her kitchen. Harper just watched her but didn't say more. Finally, Hattie stopped and explained, "Dante wants our help in locating Celeste. He thinks that whoever is killing those people is trying to send him a message."

Harper read off the text from Jackson that he'd be over within the hour. "What kind of message?"

"He doesn't know. He doesn't think Celeste is killing those people, and he's not even sure that it was her who left voodoo in my yard, but he is sure it's all connected. That's part of what he wants us to sort out."

CHAPTER THREE

"I don't know how we'd help him with that. This isn't Little Rock. I annoy the cops here enough. They aren't going to let us get involved in a serial homicide case in New Orleans." Harper sat back, looking at her aunt with a mix of annoyance and confusion on her face.

"I'm sure we will figure it out."

"Do you believe in reincarnation?" Harper asked, abruptly changing the subject.

Hattie wasn't sure. "I'm inclined to believe it's possible. I think if it's real then we have soul lessons to learn over each life, and we keep coming back until our souls have evolved. I have a hard time believing we die and sit around in heaven. What does this have to do with anything?"

"Do you believe in..." Harper stopped talking.

Hattie turned to see Dante standing in the doorway. She waved him in. "I was just telling Harper that you wanted our help."

Dante took a few tentative steps into the room. "I didn't mean to interrupt. I wanted to ask for a towel for the morning."

Hattie thought she had given Dante a towel, but maybe her memory was slipping. "They are in the upstairs hall closet, but I'm headed up that way and can get it for you."

Dante thanked Hattie. He moved toward Harper. "I know my request seems unreasonable. I know that you and Hattie aren't detectives, but you have solved murders before. I need to find Celeste, and more importantly, I need to know why she's connected to these current murder cases. My gut tells me it's personal."

Harper stayed quiet, and Hattie took that as a sign that right now wasn't the time to push her. She put her hand on Dante's arm. "Let's give Harper some time to digest everything I told her. I'm sure after she sleeps on it, she might have a better perspective. I told you I don't know how much we can help, but I'm sure Harper will consider it. Do you want me to show you where the towels are or can you find them?"

"I can find them," Dante said, and Hattie nudged him out of the room. Once he was gone, Hattie sat back down as if nothing had happened. "What were you asking me?"

Harper got up and walked to the doorway to the hallway that had the stairs to the second floor. Dante was gone. After a few beats, she walked back and sat down at the table. She leaned forward and said in a hushed voice to Hattie, "Do you believe that people can be cursed with immortality?"

Hattie's first instinct was to say no, that immortality was something made of movies and books, but she had seen enough in her lifetime to not discount anything. She told Harper as much. "It's a stretch for my beliefs, but after everything I've seen with my own eyes to be true, I can't say no."

Harper slowly recounted the story Maggie had told her about Dante and Celeste and the curses on them. "I didn't believe it at first. You know I'm slower to these things than you are, but then I started thinking about their last names. Dante La Croix and Maggie Delacroix. What if the family name evolved or changed over time or Dante purposefully changed it to distance himself?"

Dumbfounded, Hattie wasn't sure how to respond. She sat back in her chair and closed her eyes, remembering Dante in his youth and the man she knew today. He had always seemed older to Hattie in her twenties, but she took that for his experience in his craft. Dante had claimed he was close to her age, but she couldn't recall his birthday or exact age. Today, he seemed younger than her. She'd never take Dante for his sixties, and maybe that's because he wasn't.

Hattie opened her eyes to see Harper staring intently at her. "Before we jump to conclusions, why don't we see if Maggie can get us a picture of that portrait that is in her grandmother's house. We can see if there is any resemblance." Hattie paused and reconsidered what she had said. "Do that but better yet, let's also get Maggie and Dante in the

CHAPTER THREE

same place. She's seen the portrait. Let's see how she reacts when she meets Dante."

Harper texted Maggie to see if she could meet for tea at Hattie's tomorrow afternoon. Maggie responded quickly that she'd be there. "Get Dante there about two, and we will see what happens."

"What do you want to do about helping Dante?" Hattie asked tentatively.

Harper stood when the porch door opened. Jackson had arrived, stirring the dogs up in a playful frenzy. "Give me the night to sleep on it as you told Dante. We can talk tomorrow."

Chapter Four

Harper slowly opened her eyes and rolled to her side, snuggling into Jackson, breathing in his scent. Her eyes closed again as she enjoyed the warmth and safety of his embrace.

Jackson pulled her closer. "I feel like a kid who snuck into his girlfriend's bedroom and is about to get caught. It feels wrong to be here like this in Hattie's house," he whispered.

Harper giggled into his side and ran a hand across his bare chest. "You're silly. We are in our forties, and Hattie doesn't care. I'm pretty sure she'd be happy if we were here all the time. I slept so soundly. Did you hear Dante in the middle of the night at all?"

Jackson cuddled into her. "No. Everything was quiet. How long is he staying?"

"Hattie said just a night or two. Will you stay again tonight?"

Jackson pinched her side playfully. "I'd love to. Your bed is more comfortable than mine."

There was a knock on the door once and then twice. Hattie called from the other side that coffee was on if they were awake and wanted any. She called the dogs after her as she went downstairs.

"I think that's our wake-up call," Harper said, rolling onto her back. She stretched her arms above her head and peered at her hands. When she lived in New York and ran her family's magazine *Charlotte*, a week

CHAPTER FOUR

didn't go by that she didn't get a manicure. Now she couldn't remember the last time she was in a nail shop. She had forgone long painted nails for unpolished nails that were clipped short. Harper sighed happily, thankful for a simpler life than she'd had before.

Jackson sat up and slid out of bed. "I'm going to take a shower before going down. Do you want to go first?"

Harper reached for him. "What do you think I should do about Hattie and Dante? She wants me to help him with these murder cases in New Orleans."

Jackson sat back down on the bed. "What's Hattie going to do if you don't agree to help?"

"She's going to do what she always does, forge ahead on her own. You and I both know that's not a good idea. I think Hattie might be in over her head on this one."

"I agree," Jackson said seriously. "As much as I hate even the thought of it, I think you're going to have to humor her. Why don't you give Det. Granger a call today and see if he has any contacts down there in New Orleans. The first step should be to confirm some basic facts from the cops and not just rely on what Dante tells us."

Harper was equal parts friend and annoyance to Det. Tyson Granger of the Little Rock Police Department. She had wormed her way into more than one of his cases. At the end of the day, Harper helped solve the cases, but she still wasn't a welcome presence. "He might not mind if I'm some other jurisdiction's pain in the backside this time."

"Exactly." Jackson gathered up his things to shower, leaving Harper to think over a plan.

Harper didn't want to go downstairs and face Dante and Hattie until she was sure what she was going to do. She stood from her bed and went to her dresser and unplugged her phone from the charger. Harper skimmed through her contacts until she found Det. Granger. It was probably too early to call, but she clicked the call button anyway.

It rang a few times before he picked up. Out of breath, he said, "Please tell me you haven't stumbled over a dead body."

Harper laughed. "Of course not. You sound like you just ran a marathon."

"I'm down on the river trail running, but I figured you wouldn't be calling me unless it was important."

"Very perceptive, Detective," Harper teased. "I'm looking to see if you have any police connections in New Orleans."

"Are you branching out your detective work?" Det. Granger snickered. He waited for Harper to respond, and when she didn't, he cleared his throat. "No, I don't have any connections down there. What's going on?"

Harper explained about the serial murders, the voodoo connection, and Dante's request for help. "I know you won't believe this, but I don't want to get involved. Hattie, though, is full steam ahead so I don't feel like I have a choice but to protect her. I need to check some facts to see if they match up with what Dante is telling us. Jackson thought it would be good to start with you."

"Jackson was right, but I'll have to see what I can find out. Did you say that the markings on the voodoo doll that Hattie found in her yard are the same as the dolls found at murder scenes?"

Harper went back and sat on her bed. "That's exactly what I'm saying. According to Dante, the markings are rare, from a voodoo practitioner named Celeste he knew years ago. But there's a catch."

"There's always a catch." Det. Granger groaned.

Harper knew he wouldn't like what she had to say next so she said it fast. "Everyone thinks Celeste died years ago." Harper hesitated. She was still uncomfortable when she had to tell him something came from a vision.

"There's more. I know there is, so spill it," Det. Granger coaxed.

Harper let it out in one breath. "I don't know if Celeste is dead now,

CHAPTER FOUR

but back then, she faked her death."

"Explain."

"Dante gave me a pair of earrings the last time he was in town that had belonged to Celeste. When I held them, I had a vision of her packing up, setting a fire in her residence, and then leaving. Dante said they found a woman's body in her home burned beyond recognition. I don't know what, if anything, they did back then to identify her, but Dante said everyone assumed it was Celeste. I watched her set the fire and walk out. I didn't see any other woman in her home, but of course, I wasn't in every room."

Det. Granger exhaled loudly. "That's a lot to take, Harper. You have an unknown dead woman, another who faked her death, and now a serial homicide case. This would be a tough one even for me."

"You see what I'm saying then. That's why I called you."

"Let me see if I can connect with anyone at the New Orleans Police Department. They might have even called in the feds at this point. I'll get you what information I can. It should go without saying that you're in over your head with this one."

"I agree with you. I wouldn't even be thinking about getting involved if it wasn't for Hattie."

"You around later? I can meet you this afternoon and let you know what I find. Maybe I can talk some sense into Hattie while I'm at it."

Harper made a plan with Det. Granger to meet at Hattie's shop. She scheduled for the same time that Maggie would be meeting Dante. It might as well all happen at once. Plus, if Maggie thought Dante was her immortal relative, it couldn't hurt to have a cop there.

Over the next hour, Harper and Jackson finished getting ready and headed downstairs. Harper had hoped if she delayed long enough that Dante and Hattie would be gone for the day, but as she rounded the kitchen entrance their voices echoed through the room. She found them sitting at the table eating breakfast and talking. Both seemed to be in a lighter mood than they had been the night before.

"There's scrambled eggs and bacon on the stove if you'd like some," Hattie said.

Jackson kissed Harper goodbye and left. He had some work to do, but mostly he didn't want to deal with Dante. Harper found it sweet how worried he was, but the last thing they needed was Jackson losing his temper with Dante.

Harper stood at the stove and scooped scrambled eggs onto her plate and picked two pieces of nearly-burnt bacon – just the way she liked it. As she carried her plate to the table, Harper said, "I decided that I'm willing to help out, but I need to verify some facts first. I need to know exactly what I'm working with so I called Det. Granger. He's going to look into a few things for me."

Dante raised an eyebrow. "You called the police?"

Harper pinned her eyes on him. "Do you have a problem with that?"

"No, I just don't know how much help the police in New Orleans will give you," Dante said slowly, seeming to choose his words carefully. He went on to explain, "By coming to you, I thought we could bypass the police. I assume most cops won't take our gifts seriously."

"They most likely won't, but I still need to start with facts." Harper popped a piece of bacon in her mouth. "Det. Granger is looking into some information for me. I'll let you know when I know. Then we can make a plan."

"I don't know…" Dante started to say.

"Take it or leave it." Harper glared at him, showing a strength she hadn't shown in a while. She started to feel like Jackson's annoyance over the situation had become her own, and maybe, it was about time.

Chapter Five

"What got into her?" Dante asked Hattie after Harper blew out of the door after breakfast.

Hattie knew Harper's temper. She had read it on Jackson's face, too. Hattie didn't need them to say how annoyed they were, she read it on their faces and picked it up in their energies.

Hattie brushed off Dante. "Harper isn't a morning person. Plus, she's not wrong. We do need to have the facts before we can make any kind of plan to help you."

Dante shifted in his seat. It was obvious to Hattie he was still uncomfortable with the police being involved. She pressed him. "Do you have some issue with the cops? You're talking about multiple homicide cases. It's not like we can just waltz in there and take over."

"No, no of course not," Dante said. "I'm being silly. I just don't trust the cops. They are out to blame this on someone like us. Voodoo has a bad enough reputation. I'm worried about tarnishing it more."

Hattie got up from the table and poured herself more coffee. She topped off Dante's cup as well. "What if it is a voodoo practitioner who is doing this? People commit crime regardless of their religion or spirituality. Are you willing to face it if it's one of your own?"

"Yes, of course I am." Dante gripped the mug.

Dante wasn't telling Hattie something. She recalled the conversation she'd had with Harper the night before, but Hattie wasn't ready to go down that road yet. She wanted a little more information first. Hattie knew Dante wasn't going to tell her unless she had evidence he couldn't refute.

Dante touched her arm. "You look like there is something else you want to say?"

"I'm wondering how you'll feel if it turns out this is Celeste. You haven't seen her in years, Dante. If she staged her death back then and pretended to be dead all of these years, do you know what she's capable of?" Hattie had wanted to say that for a while and was glad it was finally out.

Dante tapped his heart. "There's a lot I wish I could tell you, Hattie. But I know Celeste as well as I know myself. If she staged her death, she had good reason. I don't know what it could be, but if that's what happened, Celeste didn't make the decision lightly. She's certainly not killing people now in New Orleans. And anyway, Hattie, these deaths are violent. Celeste wouldn't have the stomach for it."

Hattie nodded, although she didn't necessarily believe him. "I need to get ready to go into the shop. You're still coming in at two today?"

"I'll be there." Dante reached for her. "I know you still don't trust me, but I wish you would. There is nothing bad I'm holding back from you."

Hattie got up. She turned back to him only once. "There are things you are holding back from me, and good or bad, you are still lying. It's all the same." With that, she left the kitchen and went upstairs to grab a few things before she left for the shop.

As Hattie reached the landing on the second floor, Beau made an appearance down the hall in their bedroom. Hattie hadn't seen him since he had chastised her last night for having Dante in the house. Beau gave her a half-hearted wave as she approached.

"Are you going to scold me again?" Hattie asked as she entered the bedroom.

CHAPTER FIVE

"Would it do any good?"

"You've known me since I was twenty-five. Has it ever done any good?"

"No, you only seem to get more hardheaded the older you get." Beau looked to the ground, but Hattie could tell the corners of his lips turned up in a grin. He had never been very good at apologizing, but Hattie took it as a sign the fight was over.

She wasn't ready to be sweet yet. "Did you want something?"

"I'm glad Jackson spent the night last night. He and Harper seem happy."

"They are." Hattie moved right in front of Beau. "I'd say they are as happy as we were when we started out. Jackson is a lot like you. He's doting and protective with Harper. I can only hope that she doesn't give him the hard time I gave you."

Beau moved to her, letting their energies merge. He ran his hand over Hattie's cheek. "I'm sure she will. She's your niece after all."

Hattie felt Beau's energy against her face and moved into it. "I know there's something you came to tell me. After all of these years, I can tell when you lie."

Beau looked down into her eyes. "I heard you and Harper talking last night. She asked you if you believe in reincarnation and immortality. Do you want to know the truth?"

What Hattie wanted more than anything was to touch her husband and feel his hand against her face for real and the solidity of his body when she wrapped her arms around him. She had to settle for the energy exchange. It frustrated both of them. Hattie stepped back from his energetic embrace. "You know the truth about reincarnation?"

"You learn quite a bit on this side. Do you want to know?"

Hattie nodded and sat down on the bed. She ran her hands over the soft comforter, grounding herself back into the room. "I think it would be helpful if I knew the truth."

Beau moved and sat in the chair next to the bed. He folded his hands in his lap. "It's true. Reincarnation is real. You and I have lived many lives together. What you said to Harper last night was correct. Our souls must learn many lessons. Each time we come back we balance our karma from our previous life while learning new lessons. The goal is to advance each time, carrying with us all we have learned before. In the end, we advance on and help the living."

Hattie wasn't sure she completely understood. She had never given much credence to the idea of soulmates, but it made a certain kind of sense to her that she had known Beau for many lifetimes. When they had met in their youth, it was like they had already known each other, and, according to Beau, they had. "Is that what you're doing now, Beau? You've advanced on and helping this side?"

Beau shook his head. "No, no. I'm just waiting for you so we can reincarnate together later on. It might be our last lifetime, and we can end up like one of those old couples who are together sixty years and die at the same time or a few days apart."

Hattie looked at her husband, confusion on her face. "That isn't just a coincidence?"

"Not at all. It usually happens when two souls have merged for their last human lives before they advance," Beau explained. "See, when we come here, souls are paired. Twin flames are what some call it. They go through their lives alone and some together. Some lives they come together and back apart again each learning their lessons. As souls grow and learn their lessons, it's easier for them to be together. The last life is usually long happy marriages and deaths close in time. It's hard for the souls to live apart."

Hattie had heard the term twin flame before but she chalked it up to the same kind of credence she gave soulmates, which wasn't much. "Why are you telling me this?"

"If you're going to investigate this with Dante you need to know that

CHAPTER FIVE

reincarnation is real and so are curses of immortality. I don't know if it's happened to him, but you have to know it's real. The curses are very rare and powerful. If someone cursed him, you're dealing with someone with ancient evil powers not seen today. Tread lightly."

Hattie appreciated the insight because she hadn't taken seriously anything Harper had said the night before. Hattie stood and reached for him. "I'll be extra careful."

"If that's what happened to Dante, I feel for him. It's sad really, never being able to live a full life with the one you love. I'm sure it's just as tragic for Celeste," Beau said, frowning. "Think about it, Hattie. One of us is cursed to live forever without the other, except we do get to meet and be together for brief periods, but it never lasts. We are stuck in the same terrible cycle. I don't know how I'd manage it."

Hattie let Beau's words sink in and felt the weight of what he was saying. It was nearly unbearable for her to accept so she pushed it out of her mind. "I'll figure it out like I always do."

Beau nodded. "I'm not saying that my feelings about Dante have changed, but if this has happened to him and you want to help him, I support you."

Hattie leaned up and kissed him. She couldn't feel his lips, only his energy, but it was the best they had. "You were going to support me no matter what. You always have, and that's why I love you so much."

Chapter Six

Harper rushed to get her work done so she could be at Hattie's shop on time. Dan Barnes, her co-editor-in-chief and the one who originally ran *Rock City Life*, had been out on assignment all day. Their freelancers and photographer were also busy in the field. The office had remained quiet, and Harper was able to focus. It was nearly one and her stomach growled from hunger. The last time Harper had eaten was early that morning at Hattie's. She had worked through her usual mid-morning snack.

She'd grab something at Hattie's when she met with Maggie if she could last that long. Harper studied photos for the next layout and matched them with the appropriate stories. She was so engrossed in her work that she jumped in her seat, startled by a knock on her door.

"Sorry, Harper, I thought you'd hear me come in," Det. Granger said, taking a seat across from Harper's desk.

"It's fine. I didn't hear you." Harper looked at him suspiciously. "I thought you were meeting me at Hattie's at two?"

"I was, but I think we need to talk privately."

"That sounds ominous." Harper put aside her work and gave Det. Granger her full attention. "Is it bad?"

"It's not good." Det. Granger rubbed at his chin. "There have been six bodies found in the French Quarter so far and that's just within the last six weeks. The police have very few leads. There was a voodoo doll

CHAPTER SIX

left with each victim as you said."

Harper interrupted. "How were they killed?"

"They were shot, but this is where it gets interesting. Based on ballistics, they were shot with a Colt Model 1860 six-shot revolver.

Harper leaned forward on her desk, resting her arms. "Gun types don't mean much to me. I didn't grow up with guns in New York City. There weren't any in my home, and my father didn't hunt so if that's supposed to mean something to me, it doesn't."

Det. Granger nodded in understanding. "It's not so much the gun model that's important, but rather, the age of the gun. New Orleans has a good deal of crime, but that's a gun issued before the Civil War."

"Couldn't the killer have bought it at an antique gun dealer or had it passed down in their family? I guess I'm not seeing the significance. I know the gun is old, but there could be an explanation."

Det. Granger looked behind him and then back at Harper. "You're right. It's not just that the gun is old. In a search of records, they found that the same gun matching the ballistics was used in a previous crime in 1902. They even have an old photograph of it."

"Okay," Harper said, listening but not sure where Det. Granger was going with the story.

"The gun in the photograph had initials – DL," Det. Granger said, leveling a look at Harper. "I didn't mention it to the detective, but isn't that the same initials as Dante La Croix? I needed to tell you this because I can't tell him and certainly can't tell Hattie who might tell him. Is there any chance Dante is a killer?"

"That's a really big leap, especially for you." Harper sat back. "They aren't even sure if it's the same gun and many people have those initials."

"Right," Det. Granger said slowly, "but Dante already admitted he's tied to the case."

Harper thought back to what Maggie had told her. She shrugged noncommittally. "There's always a chance. Hattie has some history with him. I've spoken to him a few times, but I don't know him all that well."

"I knew he was here in Little Rock last spring, but then he left. Did he go back to New Orleans?"

"I'm not sure where he went. I know he wasn't here. Hattie said he showed up the other day and told her about the murders in New Orleans and asked for help. You should be proud of me, I called you immediately."

Det. Granger eyed her. "Jackson told you to call me, right?"

Harper looked away. "Well he suggested it, but I would have." She gave him a weak smile. "You know I only let myself get in a little trouble before I ask you to bail me out, but this time it isn't even about me. It's about Hattie. What I don't understand is that if Dante was killing people why he'd come up here and ask Hattie to help him find the killer?"

"Maybe he likes playing games," Det. Granger said, checking his phone. He pointed to the screen. "This is a text from the detective I spoke to in New Orleans. I asked if any of the victims were connected to each other or if they thought it was a random victim selection. He said they believe it's random. They haven't been able to find a connection among them."

"Is that good or bad?"

"I was trying to figure out if they were connected because maybe they'd have a connection back to Dante. I didn't think it would be that easy to figure out, but you never know."

"I see." Harper tapped on her desk. "Did you tell the cops your suspicions about Dante?"

Det. Granger shook his head. "It's not even a suspicion. The detective mentioned the initials and I was curious. I'd never point a finger unless I was sure or had something more to go on, but that doesn't mean we shouldn't keep our eye on him."

CHAPTER SIX

"Agreed." Harper grabbed some papers on her desk and stacked them in a neat pile. As she got ready to leave for Hattie's, she asked, "How did you leave it with the detective? Did you tell him our connection with the voodoo doll markings?"

"I did. I had to explain why I was even calling. I told him I saw a news report. He's interested if we get any leads on it. I explained that it's not an open case. That the cops here don't investigate spell work, but if we happened to come across anything, we'd let them know."

"They were okay with that?"

"They were. I don't think they know what's happening to be honest with you. The detective was good and has worked on the force for a long time, but he said he's never seen anything like it, even for New Orleans."

Harper stood. "I guess that's saying something then." Harper glanced at the time on her phone and stood. "I need to run. Are you still going to meet me there?"

Det. Granger walked out into the main area of the office with Harper. "I want to be there to talk to Hattie. I'm as worried about her as you are now."

Harper smiled up at him. "You see now why I need to be involved."

The two walked out of the office together and when they hit the sidewalk, Det. Granger asked, "Do you think you can do that thing where you touch an object and get an impression with the voodoo doll if Hattie still has it?"

Harper wasn't sure if touching actual voodoo was the best idea. Hattie hadn't asked her to do it before. Sometimes Harper's gift was more annoying than helpful, and she told Det. Granger as much. "I'd be happy to try if Hattie thinks it's okay. It doesn't guarantee I'll see anything if Hattie says the doll is okay to touch. I don't know if touching a cursed doll is the best way to go."

"I understand, but if Hattie is open to it, you should try."

Harper looked up at him. "You seem much more open to the metaphysical than you used to be." Det. Granger peered down at Harper with a sly grin on his face. Harper knew what changed. Det. Granger had been dating Jackson's sister, Sarah, who was also a medium. Det. Granger didn't have a choice but to be comfortable with it if he wanted to be with her.

"I'll meet you at Hattie's shop. I have to run an errand first." Det. Granger headed off in the opposite direction.

Harper walked to her car and left downtown. She was lucky to miss every light as she sailed up Cantrell hill on her way to the Heights. She made a right on Kavanaugh, waved to a woman she knew who was walking her dog and drove the few blocks to Hattie's shop.

As Harper got near to the shop, she eased her foot off the gas. Maggie stood in front of Hattie's shop unmoving. She had her hand up to her mouth, and her normally olive skin tone had paled. Luckily, Harper found a spot to park right across from the shop.

"I was worried I was going to be late," Harper called as she pulled her bags out of the car, but Maggie didn't seem to hear her. Harper looked both ways and crossed the street quickly. She called Maggie's name again, but still the woman didn't move or respond.

"Are you okay?" Harper asked, putting her hand on her friend's back.

Maggie pointed through the window of the shop, and Harper peered in. "That man looks exactly like the relative I told you about the other day. It can't be."

Chapter Seven

Although Harper had her suspicions, she hadn't been prepared for what Maggie said. She regained her composure from the initial shock. "That's why I asked you to meet me here. When you told me the other day about your family history, I suspected your relative might be the Dante that Hattie knows. We've had some strange things happening."

Maggie reached for Harper's hand. "It can't be, Harper. It's just a silly family legend. I never believed it was true." Maggie pressed her nose to the glass. "He looks so much like the man in the portrait at my grandmother's house. I don't know what to say. It can't be true."

"Maybe there is an innocent explanation, and he's just a long-lost relative of yours. There could be many reasons they look similar." Harper said the words but didn't believe them. She was torn because believing in immortality was a stretch for her. It was another mind-bending reality that didn't fit with Harper's worldview. She couldn't discount it or fully believe it. It created an odd dizzying feeling in the pit of her stomach.

Maggie stepped back from the glass and turned to Harper for the first time. "You don't understand. It's not just that he looks similar to the man in the portrait. Other than clothing, he's identical. I stared at that portrait for hours and hours while at my grandmother's. I was fascinated by it when I was young."

"Do you think you can still go in and face him?"

"What do I say?" Maggie asked, looking back into the shop and then at Harper. "Do we just pretend that I don't know anything?"

"I think we have to right now. Dante hasn't told Hattie anything. Maybe you can tell him you're from New Orleans and ask him some questions to see what he says. Don't press him too much because we don't want to spook him." Harper opened the door to the shop. She looked back at Maggie one last time. "You ready?"

Maggie sighed. "As I'm ever going to be."

Harper and Maggie walked in and took a seat at the table near the window. Maggie sat down while Harper went up to the counter to grab them some tea and treats.

"Where's Hattie?" Harper asked Sarah who was finishing with a customer.

"Hattie had a customer who wanted a reading. She's been back there for nearly thirty minutes, so she should be done soon." Sarah shifted her eyes in Maggie's direction. "Is that your friend who might know if Dante is a vampire?"

Harper nearly dropped the teacup but caught it before it shattered on the counter. "I don't think anyone said he's a vampire."

Sarah rolled her eyes. "You know what I mean. New Orleans. Immortal. What else am I supposed to think?"

Harper laughed. "I don't think anyone has suggested he's the undead. He hasn't died. Isn't that kind of the opposite?"

"How am I supposed to know?" Sarah asked incredulously. "I barely even knew talking to the dead was a thing even though I've done it nearly all of my life. I get here and suddenly there's voodoo, psychics, immortality, and more. I can't wrap my head around it."

"You and me both, sister," Harper said, playfully bumping Sarah's hip. She finished getting the tray of tea and treats and carried them over to Maggie. "You still think Dante looks familiar now that you're

CHAPTER SEVEN

closer up?"

Maggie nodded slowly. "He hasn't even glanced up from the newspaper yet. If it's him, I don't know if he's kept up with his family line or not. I'd be a great-niece to him."

Harper planned to approach Dante when Hattie finished with her reading, but right after Maggie mentioned that Dante hadn't even so much as glanced their way, he gave Harper a wave. Harper waved back as her lips turned up into the fake smile she had perfected at New York society events years ago. Turning to Maggie, Harper asked, "You ready to chat with him?"

Maggie didn't respond or look ready, but she stood when Harper stood and followed her over to Dante's table.

"Mind if we join you?" Harper asked, setting her tea and plate of treats down on the table.

"It would be my pleasure." Dante folded his newspaper and tucked it away at his feet. "Hattie is with a customer, but she said you'd be stopping by." Dante smiled up at Maggie and introduced himself.

"Oh, that's right you haven't met," Harper said dramatically. "This is Maggie Delacroix. She's a famous interior designer from New Orleans. Her work can be seen in homes across the south. Maggie and I went to college together."

Dante's eyes roamed over Maggie's face. "New Orleans is my home, too. Do you live in Little Rock now?"

"I do," Maggie said, her voice uncharacteristically breaking. She cleared her throat and smiled shyly. "Where are you from in New Orleans?"

"My family has lived in the French Quarter for generations. I still own the original family home. I'm just up here for a visit. What about you?"

"My grandmother owns a home in the French Quarter on Burgundy Street. It's been in my family since it was built in 1830. My parents live in the Garden District, which is where I grew up."

Dante took in a deep breath and exhaled it loudly. "There's only a handful of families that go back that far in New Orleans. I'm wondering if I might know your grandmother."

"Viviane Delacroix. Do you know her?"

Harper wasn't sure what was happening, but Maggie sat up a little straighter. She pinned her eyes on Dante, and her confidence grew. Harper wasn't sure if she should slow the exchange or let the chips fall where they may.

Before Dante could answer her question, Maggie pushed harder, "It's funny, but my grandmother has a portrait in her home of..."

Hattie interrupted. "Ladies, you're here!"

Harper made a quick introduction as Hattie and Maggie had never met.

Hattie put her hand on Maggie's shoulder and squeezed her. "Harper has told me so much about you over the years. It's lovely to finally meet you. I've heard wonderful things."

Maggie rested her hand on top of Hattie's. "When we were in college, Harper was always going on and on how much she loved her Aunt Hattie. She built you up so much I wondered if you were real. Your shop is wonderful. I should have stopped in sooner."

Harper caught Hattie's eye and communicated a message without words. Then she said, "I want to show Maggie your reading room. Is it all clear to do that?"

Hattie nodded. "Feel free. I'll walk you back."

Dante remained quiet, but Harper knew he was suspicious of what Maggie had started to say. He let them walk away though without saying another word.

Harper and Hattie walked Maggie back to the reading room as casually as possible, but Harper was bursting with excitement to talk to Maggie out of Dante's earshot. It was Hattie though who practically pulled

CHAPTER SEVEN

Maggie down the hall and into the reading room, shutting the door behind them.

Hattie gripped Maggie by the arms. "I have to know. Is it him?"

"I can't be sure," Maggie started, stumbling nervously over her words, "but if it's not then he's my ancestor's identical twin."

"It's that close?" Hattie asked, letting Maggie go and stepping back.

"It's uncanny, really. I've never seen anything like it. You have to know, Hattie, it was just a story, a legend in my family. I don't think anyone believed it. How would he get away with it all these years? He said he still lives in New Orleans. Someone had to know or at least suspect after all of these years."

Hattie paced around her small reading room, talking to herself. She'd stop as if she wanted to say something but shake her head and walk in a circle again. Maggie and Harper sat on the couch looking up at her and waiting.

"Hattie, what do we do?" Harper finally asked when she couldn't wait a second longer.

Hattie threw her hands up. "I have no idea. If we ask him, he might just deny it. If we blow his cover, he might run underground."

Harper bit at her lip. "We have another issue. Please sit so I can tell you. You're making me dizzy."

Hattie sat down on the chair across from her. "What could be worse than this?"

"The cops believe the gun used in all six homicides in New Orleans is a revolver made in 1860. It had the initials DL carved into the gun."

"Dante La Croix," Maggie said softly.

Hattie let out a string of curses, the likes of which Harper had never heard.

Chapter Eight

Harper stared at her aunt waiting for her to work herself out of her meltdown. When Hattie was done, Harper let out a soft laugh. "I've never heard you curse like that."

Hattie smoothed down her skirt. "This situation is ridiculous. What do you want?"

Harper smiled. "No judgment. But we have to figure out what we're going to do."

"What time does Det. Granger get here?" Hattie asked.

"Soon. Det. Granger told me he was running an errand first. He could be out there now." Turning to Maggie, Harper asked, "What else was in your family legend? Was Dante a good guy? Any rumors of him being a homicidal maniac?" Harper sounded like she was being sarcastic and maybe she was a little, but it was a serious question.

"Definitely not that," Maggie said, looking down at her hands. "Dante and Celeste were always described as a very loving and devoted couple. The tale was sad, not criminal. I've never heard a bad word uttered about him. Dante was described as a successful merchant in his day who amassed a good deal of wealth, but he took care of his family and even his community. They had no children although as the story goes both longed for a family. There was never any reason given why they never had children. Celeste was active in setting up some of the first schools in the city."

CHAPTER EIGHT

It was like a light went on in Hattie's eyes. "Who cursed him?"

Maggie frowned. "That part of the story was never clear. I've heard both a scorned love and a business deal gone bad. I tend to think it was a scorned love since the curse brings them back together each lifetime only to pull them apart again. That seems like the kind of revenge born out of jealousy."

"I'd agree with that." Hattie tapped her finger on her knee. "If the curse is real then it's likely that the gun could be Dante's, but who even knows if he's kept it all of these years. I just can't see him being behind murders like that so it makes me wonder if he's right and someone is sending him a message. This is far too much coincidence for me."

"That brings us right back to what do we do about it." Harper checked her phone for the time. "We don't have a lot of time to decide. Dante wants our help, but I think in exchange for that he needs to be upfront with us about what's going on."

Hattie stood. "That's what we'll do then, but I don't think we should tell Det. Granger anything quite yet."

"I don't think we should tell Det. Granger anything about a curse or that Dante might be immortal ever," Harper stressed. "He's had to wrap his mind around a lot lately, and I don't know that he can handle it. I can barely handle this."

"It might not be avoidable, but let's hold back unless it's necessary. I'm going to get Dante. We can talk back here. If Det. Granger is out there, what do you want me to tell him?" Hattie asked.

Harper followed Hattie out of the reading room, leaving Maggie to wait. "I'll handle him. Just bring Dante back and then we can talk."

Harper and Hattie walked to the front of the shop and were relieved Det. Granger hadn't arrived yet. Dante remained sitting at the table reading the newspaper. Harper went to speak to Sarah while Hattie got Dante's attention.

"Have you heard from Det. Granger?" Harper asked Sarah.

"I talked to him this morning but not recently." Sarah set down the dish she was drying and grabbed for her phone on the back counter. "I have a text from him. He told me to tell you he's running late."

That was good. Harper debated for a moment if she needed him there right now. It was probably best that he wasn't, and she didn't want to waste his time. "Could you text him and let him know we don't need him right now and I'll call him later?"

"Sure." Sarah stood there rapidly clicking the screen of her phone. When she was done, she picked her head up. "What's happening?"

"Maggie is fairly certain Dante is her long-lost relative. We need to confront him about that and I thought it better that Det. Granger wasn't here for it. We bend his mind enough. Could he handle immortality curses?"

Sarah laughed. "Tyson can't handle that I talk to spirits. I think he'd run for the hills if we start telling him people are immortal. Given his upbringing, he might start dousing us with holy water."

"Exactly my thinking." Harper waited a moment while Hattie talked to Dante and then followed them back into the reading room. Dante sat down next to Maggie on the couch. Hattie grabbed her chair and Harper perched on the arm of the couch.

"I feel like I'm in an interrogation room." Dante laughed nervously. "All that's missing is the bright spotlight and the detective who is threatening to arrest me. What's going on, ladies?"

Hattie gave Dante the sternest look Harper had ever seen. "I spoke to Harper and we've agreed to help you, but first you have to help us."

"Okay," Dante said quickly, slapping his hands to his knees. "What do you need?"

Hattie shook her head. "It's not that easy. We need to know the truth about your situation and your relationship with Celeste. We know that you're lying to us."

Dante took a breath and sat back on the couch. He glanced at each of them. "The truth about what exactly? I can tell you all about my life with Celeste. That hasn't been a secret. I already told you she broke off our engagement and was presumed dead in a fire. Harper said she had a vision that Celeste was still alive. What more do you want to know?"

Harper looked at Maggie, who cleared her throat. She turned to face Dante and explained softly, "When I was growing up in New Orleans, my grandmother had a painting of a man and woman that hung in the dining room. As a kid, I stared at that painting all the time. It's permanently imprinted in my memory. There's a legend that goes with that picture." Maggie spent the next few minutes detailing the entire story to Dante, who sat stone-faced listening.

When Maggie was done, Dante smiled. "Now that's some tall tale. I've heard a lot of wild stories growing up in New Orleans, but that's one of the best. I've not heard of immortality curses unless you're talking about vampires. But what does any of this have to do with me?"

Hattie raised her eyebrows. "Maggie believes that you're him."

Dante pointed to his chest. "Me? You think I'm your immortal relative? That's crazy. I've never heard of such a thing."

Maggie shook her head. "I know it's you. You look exactly alike. Your missing fiancée is Celeste. My relative's wife's name was Celeste. I never believed the story was true until I saw you."

Dante shifted again in his seat, and Harper could tell he grew more uncomfortable by the second. "You're mistaken," Dante said firmly.

Maggie dug in. "I'm not. I wasn't sure at first, but sitting here right next to you now, I know you're him. You both have the same small beauty mark under your left eye. There's no question in my mind it's you. You can tell me. Nothing bad will happen. I'd be happy to hear what you've been doing all of these years."

Dante didn't say anything. He gave no outright denial. He never said he wasn't the man. Dante danced around it, said Maggie was mistaken, but never outright said he wasn't him.

"There's more, Dante," Harper said as he squirmed.

"More than being told I'm Maggie's immortal relative?" Dante asked incredulously.

"There's more," Harper started. "You know I called Det. Granger because I wanted to know what he knew about the case or if he had any connections in New Orleans. He called the detective in New Orleans, Dante. They said they believe the murder weapon is a gun from 1860 and had the initials DL."

Dante's eyes flew open and he stood abruptly. "I need to go."

Hattie stood too and reached her arm out to stop him. "We can help you, Dante. You have to trust us and be honest with us."

Dante shook off Hattie's arm and opened the door to her reading room. He did turn back just once and said, "I'm in more trouble than I realized. No one can help me, Hattie, not even you." With that, Dante blew out of the room.

Harper slumped down on the couch next to Maggie. "That went well," she said dryly.

Chapter Nine

Later that evening, Hattie stood at her stove stirring a pot of chicken soup. The interaction with Dante weighed heavily on her. What she most wished for was to speak to her grandmother, Fiona, but she was long since passed and had never come to Hattie in spirit. None of her relatives ever had, not even her mother.

The line of Ryan women with magical abilities went back generations – all the way back to their Celtic roots in Ireland. Fiona had been born and raised in Tipperary and only came to America much later in life. The roots for magic ran deep in her family line. Ancestry records dating back to the 15th Century had been passed down from one to the other. History was important to the Ryans, especially their magical knowledge.

All of the women developed their own magical gifts, but the knowledge was always paid forward. Never once had there been any mention of an immortality curse. That afternoon, Hattie had left her shop and come home to read her grimoire and her grandmother's letters that she had written to help Hattie when she was young. There was nothing even remotely close to an immortality curse. Of course, the Ryan women practiced magic for good. They had known of curses for the sole reason to know how to break them. But immortality, never.

Hattie's grandmother had been particularly adept at fertility spells, helping women who could not conceive, which was ironic given Hattie's childless fate. Hattie worried about what would happen to the Ryan line.

Sure, there were cousins and distant relatives probably still practicing their magic in Ireland, but Hattie didn't know any of them. Hattie only had one brother, Harper's father Max, and he only had Harper. Harper had crossed the threshold of forty and was fairly adamant she'd never be a mother either. It looked like their family line might end with Harper. That weighed heavy on Hattie, too, but it was too much to take on tonight. Hattie truly wished she had someone with deeper knowledge than hers to help her sort out this mess.

"You look weary, my love." Beau energetically nudged Hattie's side. "Let's talk it out. That usually makes you feel better."

"I don't know if you're going to want to hear this, Beau. I know you don't approve."

"Approve or not, I'm always here for you."

Hattie poured herself a bowl of soup and pulled a warm loaf of bread from the oven. She tore off a piece and slathered it with butter. She carried her dinner over to the table and sighed heavily. "You were right to worry about Dante, Beau. I'm in over my head and not sure what to do."

Beau sat across the table from Hattie. "Dante has always caused you stress. You're not twenty-five anymore. It's going to take its toll on you. You've decided to go down this path so all I can do is support you."

Hattie took a bite of bread and savored the flavor. At least her grandmother had left her some good recipes. "It's not just Dante weighing on me tonight. I can see spirits, but I never see my family. My grandmother or mother could come to me easily, especially now when I need them most. I'd be so happy to spend some time with them again. Do you ever see them, Beau?"

Beau nodded. "They are all around you, dear. I don't know why you can't see them the way you see me, but they are here. You are never alone. I know you're a bit stumped right now, but ask them for help and guidance and you'll receive it. I promise you that."

CHAPTER NINE

Hattie wanted to believe that, but it frustrated her that she couldn't see them. "Do you ever regret that we didn't have children?"

Beau raised his eyebrows. "Is that getting you down? You finally have a maternal instinct kicking in now in your sixties? That doesn't sound like you at all."

Hattie smiled. "It's not so much wishing we had children as it is wishing that our family line wasn't ending with Harper." Hattie reached her hand out to Beau and he placed his hand in hers. "I loved our life together. I couldn't have asked for anything more. We both chose not to have children, and it suited us just fine. Please don't think I have any regrets about that."

"There's still time for Harper. It could happen." Beau looked away and wouldn't meet Hattie's gaze.

Hattie's excitement grew. "You mean Harper will have a child?"

"I didn't say that," Beau cautioned. "You know I'm not supposed to give you information like that. I'm just saying I wouldn't give up hope just yet."

Hattie shook her head at him, laughing. "It's no different than when I read my cards. Information about the future comes to me all the time. There's no difference in my readings and you telling me outright. It just saves me a step."

Beau shrugged, but the grin on his face told Hattie all she needed to know. Harper would have a child. Hattie immediately perked up. "While you're telling me things you shouldn't, did you find out anything about immortality curses?"

"I've been asking around on this side. They are real but rare, and only the same kind of magic used to curse can reverse it."

"But it is reversible?" Hattie was glad to hear that.

"It is, but it's not easy." Beau turned his head slightly to the side, glancing out the kitchen window. "You have a guest, my love, so I'll leave you to it."

45

Beau disappeared, and sure enough, not even ten seconds later a loud rap reverberated on Hattie's porch door. She got up to answer and took a step back when she saw Dante's face. He had been crying. His face was puffed out and his eyes were watery.

When Hattie opened the door, he frowned. "I'm embarrassed I ran from the shop like that today."

"I had hoped you'd be back. When I came home from work and saw your things still in the room, I was relieved that you hadn't left town completely." Hattie stepped out of the way so Dante could come inside. "There's soup on the stove and fresh bread if you want some."

"I don't think I could eat." Dante walked into the kitchen and sat down at the table. He dropped his head low, looking at his hands in his lap.

Hattie sat and left him in silence while she ate. She wasn't going to participate in his pity party but knew just by him being there that he wanted to talk. When Hattie finished her last spoonful of soup, she pushed the bowl to the side. "Are you ready to talk?"

"I don't even know what to say to you."

Hattie leaned back in her chair. "You can start with the truth."

"It's not that easy."

Hattie eyed him. "It's as easy as you want it to be. I've put up with a lot from you over the years, Dante. If you want my help, and more importantly, Harper's, you have to tell me. Are you Maggie's cursed relative?"

Dante nodded once but didn't say a word.

Hattie dropped her angry, icy demeanor and softened almost immediately. If it were true, then she felt bad for Dante. A cursed life is not a life at all. She reached her hand out to him. "Dante, I truly want to help you. We have to know what we're dealing with. There are already six people dead in New Orleans."

Dante picked his head up. "You're right. I know you're right, but it

CHAPTER NINE

doesn't mean telling the truth is easy. It's a long, complicated story that sometimes even I don't understand."

"The truth is never easy to say, but in the long run it's easier than living a lie."

Chapter Ten

Dante sat back in the chair and reached for Hattie's open hand. "I was cursed and so was my wife by a man who wanted to marry her. She chose me, and we have been forced to live this life ever since. I hope after you hear this story some of my past actions will make more sense to you."

Hattie started to ask a question, but Dante waved her off. "Let me tell you the whole story from the beginning, and then we can talk." Dante took a deep breath and closed his eyes. "I was born on the outskirts of New Orleans in 1768. My father was a merchant, and I followed in his footsteps. I went to New Orleans in 1788 just after my twentieth birthday and the first fire that destroyed the city. We knew the city would rebuild and grow, and there was great wealth to be made. I went to set up our shop. I built a home on Chartres Street near what is now Jackson Square. Celeste and I met shortly after and fell in love immediately. It was instant, like we had known each other forever. We knew immediately that we'd be wed. Celeste had another suitor, Pierre Lacourt, a man her father wanted her to marry. But Celeste had no interest in this man even before she met me. He vowed revenge when she rebuffed him. I honestly thought it was all bluster because he left the city soon after."

Dante sat back in his chair. "We were married in 1790. The home I had built was burned in the second great fire in 1794, but we rebuilt.

CHAPTER TEN

That is the home where I live now. Celeste and I never had children. It just wasn't fated for us, which in the grand scheme of things was probably a blessing." Tears formed in Dante's eyes as he tried to choke back the emotion.

Hattie got up and poured him a glass of water from the pitcher in the fridge. She set it down in front of Dante with a box of tissues. "Take your time."

Dante calmed himself down. He thanked Hattie for the water and took a sip. "Children or not, we had a good life," he started again. "It was an exciting time. The city was blossoming. I watched it build up around me. My shop brought us wealth. Celeste was teaching, setting up the first schools in our community. For several years, it was bliss. Then, in the summer of 1813, when I was forty-five, Pierre came back. He came into my shop, and right away I knew who he was. He was different though. He seemed calmer and nicer. Pierre told me that he had met and married a woman named Marie and while he was in New Orleans, he wanted to wish us well. He invited Celeste and me to dinner."

Dante shook his head in disgust. "I was so stupid, Hattie. I believed him. Celeste didn't want to go to dinner, but I convinced her. I told her it was good to mend fences. Pierre Lacourt still held a lot of power in New Orleans. I thought it would be better to make peace. I forced her to go."

Hattie reached for him. "You didn't know."

"I know, but I should have." Dante took another sip of water and fought back tears. "We met Pierre at his family's home not far from our own. Celeste was angry with me, but she had never looked more beautiful. She had worn her best dress. Her hair was done perfectly. But right away I felt something was off. Pierre said his wife was tired and didn't join us for dinner. The meal tasted strange and soon we were both tired. At one point, I said that we should go. I tried to stand, but collapsed on the ground."

Hattie knew that this had happened more than two hundred years ago, but her heart ached for him like it happened last week. Dante's face showed his pain.

He recounted, "When I came to, I was on my back on the floor. The wood was rough under me, and the only light was a candle off in the corner of the room. Celeste was right next to me. Hattie, I was so scared. You have no idea. When I turned to look at Celeste to see if she was okay, I thought she was dead. She had strange markings in blood all over her face. That's when I reached up and touched my face. I came away with blood on my fingers. I was frantic, but I soon discovered it wasn't our blood. I roused Celeste finally, and I was never more relieved to hear her voice. We both sat up and that's when we realized there were strange markings on the floor all around us. They were voodoo symbols I came to learn later. Pierre was nowhere in sight. I grabbed Celeste and I got us out of there as quickly as I could. It was only when we were heading for the front door that Pierre showed himself to us."

Dante became more animated with his hands as he spoke. "Pierre told us right then that he had cursed us. He said that I was to live forever, never growing older than my forty-five years and that I'd never die. Celeste would lead her natural life but was cursed to find and love me over and over again only for me to lose her in death, live without her, and then meet on her twentieth birthday and fall in love all over again. Hattie, we laughed at him. We left his house feeling strange but relieved to be alive. We didn't believe in curses."

"Until you did?" Hattie asked with her eyebrows raised.

Dante nodded. "Probably no more than a week later, a man came into my shop to rob me. He shot me right through the heart. I felt the gunshot, collapsed on the floor, and woke up fifteen minutes later completely healed. I lived with no medical intervention. Celeste lived only a few more years and died on her forty-eighth birthday. Like

CHAPTER TEN

clockwork twenty years later we met again."

Hattie's hand flew to her mouth. "How many times has this gone on?"

"More times than I care to count. It's like this vicious cycle we cannot break. I've seen the woman I love die in various ways throughout the years. I've tried to kill myself time after time. I joined wars to die. I was injured in battle but never died."

Hattie looked up at him. "Does Celeste know what is happening to her in each life?"

Dante frowned. "No, not until I tell her. That's been the hardest part. I've tried to stay away from her, but the pull between us is too great. This last time, Celeste left me. She's never done that before. We usually get through it together. I don't know what changed."

"Is this why you studied voodoo?"

Dante sighed. "I studied everything I could get my hands on. That's when I came to learn what was used against us was a form of voodoo. Not what most people practice but a distorted vengeful form. After that, I decided to become a voodoo practitioner. I immersed myself in the culture, learned spells, and tried to become as powerful as possible in the hopes of reversing it."

Hattie pinched the bridge of her nose. "How did I factor into all of this?"

"Celeste had recently passed, and I knew it would be years until I met her again. I was honestly very drawn to you, Hattie. Loved you even. You were powerful. I could tell that right away, and I thought you might be able to help me. This way when I did meet Celeste again, we could have a normal life and death this time around."

Guilt washed over Hattie. She wished she had known then. It might have changed the dynamic between them. "Why didn't you just tell me?"

"Would you have believed me?" Dante asked skeptically. "I'm not even sure you believe me now."

"I believe you. I don't know what to do about it," Hattie said sadly. "You know, I might have believed you then if given time to accept it, but you're right, it would have been a stretch for me. What have you done to try to reverse it?"

Dante shook his head regretfully. "Everything, Hattie. I've sought out voodoo practitioners, some of the strongest I've ever met. I traveled to the Caribbean, Haiti, and Africa, looking for anything that might break the curse and nothing. I've tried everything. That's why when Harper held my hand and picked up my energy a few months back I was hoping she saw the future. I was hoping she saw me finally die." Dante pointed to his heart. "I've had this constant pain in my chest for months now. I've been praying for a heart attack."

"I need to think." Hattie got up and dropped her bowl in the sink. She had no idea what to say to Dante or how to help him, but she had a million questions running through her head. As Hattie washed dishes, she asked, "How did you get away with this for so long? You're living in the same house. People must have noticed."

Dante came and stood beside her. "People only see what they want to. Sure, there have been rumors about me. I've left New Orleans at times after Celeste passes only to return right before she turns twenty. There was one time I had hoped to avoid it completely and I left for Europe. She went on a trip with her family, and we met in Paris. The curse or fate keeps bringing us back together."

"Dante, I have no idea how I can help you, but maybe we can at least work to find Celeste."

Dante nodded sadly. "I understand. Whatever you can do." He placed his hand on hers and kissed her cheek. Dante left the kitchen and headed to the guest room for the night.

Chapter Eleven

The next morning Harper stopped briefly at Hattie's bedroom door wanting to talk to her aunt before they both left for work. She stood there for a moment listening to see if her aunt was awake, and when Harper didn't hear anything, she figured Hattie might still be sleeping. Harper had arrived home late the night before and Hattie had already gone to bed. Dante's bedroom door had been closed as well. Harper didn't know if Hattie had shut the door or if Dante had come back. That was partly what Harper wanted to discuss. It would have to wait. She showered and finished getting ready, thinking she'd catch Hattie later.

As Harper hit the landing to the first floor, she pulled up short when she saw her aunt sitting at the kitchen table. Dark circles had formed under Hattie's eyes and her coloring was off.

"Are you okay?" Harper asked as she pulled yogurt from the fridge.

"Not really. It was a long night, to say the least." Hattie sipped her coffee and rested her head on the palm of her hand. "Sarah is opening the shop for me this morning. I'm not sure I'm even going in. I've asked her to reschedule the readings I had for today."

Harper didn't have time to sit and talk with Hattie like she wanted to. She had a meeting with an advertiser with the magazine first thing. Dan was busy working with another. Bringing revenue into the magazine had been a priority so they could expand. "I don't have a lot of time this morning, but is there anything I can do?"

Hattie nudged a newspaper in Harper's direction. "There's been another murder in New Orleans. It's even made the paper here. At least we know it's not Dante since he's been here with us."

Harper dropped her bag to the floor and set her yogurt on the table. She picked up the paper and skimmed through it. A thirty-year-old man was found in an alley in the French Quarter. A similar voodoo doll and strange markings were drawn around the body. "Is this like all the others? We knew about the doll, but I don't remember hearing about the markings around the body."

"I'm not sure. This is the first real official account that I've read. As you can see, it doesn't detail the other murders. It only mentions that it's connected to six other similar homicides." Hattie turned on her chair and said in a whisper, "I talked to Dante last night. He confirmed that he's Maggie's relative. The curse is real."

Harper took a step back. She had suspected it was but had been holding out hope that it was nothing more than a silly family legend. "What happened?"

Hattie waved her off. "It's far too much to get into right now. We need someplace to meet later out of the way. I don't want Dante around when we discuss things."

Harper set the paper back down on the table. "Sure, come to my office. I have a meeting in about twenty minutes but will just be working on articles after that. Do you want me to ask Jackson to come? I told him last night to sleep at home to shield him from potential drama, but I think he's free today."

"Yes, please do." Hattie rubbed at her eyes. "I think it's too early to tell Det. Granger. I'll have Sarah watch the shop and fill her in later with the details."

"Anything you need, we can handle," Harper said seriously, reading the concern on Hattie's face.

CHAPTER ELEVEN

Hattie stood. "I hate to even ask you this, but I want to know if you'd be willing to touch the doll that was buried in the yard to see if you can get an impression."

"I will if it's safe. Det. Granger asked me the same thing. You hadn't asked before so I didn't bring it up. I wasn't sure how safe it would be to touch actual spell work."

"I don't know the answer to that, but I won't have you do anything unsafe. I'll look through the family grimoire before we meet. I can check with Dante, too."

"Are you going to bring the doll to my office?" Harper wasn't sure that was a good idea. She didn't even like that it was in the house.

Hattie nodded. "I don't want you to do this in front of Dante or have him around when you're doing it. Your office seems like the safest space unless you can think of somewhere else."

Even though Harper thought better of it, she agreed. "That's fine. I'll try to clear the office out for our meeting, but Dan will probably be there."

"It's okay. We trust him."

Harper left for her office filled with mixed emotions. Her gift of psychometry grew stronger and stronger with each passing day. Like a muscle, the more she used it, the stronger it became. Harper wasn't sure how she felt about touching actual spell work, particularly voodoo if that's even what it was. Since Hattie didn't know the actual practitioner, they didn't know the type of magic behind it.

After the meeting with Dante yesterday, Maggie told Harper more about growing up in New Orleans and her exposure to voodoo, which wasn't all bad. No one in her family practiced it, but she had several friends who did. None of the voodoo rituals and spells they conducted were bad or anything similar to what was portrayed in the movies. But like with anything, there were darker forms of voodoo some practitioners used.

Hattie had said the same about her spell work. The Ryan family grimoire was filled with all kinds of spells, the majority for good, some curse-breaking, and protection spells, but there were other spells that Hattie never used and said she never would. Harper wasn't sure if she was comforted by knowing she had access to darker spells if needed or not. She couldn't imagine ever using them. Besides, spell work hadn't been her gift. Harper assumed she could learn it if she desired, but she hadn't felt the need yet, and she hoped she never would.

Harper parked near her office, walked the few blocks to the building, and trudged up the stairs to the second floor. As she hit the landing, she was surprised to hear Det. Granger's voice filling her loft office space. Harper walked straight to Dan's office concerned.

Harper poked her head in the doorway. "Is everything okay?"

Dan waved her in. "Det. Granger was looking for you this morning so I told him to wait with me until you arrived."

Harper looked up at the clock. "I don't have much time. I have a meeting with an advertiser in five minutes."

"No worries," Dan said. "They rescheduled until next week, but whatever you said to them on the phone worked. They are placing a few ads. They will be in next week to finalize details."

Det. Granger patted the seat next to him. "I didn't get a chance to talk to you after you met with Dante and your friend yesterday. I found something you need to see."

"I'll be right back." Harper went into her office, put her bag down on the floor next to her desk, and left her purse on her chair. From her office, she yelled, "Does anyone want any coffee?"

"I grabbed you one at the deli about ten minutes ago. It's still hot." Dan held the cup out to Harper as she returned to his office. "Take a breath. You seem frazzled."

"I am. Hattie caught me on the way out of the house and told me about another murder in New Orleans. I rushed here to meet the advertiser

CHAPTER ELEVEN

on time. I haven't had a chance to catch my breath." Turning to Det. Granger, she asked, "The meeting yesterday went horribly, but are you sure you want to hear this? You're not exactly comfortable with our world. Hattie and I talked about not telling you yet until we had a few things sorted."

"I can handle it. At this point, I'd like to know everything even if it's not immediately believable to me."

Harper took a sip of her coffee and sat back in the chair. "I'm going to say it and not sugarcoat for you because I have no other way to say it. Yesterday, Maggie was convinced Dante was her long-lost relative. Dante denied it and stormed out of the meeting, but he spoke to Hattie last night. He confirmed that he was cursed and is immortal. Hattie didn't get into it with me this morning so I don't know any details of how that happened. I'm having trouble believing it's real, but like you, it takes convincing. You can tell me it's all crazy now."

Det. Granger didn't argue with Harper at all. He simply placed a photo on her lap. "Take a look at that. I nearly called you at midnight when I found this. I didn't sleep a wink last night."

Harper picked up the photo, which had been printed from the internet. Dante sat ramrod straight in his Civil War military uniform. His hair was different and he had a full beard, but there was no denying it was him. Harper swallowed hard. "I'd say that's some solid proof or every male relative of Dante's looks exactly like him."

Det. Granger glanced between Dan and Harper. "I don't even know what to say. I don't know how he grew up in New Orleans and ended up fighting for the Union, but that's the least of things I'm curious about."

Chapter Twelve

Harper called Hattie immediately after seeing the photo Det. Granger had found and asked her to come to the office as soon as possible. She sat with Det. Granger and Dan waiting for Hattie's arrival.

"Doesn't the fact that we have a photo of Dante from the Civil War, and a gun issued right around that time with his initials on it, point to him as a suspect in the murders in New Orleans?" Dan asked, staring down at the photo after Harper let him have another look.

"It would, but there was another murder last night and Dante was at Hattie's the whole night."

Det. Granger shook his head. "Is there any way he can fly or transport himself there by means not human?"

Harper scrunched up her face. "I don't think that's a thing."

"Well I didn't think being immortal was a thing until late last night."

"True," Harper admitted, unsure of what else to say. In reality, she had no idea the extent of Dante's powers. "Let's wait until Hattie gets here and she can walk us through everything. She also asked me to hold the doll from the voodoo found in her yard to see if I get an impression. She's bringing it with her."

Dan raised his eyebrows. "Voodoo in the office?"

"I'm not creating a spell. I'm just touching the doll from someone else's spell that no longer holds any power."

CHAPTER TWELVE

"I'm here. I'm here!" Hattie yelled from the main office space. She got to Dan's doorway and caught her breath. She had the box with her that had been dug out of the ground. "Those stairs aren't fun for an old woman."

Det. Granger stood up and let Hattie sit down. "I'll go grab another chair," he said, walking out of the office into Harper's. He came back with a chair and sat down next to Hattie.

Hattie set the box on the floor next to her feet. As soon as she calmed herself, Dan slid the photo across his desk to Hattie. "What's this?" she said, picking it up. As Hattie peered down at the photo, her eyes got as wide as Harper's.

Hattie looked up from the photo, shaking her head. "Apparently, Dante didn't keep his immortality as much of a secret as he thought he did. This is definitely him."

"Dante is immortal then. It's confirmed?" Det. Granger took the photo back from Hattie as she handed it to him.

"It's confirmed. He told me last night, and it's as wild a tale as I have ever heard." Hattie spent the next fifteen minutes explaining everything Dante had told her the night before.

Harper listened intently to the story, captivated and horrified at what Dante and Celeste had been through. Dante's desperation when he met Hattie earlier in life now had a context to it that made sense for Harper. It still didn't give Dante a right to treat Hattie so poorly, but if he thought she was his only hope of breaking the curse, Harper could understand the acts of a desperate man.

Harper had no desire to live forever. She wasn't even sure she wanted to be reincarnated over and over again. She was pretty sure once was enough for her.

When Hattie was done, and Dan and Det. Granger were shocked into silence, Harper asked, "How did Dante go this long undetected? He was living right there in his family home. There was a portrait at Maggie's grandmother's house. Didn't someone from the family notice him?"

"You would think," Hattie said. "Dante didn't have a good explanation. He changed up how he looked from time to time. He'd leave the city for years sometimes and then return. I'm sure there had to be rumors, but people die off through the generations. If you're not looking for it, I guess it's not that hard to hide it."

"Are you sure Dante isn't the one responsible for the murders?" Dan asked.

"I'm positive," Hattie assured emphatically. "There's no way it can be him if the murder last night is tied to the others. He's been in Little Rock the last few days and sat with me in my kitchen last night talking for hours. He went into the spare room at the same time I went to bed."

Hattie remained quiet for a moment seemingly mulling over her thoughts. "We are looking for someone who has either found out Dante's secret and is trying to draw him out or something else is going on entirely."

Det. Granger sat back in his chair and folded his large muscular arms across his chest. "There is no way I can go to New Orleans police with this story. I'm sure they have heard far more than I ever will about voodoo, but they are going to think I've lost my mind. Hearing this, I'm questioning my sanity."

Hattie reached her hand over and patted his leg. "You're as sane as the rest of us."

Det. Granger offered a half-hearted smile. "That makes me feel better," he said sarcastically. "But really, what do we do now that we know?"

"We need to help Dante break the curse, but first we have to find out who is trying to set him up to take the fall for these murders. His immortality gives new meaning to a life sentence." Hattie reached down on the floor and picked up the box. She turned to Harper. "Are you ready to see if you can get a vision?"

CHAPTER TWELVE

Harper reached her hands out and took the box, careful not to fully wrap her hands around it. "Do I hold the box or should I take the doll out and hold that?"

"Everything I've read and from what Dante said, the spell is broken. There is no more magic in it. This is no more dangerous to touch than that pen on the desk."

Harper relaxed into her chair and opened the box. She took the doll out and removed the cloth that had been placed around it. She locked eyes with Hattie. "If I seem upset, please shake me out of it. This is the first time that I've been a bit scared to try this."

"We are all right here with you." Hattie reached over and patted Harper's arm.

Harper wrapped her hands around the doll and closed her eyes. Normally, she'd take a few breaths to get into a vision, but this time she was catapulted through time and space without any effort at all. She stood at the edge of Hattie's driveway surrounded by darkness. Harper didn't know the exact time but given the stillness and moon overhead, it was sometime in the middle of the night. A sound caught Harper's attention and she moved toward it across the lawn to the back of the house.

Harper stopped dead in her tracks when she saw the hooded figure on their knees burying something in the dirt. She stood there for several moments watching the person, afraid to move closer. Harper summoned the courage and walked toward them, but they turned sharply and looked around as if they heard her. That wasn't possible or at least that's what Harper hoped. She swallowed hard and continued when the person turned back to what they were doing.

Harper took one tentative step after another until she reached them. The energy they gave off was stronger than she had ever felt. The person chanted words Harper couldn't understand. She wasn't even sure what language it might have been. It almost sounded French but not quite.

From behind the person, Harper couldn't see their face with the dark hood from a cloak pulled over their head. The garment looked old, something not worn in this century. Harper stepped around them and could finally see their face. It wasn't a woman as they all had suspected. It was a man. Harper could barely make out his face, but dark hair hung over his forehead. After the man chanted a few more words, he covered the items with dirt using his bare hands.

He stood and brushed his dirty hands down his pants, wiping them free of soil. He glanced up at Hattie's house and chanted a few more words. Harper finally got a good look at his face. It wasn't a man she had ever seen before. She memorized his high cheekbones, thin lips, and dark brown eyes. His jawline was strong and face full. If Harper had to guess she'd put the man in his mid-forties.

As he turned to leave, Harper tried to follow, but she was brought back to the present. Harper sucked in a few sharp breaths as she reoriented herself back in Dan's office. She blinked rapidly and looked around. Dan, Det. Granger and Hattie sat on the edges of their seats watching her intently.

"I'm fine," Harper said softly, placing the doll back in the box. She closed the lid and set the box down on the floor. "I didn't see a woman. It was a man."

"Are you sure?" Hattie asked, confusion in her voice. "I was told the person who cursed me was named Celeste, and Dante said the spell work had her mark. I was sure it would have been a woman."

"I watched him. It was a man." Turning to Det. Granger, Harper said, "If you can do me a favor and put me in front of a sketch artist, I think I can give a pretty good description."

Chapter Thirteen

Later that evening, Hattie sat at her kitchen table, pushing around chicken marsala on her plate. Hattie stabbed a mushroom and popped it in her mouth. "This wait is killing me," she said to Dante who hadn't eaten any more than her.

His full plate still in front of him, Dante asked, "What time did Harper say she'd be done with the sketch artist?"

"Det. Granger told Harper he'd be there at four, but that was nearly three hours ago. How long does it take?" Hattie dropped her fork and shoved her plate off to the side. "I was sure it was a woman. I was positive Harper would have seen Celeste."

Dante set the fork down. "I can't explain it any more than you can. We won't know anything until Harper gets back so we should try to just stay calm."

Hattie shot him a dirty look. "I guess that's easier for you since you've been dealing with this for a couple of centuries. I need answers now."

"Welcome to my world," Dante said, holding out his arms. He looked at her sympathetically. "Yes, I've been dealing with this a lot longer than you have, but not quite like this. I've not had anyone out there killing people trying to frame me for it." Dante shoved his chair back. "I've been sitting on the edge of my seat waiting to be arrested. If that happens, I could spend an eternity in prison. You can't exactly hide immortality there. What will happen then? I'll be stuck in some lab as a test study."

Hearing that, Hattie realized how ridiculous she sounded. She'd only been waiting a couple of hours. It didn't compare to Dante's plight. "We are going to make sure that doesn't happen."

Hattie brought her plate to the sink as Harper came through the back door. Hattie dropped her dishes and met Harper just as she crossed the threshold into the kitchen. "Do you have it?" Hattie asked, blocking Harper's path.

Harper laughed. "I have it. Calm down. Sorry it took me so long. The sketch artist was thorough and then Det. Granger stopped back down to my office to see it when I was done. He said we can keep this since he doesn't have an open investigation." Harper walked around her aunt into the kitchen. She spotted Dante at the table.

"I guess we can all see it together," Harper said with an edge of uncertainty in her voice.

Dante stood. "I can't thank you enough for using your gift to see who spelled Hattie. I'm sure by now you know my story. I'd be happy to answer any questions for you. I was so caught off guard yesterday when I saw your friend and then what you were asking, I just had to get out of there."

Harper nodded in understanding. "It was hard for Maggie, too. She thought your story was just a family legend. She had no idea until yesterday it was real. I hope you'll be willing to sit down with her at some point and discuss it. Maggie would like a chance to get to know you and learn more about her family."

"I'd like a chance to get to know her, too. She seems like a lovely young woman." Dante smiled and waited while Harper dug through her bag and pulled out a folder.

Harper opened the folder, took out the sketch, and handed the thick drawing paper over to Hattie.

Hattie took it from her and carefully scanned over the chalk-drawn

CHAPTER THIRTEEN

image. Dark almond-shaped eyes stared back at her. His thin lips were drawn into a straight stern line, and he had a clump of hair that cascaded over his forehead. The cloak covering his head shielded the rest. The man looked ordinary, if not attractive, to Hattie. She wouldn't have crossed the street if she saw him at night or thrown him out of her shop. He did not look like the monster his actions implied him to be. Not that they ever did. Many got away with the evilest deeds because they blended into society so well that even when they were found out, it was still hard to fathom. The man did not look familiar to her in any way. Hattie told them as much as she handed the paper to Dante.

Careful not to smudge the image with his finger, Dante gripped the sides. He dropped his head to look and immediately stumbled back to his chair. His hand flew to his mouth and the paper dropped to the table. "This can't be. It can't be him. He's dead."

Harper moved towards him. "Who is it, Dante?"

Dante looked up and shifted his eyes between Harper and Hattie. "It's Pierre, the man who cursed me, but it can't be. I assumed he was dead long ago."

Hattie went and sat next to him. "Dante, if he cursed you with immortality, then he might have done the same to himself. It could be that he doesn't see living forever as the curse you've found it to be."

Dante shook his head. "Don't you think I would have seen him over the years? He never sought me out. I never even saw him again after that night he cursed us. I tried so many times to find him later after we realized it was real to beg him to undo what he did, but I never found him again. I heard he had died."

Harper stepped forward. "Are you sure it's him? Could it be a relative of his who looks like him?"

"No," Dante said adamantly. "That's him. I'm sure of it."

Harper sat at the table with them and put her head in her hands. "This doesn't make a lot of sense to me. Dante, how would he know to use voodoo against Hattie? Matthew Inslee told Hattie the person he used to spell cast Hattie was named Celeste. If it's him, he had to have been watching you for a long time to know where you were and who you were interacting with."

"I wish I had some explanation, but I have nothing." Dante sat back dumbfounded, unable to say much more.

"What do we do?" Harper asked, looking to her aunt for help.

Hattie sat for several moments without responding. The truth was she didn't know. In all her years practicing her craft and learning from her mother and grandmother, Hattie had never come across a situation like this. It was so far out of her range of knowledge she didn't even know where to start. The only thing Hattie could do was what she'd always done. Use her intuition and call on her ancestors for guidance.

Hattie took a deep breath and exhaled slowly. She closed her eyes and repeated the same breathing over and over again until she cleared her mind. Harper and Dante remained quiet just watching and waiting. Hattie settled and mentally asked for guidance on how to improve the situation and help Dante. Then Hattie simply waited for the answer. After a few moments, it struck her out of the blue. Hattie questioned it because the thought seemed ridiculous, but it persisted, which is how she knew it was the right answer.

Hattie opened her eyes but didn't make eye contact with either of them. She stared straight ahead determined. "We have to go to New Orleans. It's the only way we can find and stop him."

"We can't do that!" Harper yelled suddenly. "There is no way we can go down there and dig around in this investigation. It's a serial homicide. I'm not afraid of stepping on Det. Granger's toes. He loves us, but we can't bother cops who don't know us. They will arrest us for interfering."

Dante shook his head. "Hattie, I have to agree with Harper. If I'm up here, I'm well outside of the city and they can't possibly accuse me of these murders, but if I go back down there to the lion's den, I'm done for."

"It's the only way," Hattie said adamantly. "If he's trying to draw you out, Dante, or frame you for these murders, Pierre is not going to stop killing people. We have to find him and put a stop to it. Plus, if I'm going to help you break this curse, I need access to real voodoo. I'm not going to get that here. I'm going with or without the two of you. I'm leaving tomorrow afternoon. Sarah and Beatrix can watch the shop."

Chapter Fourteen

"Tell me again about Hattie," Jackson said as he sat on a chair across from Harper's desk the next day. He had stopped into Harper's office after she called him.

Harper recounted the events of the previous day. "Hattie is convinced that to help Dante we have to go to New Orleans. Dante said we could stay at his house, but I'm not sure what she thinks she's going to do. It's not like here. New Orleans police aren't just going to let her get involved in their serial homicide investigation."

Jackson rolled his eyes. "I love Hattie so don't get me wrong, but she's out of control this time. Someone needs to talk some sense into her."

Harper laughed. "Why do you think I called you?"

Jackson pointed to his chest. "You think Hattie is going to listen to me? She's never listened to me before. She's not going to start now."

Harper drummed her fingers on the desk. "We have to do something. If not, I'm going to New Orleans."

"Good luck with that." Jackson laughed.

She pouted. "Seriously, you won't help me?" Harper hadn't thought he would, but she had called Jackson anyway, hoping he'd have some sage advice or warning not to get involved. At this point, Harper assumed he had stopped fighting her and Hattie on the crazy things

CHAPTER FOURTEEN

they did.

Jackson sat still for a few moments, then like a flash, he had an idea. "Let's both go to New Orleans with her. I haven't been to New Orleans in a while and it would be fun to explore the city with you."

Harper narrowed her eyes at him. "While there is a voodoo serial killer on the loose? It hardly sounds like a vacation."

Jackson shrugged and smirked at her. "Do you think either one of us is going to talk Hattie out of going?"

"No," Harper said resigned. "I was hoping you might have had some advice for me."

"I have nothing. But we can go with her and make the best of it. Neither one of us understands all this voodoo stuff so we won't be much help. The detective on the case definitely won't listen to Hattie so she'll be down there spinning her wheels. We can at least distract her from getting herself into too much trouble." Jackson sat back, pleased with his plan. "When do we leave?"

This is why Harper loved him so much. He was willing to make the best of a completely crazy situation. Jackson was willing to be there no matter what she needed.

"I love you," Harper said softly, not realizing until after the words were out of her mouth that she had said it aloud. They hadn't said the words before. The closest Jackson had come was saying he adored her. Harper looked down, feeling momentarily uncomfortable like she'd said too much and the bubble of happiness they had created might burst at any moment. Jackson wasn't letting her off the hook so easily.

"Harper," Jackson said and a rush of nervousness ran through her. "I love you, too."

Harper raised her eyes and looked at him. Jackson smiled sweetly, and she knew she hadn't made a mistake.

He laughed nervously. "This isn't exactly how I thought we'd say it to each other for the first time. I had pictured something a bit romantic, but I don't think if the feelings are real, the time and place matter."

Harper fell in love with him all over again at that moment. With a sheepish look on her face, she offered, "I didn't mean to blurt it out like that. I'm grateful for you. You're there no matter what I need or how crazy it might seem. You do it without even flinching. I don't have to talk you into it or anything."

"You're important to me. Hattie is like a second mother to me. When I arrived in town, I didn't know anyone, and I wasn't in the best frame of mind. Retiring from the Army had shaken my identity. My divorce had taken a toll emotionally, and Hattie was there. She didn't push me to talk. She didn't offer unsolicited advice. No questions were asked. Hattie jumped in making sure I felt like I was at home."

Jackson's eyes got soft as he looked at Harper. "Most importantly, Hattie introduced me to you. She told me about you before you even moved to Little Rock. She knew even then we'd be together. There isn't anything I wouldn't do for the both of you even if it means going to New Orleans to hunt down a voodoo serial killer." Jackson said the words and then chuckled. "Now that's a sentence I never thought I'd say."

"Right?" Harper said, shaking her head. She leaned her arms on her desk. "If you told me back when I lived in New York I'd be helping Hattie track down a voodoo serial killer because her old nemesis was cursed with immortality, I'd have thought you were crazy. Now, look at us!"

"Look at you doing what?" Dan asked from outside of Harper's door.

"Long lunch." Harper gave him a knowing glance. "How was your date?"

At hearing Dan had a date, Jackson beamed. He nudged the chair next to him. "Come sit down and tell us about this mystery woman." Jackson couldn't be more obvious if he tried. His jealousy over Dan and Harper's working relationship early on was well-known. It hadn't helped that Dan had asked Harper out shortly after they met.

CHAPTER FOURTEEN

Dan took the seat and chuckled, clearly embarrassed. "It was nothing," he said coyly. "We went out to dinner last night, too."

"You had sex!" Harper yelled.

Dan opened his mouth to speak, but no words came out. He looked to Jackson for help, but he just shrugged and laughed.

"Harper isn't wrong," Jackson said, slapping Dan on the back.

Dan rubbed his face. "I didn't realize it was obvious."

"You look happy, and we are happy for you. See what happens when you leave the office and venture out into the world?" It had been a running joke since Harper started working with Dan how little social life he had. Dan insisted he was happy, but Harper knew better. No man was an island, even Dan.

"All right, well you're embarrassing me so let's change the subject." Dan leaned back in the chair and kicked his ankle up on his other knee. "You're not usually here in the office, Jackson. I assume you're here for the same reason Hattie was this morning."

Harper explained their impending trip to New Orleans. She expected Dan to caution her or tell her he couldn't do without her in the office, but Dan said none of that.

"I think it's a good idea," Dan said firmly.

"You think it's a good idea?" Harper asked skeptically.

"Yeah, I do." Dan sat forward, planting both feet on the floor. He locked eyes with Harper, which let her know he was serious. "There's something nefarious going on with Dante beyond his curse of immortality. Dead bodies are piling up in New Orleans. If this killer figures out Dante is up here, do you want the killer coming up here and doing the same?"

Harper hadn't thought about it like that, but Dan was right. This killer was trying to frame Dante or get his attention. The less Dante paid attention to it, the more the killer upped his game. To keep him out of Little Rock, they had to go to New Orleans. Harper caught Jackson's expression. She knew he was mulling over the very same thing.

"You'll be okay without me in the office for a few days? I have no idea how long this will take."

"Take as long as you need," Dan said evenly. "The last thing we need up here is some deranged killer who can also curse people. I've seen enough horror movies to know it's not going to end well."

Harper gestured to the mess of files and photos stacked on her desk for the next issue of *Rock City Life*. "What about all this work?"

"I can handle it. I handled it all before I brought you on, and I was fine. I can handle it now." Dan paused, his face giving the look he had when he was hitting on an idea that hadn't quite formed yet. Finally, he pointed at Harper. "You should write a travel article about your visit to New Orleans."

Harper started to say no, but Dan cut her off. "Instead of a typical travel article, you can focus on the voodoo culture. You can take a look at it from a cultural and even historical perspective. It would have to fit with the current vibe of the magazine, but I think it would be interesting to people here. Many people visit New Orleans and they want a taste of the real city and culture instead of the tourist and tacky fake voodoo shops. You can give the readers something real."

Harper wasn't sure anyone wanted to hear about that. She wasn't even sure she wanted to know about it, but if it made Dan happy and gave her time to go with Hattie to New Orleans, she'd do it. "If you think our readers would like it, I can write it."

Chapter Fifteen

Hattie rushed around her bedroom grabbing the last few things she needed to pack into her suitcase. Dante had been skeptical when Hattie had told him she was going to New Orleans to look for Pierre. He tried to argue, but it got him nowhere. Dante left for New Orleans right after Harper had called home to tell Hattie that she and Jackson would go with her. Dante said he'd go ahead of them and get his house ready for guests. Hattie told him they'd be more than happy to stay at a local hotel, but Dante insisted. He had a six-bedroom home and no one staying in all those empty rooms. He told Hattie he had a housekeeper who would make sure the fridge was stocked and everything was ready for their arrival. Dante had expressed great doubt about the entire situation and whether anyone could reverse the curse or stop Pierre, but Hattie would not be deterred.

"Are you ready, Hattie?" Jackson called from the bottom of the stairs. "I'll carry your suitcase down."

"I'll be right there." Hattie finished putting the last of her things in the case and zipped it closed. She carried it to the edge of the stairs. "You can grab it now. Did you drop Sparkle and Shine off with your sister?"

Jackson turned the corner at the landing midway up the staircase. He jogged up the rest of the stairs to where she stood. "They are all set. Sarah is happy to have them, and Anabella is over the moon to have dogs in the house. She has been asking for a dog for months, but Sarah keeps putting her off. It's a good trial run in responsibility for her."

Hattie had fretted over the dogs. The last time she went away, she had a dog sitter come to the house, but she didn't have time to set that up this time. Sarah had offered, which brought Hattie great relief, but still, she worried. "I'm glad, but they are still my babies so I'm going to worry like an old mother hen."

Jackson grabbed her suitcase and carried it down the steps. "They are fine, I promise you," he called over his shoulder. "Anabella gave them treats and belly rubs, and they were in heaven."

Hattie grunted. "They probably will get so spoiled they won't want to come home." As Hattie started her descent down the steps, familiar energy radiated protectively behind her.

"You know I'm not letting you go alone," Beau said quietly, which was silly because no one but Hattie could hear him.

"Do you think that's a good idea?" Hattie whispered back.

"Why, my love?"

"It's New Orleans. Who knows how many people have this gift? Are you willing to be seen?"

"I'm going to do whatever is necessary to protect my wife. While I'd love nothing more than to have you in my arms again, you have a lot of life left in you. I know Harper and Jackson will be there, but I can see what they can't. I'll feel better if I'm there."

Hattie turned her head to gaze up at him. "I'd marry you all over again." Hattie gave him Dante's address and said she would see him later. While Hattie had nearly a seven-hour car ride in front of her, Beau's method of spectral transportation was a little more efficient.

Buckled into the back seat of Harper's SUV, Hattie asked, "Are you sure you want to go with me? Once we are down there, it could get messy."

From the passenger seat, Harper reached her hand back to Hattie.

CHAPTER FIFTEEN

"We are sure. There is no way you are doing this alone. Besides, Dan gave me an idea for an article so I'm multi-tasking."

Jackson started the SUV and pulled out of Hattie's driveway. She had wondered if Harper would argue with him about driving her car, but there wasn't even a discussion. Harper simply handed over the keys and that was that.

Hattie reached into her bag and found the silk pouch she had brought with her. Inside, she slid her fingers across the smooth tiger eye stones. She reached her hand between the seats. She had two stones, one for each of them. "Here you go. Take one and carry it on your person at all times."

Harper picked up both stones from Hattie's hand. She stared down at them taking in their gold and dark brown hues. "Is this tiger's eye?" she asked her aunt.

"You're getting better at identifying the stones. Studying up?"

Harper glanced back at Hattie. "You gave me the book of gemstones and told me to learn them, their properties, and uses. I did what you asked."

"Good girl," Hattie said happily. "Yes, that's exactly what they are. I've done a spell over them. They are naturally protective stones. I gave them an extra boost, super-charged them so to speak. You must carry them with you at all times. Understand?"

"I can carry it, but I don't understand what it will do?" Jackson asked as he navigated onto the interstate.

"There's more we will need to do down there to protect ourselves. The stone is just the first step, but it will work to create a shield around your energy field. You still need to make smart decisions, but think of it as a little spiritual protection."

Jackson held his hand out to Harper and she dropped one of the stones onto his palm. He slid it into his pocket without another word. Harper did the same.

Pointing to Hattie's bag where she had carried the stones, Harper asked, "What else do you have in there?"

Hattie patted the side of it. "I have a few things we will need for protection as well as the grimoire and some supplies. I don't know what we will encounter down there, but I wanted to be as prepared as possible. We aren't dealing with a serial killer in the typical sense. We are dealing with someone who is using very dark magic and killing for the sport of it. Those people did not have to die for Pierre to make his point, whatever that may be. He is showing his power, and I believe with everything in me, he'd use it against us if he finds we are helping Dante."

Jackson changed lanes and glanced at Hattie in the rearview mirror. "Hattie, correct me if I'm wrong, but we don't know that it's Pierre who is killing people. We know from Harper's vision he was the one who put voodoo in your yard, but we have no confirmation he's the one killing people or even why."

Harper reached across the console and put her hand on his thigh. "I have to agree with Hattie. No, we don't have proof it's him, but Pierre used Celeste's voodoo symbol on the voodoo left in Hattie's yard and now it's on the dolls left at these crime scenes. I think we can assume at this point, it's all Pierre."

Jackson looked at her skeptically. "I think we should keep an open mind."

They settled into the car ride without much conversation at all. Hattie spent the time searching her memory for every interaction with Dante. Now that Hattie knew the truth, she had a different perspective on her past. Dante's desperation for her to be a part of his life and share her power with him made perfect sense. He had been desperate. A tinge of guilt worked its way up her spine, but Hattie shut it down quickly. She had never been one to live with regret. Her life could have turned out completely different if she had given in to Dante back then, and Hattie

CHAPTER FIFTEEN

wouldn't entertain it. She loved everything about her life and wouldn't change a thing, other than having Beau live longer.

Night had long since fallen and there wasn't much to see, but as they got closer to New Orleans, the energy took on a different vibe. Hattie wouldn't say ominous, just heavier. She wouldn't be surprised if the veil between the living and the dead was thinner in the city. Until that very moment, Hattie hadn't given any thought to other spirits she might encounter. She was so used to the ones she already saw. Those experiences, while startling at times, had always turned out pleasant. Hattie wasn't sure what she would do faced with a spirit darker in energy.

As if sensing Hattie's thoughts, Harper asked, "Does anyone else feel weird?"

"I always feel weird when I come to New Orleans," Jackson said, surprising Hattie. "I never know what it is, maybe the weight of history is stronger since not a lot has changed or maybe it's just the folklore of the city clouding my perception."

"It's the voodoo and the dead, Jackson. It impacts the energy of a place," Hattie said evenly. "Even if you don't believe or don't think you have gifts of your own, we are all born with the gift of intuition. You may deny you have it, but it's still there."

They fell back into silence as Jackson drove. Hattie peered out the window noting the bayous and the small shacks that lined them. Louisiana had a culture all its own. It had been a long time since Hattie had been to New Orleans.

Jackson navigated off the interstate and delivered them onto city streets. Hattie was surprised. He didn't even need directions to get them to the French Quarter. He checked his phone only once for the address and confirmed it with her.

"If you cut down an alleyway, there is a small two-car driveway in the back of his home. It's narrow though as it was built for horse and carriage," Hattie explained.

Jackson did just that, navigating the narrow streets of the French Quarter with ease. There wasn't much traffic at that time of night. Hattie hoped at nearing eleven Dante was still awake. He had texted her a few hours ago and assured her he would be.

Passing a two-story home whose brick had been painted a sterling gray, Jackson pointed. "That's the house."

Hattie peered up, fighting off a growing sense of dread as they passed the house and cut down an alley to the back.

Chapter Sixteen

"I hope your drive was smooth," Dante said, helping Jackson with their luggage.

Jackson offered a strained smile. "It was as good as can be expected, but I think we are all a bit tired."

"Certainly, come on in." Dante took two suitcases and navigated the brick walkway through a small courtyard which featured an elegant white fountain in the center. Comfortable chairs were positioned around the patio and potted shrubs and flowers hugged the sides. Even if the space was small, Dante had created a comfortable outdoor sitting area.

Harper, Jackson, and Hattie followed Dante into the back of the home through a narrow hallway that brought them right into the kitchen. Original brick anchored one wall while the other had been painted a muted grayish-blue. The cabinets, countertops, and appliances were all fairly new. The center island with its marble countertop couldn't have been more than a few years old. It was certainly an updated space.

Dante caught Hattie admiring the design. "Being immortal gives you a lot of time for a redesign. I've tried to keep up with it through the years. I just had this done a few years ago. The space is the same, no walls knocked down, but it's nothing like it was when we first built it."

"It's lovely," Hattie said truthfully. The kitchen led into a dining room and then an open living room with comfortable furniture. The room had an original fireplace and floor to ceiling doors flanked by thick drapes on each side. It gave it a dramatic effect. The home featured exposed brick and moldings Hattie was sure were original. Dante had melded old with new in a way that impressed her.

"Those open," Dante said, pointing to the doorways. He pointed to the top. "For security, there are latches at the top and bottom. I don't open the outside shutters much though. It's so open to the street that tourists can see right in. I like a bit more privacy than that. When the home was first built, they were open all the time. Unfortunately, closed and shuttered blocks a bit of light, but it's better than the alternative. Through the years, I've often thought of taking them out and putting in real windows, but this was a feature Celeste loved the most about the home, and I couldn't bear to change it."

Harper stepped around Hattie and into the living room. She glanced in every direction. Turning back to Dante, she said, "This is the room I saw in my vision. Both of my visions. The one from back in the 1700s and the other with you sitting by the fireplace more recently."

Dante nodded. "That doesn't surprise me. This is the most used room in the home. It always has been. I have another sitting room upstairs I used often, but this room has always been about entertaining. I read in here sometimes, too."

Dante took them up the front staircase to the second floor. At the landing, the hallway forked to the left and the right. Dante carried their bags to the right to the front of the home. "I thought I'd put each of you in a room in the front of the house. Both rooms open to the wide front veranda. I thought you might like the breeze that comes in. Now that it's fall, we can stand to have the windows open. There are tables and chairs out there. It's quite relaxing."

"Where is your room?" Hattie asked as she stepped into one of the bedrooms.

"I'm in the back." Dante set Hattie's suitcase down on the floor.

CHAPTER SIXTEEN

"This room used to be my bedroom when we first built the house. I stayed in here for quite a while, but since Celeste left this last time, I couldn't bear it anymore. Too many memories. It's a lovely room though, and I hope you'll be comfortable."

Hattie offered him a sad smile. The room was lovely. It had a large four-poster bed and antique dresser and mirror. There was a comfortable-looking chair and ottoman in the corner. She stepped toward the front of the room and opened the French doors that sat behind sheer curtains. Dante was right; the front veranda was a spectacular feature. The wide-open space would be perfect for relaxing in the evening or with morning coffee. When Hattie stepped back into the bedroom, Dante was gone, but she could hear him talking to Harper across the hall. She followed their voices into the other bedroom.

"Dante, I know it's late, but I was hoping to see any information you have about Pierre," Harper said.

Hattie added, "I'd also like to see anything you have about the curse. Spells you've tried, anything you've learned. I know you, Dante. I'm sure you've kept immaculate records."

Dante stepped forward and took Hattie's hand affectionately. "I have. I'll go down and start some hot tea for all of you. Once you feel settled, come down and I'll show you everything."

Hattie squeezed his hand and went back to her bedroom. She closed the bedroom door behind her and took a big deep breath. Pulling her suitcase to the bed, she began to unpack enough to find a change of shirt. When she was done, Hattie opened the closet and dropped her suitcase inside along with her special bag with her grimoire and magical supplies.

As Hattie bent over to ensure that the bag was hidden out of view, a cold chill ran up her spine. Hattie straightened up and pivoted her body slowly to face the room. When she did, Hattie came face to face with the spirit of a man dressed in blue pants that came to his knees, white socks that covered the lower half of his legs and a brown jacket buttoned once at the chest that flowed down to mid-thigh. The clothes were common for the late 1700s. He had a cap in hand and jumped back as surprised as Hattie that he could be seen.

"Excuse me, ma'am, I didn't mean to startle you," the man said sheepishly. "I didn't know anyone could see me."

Hattie swallowed hard. "Do you make a habit of sneaking up on women?"

"Of course not." The man stepped back out of Hattie's way as she brushed past him. "You just have an energy about you that gives off the warmest strongest light. I could see it from the street."

Hattie smiled shyly at him. It was clear he meant her no harm or offense so she let down her guard and introduced herself.

The man did a slight bow forward. "I'm Louis. I was a friend and business partner of Dante's. I stop by from time to time to check on him. It's an awful thing that happened to him."

"It was," Hattie agreed. "It's actually why I'm here. Do you know about the murders happening here in the city? The ones with the voodoo dolls?"

"I've heard talk," Louis said sternly. He moved to the corner of the room and sat in the chair. "There have always been strange happenings in this city, even during my time. I've not seen the person committing these heinous acts if that's what you want to know, but there's talk on both your side and mine. It needs to be stopped."

Hattie went to the French doors which were still open to the veranda. "How do you think Dante is doing? I can't imagine having to live his life, never dying and repeating a relationship over and over again only to part in the end."

"It's no life at all, but he makes the best of it. I'm not sure he likes what he's become, using the same voodoo that cursed him. He had a hard time for a while. Anger built up inside of him, but in the last few

CHAPTER SIXTEEN

years, he has been gentler. Dante seems to have made some peace with it so all of this happening now doesn't make a lot of sense."

Hattie turned to him. "Have you seen Pierre, the one who cursed him?"

"Not in many years, but he didn't die at a normal age if that's what you're asking. I think Pierre did the same thing to himself he did to Dante or it was done to him."

Hattie raised her eyebrows. "Have you seen Celeste?"

"Not since the night of the fire." Louis glanced down at his hands.

Hattie was sure he was lying or at least had more to tell. She urged him on, but he didn't say anything else about Celeste. "Please keep your eye out for us. We need all the help we can get."

Louis readily agreed and disappeared before Hattie's eyes. She exhaled still not quite used to seeing spirits of people she didn't know. At least he was friendly and someone Dante had known.

Hattie headed out of her room and knocked once on Harper's door, letting her and Jackson know to meet her downstairs. New Orleans may have a strange vibe for Hattie, but Dante's house was warm, inviting, and comfortable. She found him in the kitchen preparing a tray of tea and treats for them.

"It's like being back at my shop," Hattie said as she entered the room and walked to the counter where Dante stood. "Let me help you with that."

He shooed Hattie out of the way, smiling down at her. "I have it." He produced a black antique key from his pocket and placed it in her hand. "Are you sure you're ready to see all I've accumulated over the years?"

Hattie held the key up, examining it with interest. She'd never held a key quite this old before. "What door does this unlock?"

Dante didn't answer but waved for her to follow him. Hattie trailed behind him as Dante went into the living room and to a bookshelf in the far corner of the room. He reached behind the books on the third shelf from the top. Hattie couldn't see what he was doing, but suddenly a narrow section of the wall next to the fireplace popped open. Dante pointed. "You'll need the key for the second door."

Hattie walked into the narrow space and saw that there was indeed a second door. She fit the key into the lock and pushed it open. Behind her, Dante flipped on the lights. Hattie's breath caught in her throat as she took in the space. Stacks of papers, books, and journals filled every corner of the room. Hattie went to speak but no words came out. She went to the stacks, running her hands over them. Old photos were tacked to the wall. "There's so much," Hattie said in a whisper.

"It's more than two hundred years' worth of information searching for a way to break the curse," Dante said sadly.

Chapter Seventeen

Harper sat up in bed, the pillows propped strategically behind her back, as she watched Jackson sleep soundly. She didn't know how he did it. Harper was a bit irrationally angry he had slept so well while she tossed and turned next to him. In total, she maybe slept four hours, but it wasn't the deep peaceful rest she was used to. After seeing Dante's room where he kept his centuries' worth of research, her stomach had knotted with an overwhelming sense of failure before they had even started.

Jackson hadn't said much. He raised his eyebrows and took it all in. After, when they finally snuggled into bed, Harper had expressed her worry and fear about helping Dante. Jackson had simply patted her arm, pulled her down into him, and kissed her sweetly, reminding her it would all look better in the morning. Except it didn't. Not even close.

It seemed Dante had tried everything to break the curse. He had consulted shamans, witches, voodoo practitioners. He had even traveled to Africa and spoken to hoodoo priestesses who were known far and wide as being the most powerful on the continent. He traveled to Haiti and did the same. Dante tried everything they told him. He sat for every ritual they performed and still nothing.

Harper had even held objects Dante had collected over the years, hoping to gain some vision of anything that might help, but so far, there was nothing. Her heart ached for the man who wanted nothing more than to stop living. Harper knew without even speaking to Hattie that she had been overwhelmed, too. Harper wasn't sure what time Hattie went to bed, but she was still reading when Harper finally had enough and had to retire to sleep.

The curse was out of Harper's depth. She had to admit it to herself right now, which meant she wasn't going to be any help to Hattie or Dante in solving the curse. Harper and Jackson would work on finding the killer, but she hoped that also meant finding Pierre.

The killer had murdered seven already. Harper wanted to make sure it wasn't eight. She nudged Jackson's side and he looped an arm over her lap. "Wake up. We need to make a plan."

He grunted. "Not a very nice way to wake me up. What about some cuddles and a kiss?"

"There's no time for that."

Jackson snuggled her closer. "There's always time for that." Harper wasn't giving in so he rolled onto his back and inched himself up into a sitting position. He leaned over and sweetly kissed her cheek. "Okay, what's so pressing it can't wait?"

"Seven dead bodies."

Jackson rubbed his bald head and yawned. "Getting right to murder so early, I see."

"I can't help it," Harper said softly, changing her tone. "I'm worried about Hattie and being here. The faster we find this guy, the sooner we can go home."

"Have you heard from Det. Granger?"

"No. I don't think there's a lot he can do for us." Harper pinched the spot between her eyes. "We are going to have to handle this on our own. Where do we start?"

Jackson exhaled loudly and kicked his legs out from under the covers. "We need to start with the victims and learn who they are, how the murders happened and see if there is any connection among them."

CHAPTER SEVENTEEN

Harper knew Jackson would come through for her. He had a logical mind like no other. No matter how much her brain might spin, Jackson knew. "Do we start with the police?"

"Not yet," Jackson said, pausing. After a few beats, he said, "Let's start with the newspaper and connect with the journalist who has written the most. They speak your language. You can use the metaphysical angle and the story you're writing for *Rock City Life* as our in. We gather as much intel as possible and go from there."

Harper smiled, leaned over, and kissed him before jumping out of bed and making some calls.

Two hours later, Harper and Jackson sat in the office of Rick Broussard, a senior reporter from *The New Orleans Advocate*, which had been in operation since 1837. Rick happened to have gone to high school with Harper's friend Maggie and was more than happy to answer any questions they had.

Rick stood close to six-three, had a solid build, and a grip like he could take down a lion with his bare hands. He had pleasant features and an easy relaxed smile. Harper liked him immediately. Jackson seemed to take to him as well.

"Maggie said you're writing an article for *Rock City Life* about New Orleans voodoo. Is that correct?" Rick asked, sitting on the edge of his desk. He had already offered them coffee, which they had declined. They had both been full from the breakfast Dante had made for them.

"It's a little more complex than that," Harper explained from across the room. She and Jackson sat on a comfortable couch across from Rick's desk. Harper had a notepad in front of her and a pen. "I'm not looking to do the typical tourist article about voodoo. I want to talk to real practitioners and better understand the culture of it. It's not a side-show attraction for me. I'm here though because Maggie said you've been covering the recent murders where voodoo dolls have been left at the scenes."

Rick's eyebrows went up. "I wouldn't think a lifestyle magazine would cover something like that."

Harper waved him off. "We cover a range of topics. I assume there's no way to tell if the person committing these murders is a real practitioner of voodoo or if it's just some sick calling card, but the angle is tied into my story. I'm sure Maggie also mentioned my aunt is a practicing spiritualist, and I have some magical gifts up my sleeve, too." Harper hadn't been sure she'd reveal this to Rick, but when Maggie called him, she had been eager to tell him about Harper and Hattie. The cat was already out of the bag. Harper didn't feel any desire to walk it back.

Rick smiled. "Maggie mentioned it, but she gets excited about these kinds of things. I wasn't sure if she was just joshing me or being truthful."

"Truthful," Jackson said wryly. He held his hands up. "No tricks up my sleeve. The Ryan women though are unstoppable, Rick. You're better off just giving in and telling Harper what she wants to know or she's going to stalk your office all day."

"Oh, I'm going to give you everything you want. I can't make heads or tails of this case myself, and between you and me, neither can the police. Seven bodies and not even the hint of a suspect." Rick hopped off his desk and went around to the back. He grabbed a stack of newspapers piled high in a corner and motioned with his head for Harper and Jackson to follow him. "Let's go down to the conference room where you can spread out."

Once inside, Jackson and Harper took a seat at the table opposite each other and each picked up a newspaper. Rick stood at the edge of the doorway. "I'm going to get you coffee. You're going to need it. I'll give you some time to read through and then you can ask me anything you want."

Harper agreed his plan was a good one. Before Rick left, Harper asked,

CHAPTER SEVENTEEN

"Have you made any sort of timeline of the crimes or what happened to the victims on the lead up to their murders?"

Rick pointed to the middle of the stack. "We just put out an article like that yesterday. It's in there." He disappeared behind the wall and out of sight.

"That was easier than I thought it would be," Jackson said as he unfolded the first paper and positioned it for better reading.

"We might as well start easy because I don't think it's getting any easier from here." Usually newspaper people had all the gossip and the real news. It shook Harper a little that Rick didn't seem to have either, which meant Rick was right – no one was close to a suspect on this one.

Jackson and Harper dug into the stories, each consumed with an article and then trading. After reading each article start-to-finish twice, Harper jotted detailed notes about each victim, including their biographical details, any known information about their lives, and information leading up to the murder and then about each crime scene. Since Harper didn't have a big dry erase board to see it all in one snapshot, her notebook would have to do. She created a page or two for each case for easier reference later.

Rick came in and dropped off two cups, a full carafe of coffee, a plate of beignets, and cream and sugar. "If you need anything else, just let me know. Come down to my office when you're done and we can go over everything." Rick gave a friendly wave and left them to do their work.

"Maggie was right," Jackson said, pouring them both coffee. "Rick is a nice guy."

Harper thanked Jackson for the coffee and took a sip, quietly pleased Jackson knew just how she liked it. Setting the cup down, she said, "I could be wrong, but I think Maggie has a bit of a crush on him."

Jackson laughed. "Are you going to play matchmaker while you're here?"

"We have enough going on without getting involved in Maggie's love life, but I approve if she wants to go for it."

"Does Maggie approve of me?"

"Of course she does. She might even have a little crush on you, too, but don't get any ideas."

Jackson grinned ear to ear. "I am quite lovable," he teased.

Chapter Eighteen

Soon after Harper and Jackson had left in the morning, Hattie and Dante did, too. Hattie wanted to see the city and feel its energetic hum firsthand before she did anything else. She had told Dante she wanted to click her heels against the gravel under her feet, smell the scents wafting through the air, and see for her own eyes the narrow streets and alleyways that made up the French Quarter. It was more than just a tourist jaunt through the city. Historical landmarks, voodoo shops, and the swath of bars and restaurants weren't what Hattie was after. She wanted to absorb the energy around her, feel its pulsating vibe.

They walked for blocks, going from Dante's home on Chartres Street back to Rampart Street to Louis Armstrong Park, traversing up and down the main and cross streets making sure to cover nearly every inch. Hattie couldn't quite explain the sensations shimmering through her body as she and Dante walked. For moments, it was almost like she had Harper's gift of slipping back in time. Hattie could have sworn the people she passed were from a different era. At times, it seemed instead of concrete under her feet, she could feel the dirt that once marked the roadways. If Hattie had to describe it to someone, it was like she slipped back and forth between present and past.

Quite possibly, the people she passed were from a different era because the people she was seeing were spirits who roamed the city.

New Orleans often landed on the blogs, articles, and maps as one of the most haunted cities in America and that was before Hurricane Katrina. These spirits were different though if that's what was happening. The thick veil between the living and the dead Hattie experienced in other places seemed to vanish in New Orleans. The dead walked among the living as if they were still alive, taking up the same space, separated simply by time. Hattie had a vision into both worlds at once, and it was as wondrous as it was disorienting.

Hattie had been so quiet that Dante eventually grew concerned. "Are you okay?" he asked as they hit the corner of St. Louis and St. Peter's streets right near Jackson Square. Dante directed them into Jackson Square to walk along the well-manicured lawns.

"I'm fine. It's just a lot to take in," Hattie said quietly. She was telling the truth. It was a lot to take in – the sights, smells, sounds, and energy both good and bad.

Dante walked next to Hattie, his hands clasped behind his back as if they were out for an leisurely stroll. It was clear to Hattie just how comfortable Dante felt in the city. It was after all his home for hundreds of years. He and his wife were among the first to open a shop as the city grew up around them. New Orleans was as much a part of Dante as he was a son of the city – linked forever, literally.

Dante kept taking glances down at Hattie, and she knew how pensive she must look. Hattie relaxed her face and tried to smile. The most she could accomplish was a slight upturn at the corners of her mouth. She turned her head to look up at him, the sun blinding her as she did.

Hattie held her hand up to shield her eyes. "I'm really okay. I promise you. I'm just trying to get a feel for the city so we can get to work. I really think..." Hattie didn't finish her thought because she was stunned into silence by the intense white light pulsating above Dante's head. It was more than the sun.

Hattie blinked again and tried to adjust her eyes. It was the third time

CHAPTER EIGHTEEN

she blinked when she saw him. Hattie couldn't quite believe her eyes, but she also couldn't look away. Appearing before her was an angel or at least that's what Hattie thought it was. He came to her in the image she most associated with angels during her endless years of Catholic school. While she couldn't quite make out the details of his face, the light was so blinding, he was cloaked in blue and had wings the shiniest gold she had ever seen coming from his back. In his hands, he held a long silver blade. As she took him in, her whole body warmed. The anxiety she had been carrying around, weighing her down for the past few weeks, eased away and was replaced by a radiating peace she had never quite felt before.

Hattie went to speak, but no words came out.

Go back to your roots to save his soul.

Hattie wasn't sure if the angel spoke those words aloud or if it was something she just heard in her head, but the words repeated and then repeated again. The angel left as quickly as he appeared. Hattie stumbled back several feet and nearly fell, but she found her footing and righted herself.

When Hattie finally adjusted her eyes, the concern on Dante's face startled her. He rushed towards her. Gripping her arms, he asked, "Hattie, my dear, are you ill? Are you okay? Speak to me."

Hattie shook herself out of the fog. "I'm fine. I'm fine," she reassured.

"You startled me. I thought you were having a stroke." Dante exhaled several breaths loudly as he, too, tried to regain his composure.

Hattie laughed. "Nothing quite as dramatic as that. I saw a vision of...an angel, I believe."

Dante blinked rapidly as he took in what she said. He asked Hattie to repeat it so she told him about her vision. When Hattie was done, Dante said, "I don't know about your world, but seeing angels sounds pretty dramatic to me."

"It was just one angel," Hattie corrected. "He gave me a message. He said, 'Go back to your roots to save his soul.'"

"What does that mean?"

"I'm not quite sure, but I was raised Catholic. Those are my roots. My family has blended Catholicism and our spiritual gifts through the centuries."

Dante raised his eyebrows. "I was raised Catholic, too. Maybe it's time we both got back to our roots." Dante pointed across Jackson Square. "St. Louis Cathedral is right there. We should stop in."

Hattie simply nodded and followed him through the winding path. As they stood across the street taking in the beautiful architecture, Dante said solemnly, "I watched every phase of construction of this church. There has been a church on this spot of land since I came to this city. The first church burned in the great fire, but they rebuilt again soon after – stronger and better than before."

Hattie reached her hand out and laced her fingers through his. It wasn't a romantic gesture on her part, but one made in friendship and support. She said jokingly, "I've never been inside. Hopefully, when we both enter, the whole church won't collapse around us."

Dante's lips curled up in a smile. "I come here sometimes and pray. Never for mass but on my own. I think I'm good, but let's be careful of you – you heathen."

Hattie squeezed his hand and they walked across the street and into the entrance of the church. Cold air washed over Hattie as soon as she entered. It was almost like feeling a blast of the air conditioner but none was on. She imagined on a hot New Orleans day it was a welcome relief. Hattie wasn't sure what to look at first. Her eyes wandered over the architecture and grandness of the cathedral. As they stepped down the main aisle of the church, Hattie strained her eyes to see the flags overhead. She wasn't sure what they represented, but she identified among them flags from other countries and those from other Catholic dioceses.

Dante sat in a pew midway up the aisle and Hattie slid in next to him. They blessed themselves and said the Lord's Prayer, Hail Mary and Glory Be together. It had been a long time since Hattie said the words, but they flowed from her as if she said them every day. She had never thought about Dante being religious before. He had been so steeped in voodoo the entire time she knew him that Hattie assumed the church would have been off-limits. She said as much.

Quietly, Dante explained, "The history of voodoo and Catholicism has always been intertwined. Back during the time of slavery even, voodoo was not permitted on the plantations so slaves would cloak their activity in Catholicism. Altars they set up to pray to the voodoo Loas would feature Catholic saints. As the city grew and voodoo leaders became more widely recognized, culture intertwined. You'd never find voodoo practiced in a Catholic church. It hasn't been sanctioned by the Vatican, but there have been many Catholics who sought out voodoo prayers and blessings. It's an odd blend, but so is New Orleans."

Hattie thought about what Dante said. She remembered her schooling and novenas including candle lighting and prayers for the intercession of saints. In truth, it wasn't all that dissimilar to spell work – the intention being the crux of it all. She looked up at Dante. "Maybe there is something to my vision after all."

He glanced down at her. "It is the one thing I've never tried."

"Then we should," Hattie said, settled on the idea. "We need help though. Is there a parish priest here we can speak with?"

Dante sat still for several moments. "Not the parish priest here, but I know someone who might be able to help. I probably should have gone to him a long time ago."

Chapter Nineteen

As Hattie and Dante stepped back out of the church onto the road, Hattie asked, "Where are we headed?"

"To see Father Ignatius Cormier."

"That's a mouthful. Why not the parish priest?"

Dante shook his head. "The parish priest is fairly new and not from here. I think the diocese moved him in from out of state. From what I heard, he's not too favorable to voodoo. We need someone who will not only believe my story but who is steeped enough in New Orleans to understand voodoo and its history."

What Dante said made sense to Hattie. No point seeking out the help of someone who would just think they were crazy or worse judge Dante. It was the last thing they needed especially because they needed answers and help as soon as possible.

"Fr. Cormier is such a man?" Hattie asked.

"He will believe. I don't know that he'll be able to help, but he's been steeped in the supernatural for as long as I've known him. He's an exorcist who worked directly at the Vatican. He's retired now but hasn't lost his edge."

Hattie furrowed her brow. "You're not possessed though? Are you?"

When they left the church, they had taken a right back onto Chartres Street. Before getting back to Dante's house, they ducked down an alleyway and then another until they came upon a small entrance to a narrow three-story home.

Standing at the door, Dante shook his head. "I'm not possessed, but Fr. Cormier knows dark practices and how to counter them. He was a priest here many years ago. I knew him well. He comes from a long line of Catholic priests in his family. I knew a great-great uncle of his back in the 1860s." Dante smiled. "Of course, I never told him that. Fr. Cormier was chosen by the Vatican to go to school to become an exorcist many years ago. He is world-renowned for his work."

Dante paused, a slow smile turning up the corners of his mouth. "He's also a bit of a character."

Hattie tried to do the math to figure out how old the priest might be, but her brain wasn't firing on all cylinders right now. "How old is he?"

"Well into his eighties, but you'd never know it."

"Why haven't you sought his help before?" Hattie asked.

"I don't know why it never occurred to me. Fr. Cormier has been gone from here for much of his life. He's only been back a few years, and by then, I had given up hope my condition could be helped." Dante reached his hand up to knock but stopped short of laying his knuckles against the door. "You know possession is rare, right?"

"I never gave it much thought, to be honest with you. I assumed most of it was misunderstood mental health issues and drug addiction. Others blame everything that doesn't agree with their religion on the devil. I guess I've never quite believed it was real."

"Oh, it's real, but very rare, thankfully." Dante rapped on the door hard enough to shake the whole house. When Dante saw the way Hattie looked at him for pounding on the door, he explained, "Fr. Cormier is a bit hard of hearing these days and refuses to put in his hearing aid. If I were him, I'd probably want to drown out the world, too."

Hattie took a deep breath. The peace she had felt in the church had passed as the anxiety crept back in. Dante had to knock again, but soon after, an older man yelled from inside the home that he was on his way.

Hattie wasn't sure what to expect, but the man who pulled open the door and asked what the heck they wanted looked nothing like she had imagined.

Fr. Cormier stood close to her height and had a head full of messy white hair. He had hazel eyes with a ring of dark brown around the pupil and a ruddy complexion.

"Dante," he said with an affable smile plastered ear to ear. "Why didn't you say it was you? You know those darn kids frequently knock and run. I thought it was them. Come on in. Who is your lovely companion?" Fr. Cormier stepped out of the way and let them enter his house.

Hattie introduced herself as Fr. Cormier nudged them down the hall into the kitchen. "Let's sit and have a drink." He moved around the kitchen with an ease Hattie didn't often see for a man his age.

Looking over his shoulder, he winked at Hattie. "I much prefer the bourbon I was drinking before you arrived, but if you want the tea, I can oblige."

"It's eleven in the morning," Hattie shrieked, looking between Dante and Fr. Cormier.

Wide-eyed, Fr. Cormier hitched his chin toward Dante. "Where'd you find this one – a convent?" He had a good laugh at himself as he puttered around the kitchen. He glanced back at Hattie. "What will it be? I can mix the bourbon with ginger ale or soda water if that makes you feel better." He picked up his glass. "I prefer it exactly as God intended though and so does Dante." The priest slid a glass over to Dante.

"Tea will be fine," Hattie said stiffly.

"Don't get your panties in a bunch. I'm retired." He held out his arms. "I haven't even worn a collar in three years. Those old black frocks are hung up for good. Let your hair down, sister."

Hattie narrowed her eyes at him, feeling a little put out. He wasn't

CHAPTER NINETEEN

like any priest she had ever met. Nicely, she said, "Tea, please, will do just fine. Thank you, Father."

Fr. Cormier pointed and shook his finger at her. "None of that Father crap either. Just call me Iggy. Everyone else does."

"Iggy?" she asked, her voice dropping in surprise.

"It's my name. It's what my mother called me. Iggy is good enough for me." He went back to making tea for Hattie.

Dante nudged her side and whispered, "I told you he was a character."

"Are you sure he can help?" Hattie asked quietly.

Dante just shrugged and took a sip of his bourbon. After a few minutes, Iggy slid Hattie's tea in front of her and sat down.

"Is this a social call?" he asked, leaning back in his chair and drinking his bourbon.

"Not exactly," Dante started cautiously. "Hattie had a vision earlier today, and it led me to believe you might be able to help us."

Iggy shifted his eyes to Hattie. "What kind of vision?"

Hattie swallowed. She had known she was going to have to tell him, but right at the moment, her throat felt dry and the words didn't come. Hattie took a sip of her tea and set the cup back down. "It's all a bit more complicated than the vision..." she started.

"It usually is." Iggy gave her a knowing look.

Hattie rested her arms on the table. "I had the vision while I was walking through Jackson Square. Suddenly, there was an angel overhead giving me advice about what I should do about a challenge I'm facing."

Iggy nodded. "An angel, huh?" He got up and walked out of the room. Dante and Hattie watched him go down the hall until he disappeared out of sight without another word.

"I don't see how he's going to be much help if I scared him off that easily," Hattie said.

Dante pointed as Iggy moved back into the hall and shut a door behind him. He had a thin maroon-colored book in his hand. Iggy came back to the table, took the last swig of his bourbon, poured himself another, and then sat back down.

He slid the book toward Hattie. "Look in there and tell me who you saw."

Hattie took it and opened the first page. It was a book on angels, including pictures, descriptions, specialties, colors, and more. Archangel Raphael, Hattie read, often comes to people with a green glow or light around him. His healing energy has been known to miraculously cure people. Archangel Chamuel was the angel of relationships. Hattie's eyes scanned over the pictures and texts completely mesmerized. She had no idea there were so many named angels.

Hattie looked up at Iggy. "Is this sanctioned by the Catholic Church?"

"Not officially, but you're going to have to trust me on its veracity. Keep reading and find who showed themselves to you."

Hattie dropped her head back to the book, growing more and more distrustful of the strange priest. She tried to block out her unease as she skimmed the pages. Hattie's stomach dropped when she came upon the image from her vision.

Pointing to the page, Hattie said excitedly, "This is it. This is who I saw." She pushed the book towards Iggy.

He glanced down and then looked up quickly at her with a smirk on his face. "You must have something very dangerous happening in your world for Archangel Michael to visit you. He's around but rarely shows himself. Care to explain?"

Hattie did not care to explain because she didn't believe him. "Archangel Michael? Really? You expect me to believe the Archangel Michael visited me?" She believed in Archangel Michael, many religions and spiritual and non-spiritual folks alike did as well. It wasn't that Hattie didn't believe in angels or Archangel Michael's power. Hattie simply couldn't believe he had chosen to show himself to

CHAPTER NINETEEN

her. Hattie looked between Iggy and Dante for one of them to explain themselves but neither said a word.

"You saw with your own eyes," Iggy said finally, leaving no room for debate on the matter. "What did he tell you?"

"To save a soul I had to go back to my roots," Hattie said dryly, a lump forming in the back of her throat. "I took that to mean to go back to my roots of Catholicism. I currently practice another brand of spiritualism."

Iggy pinned his eyes on her. "You're a psychic and can cast spells. Good ones though. You're a pure soul." Iggy stared hard at Hattie for a few more seconds. "You can see the dead, too."

Hattie was left speechless. How could this man know so much about her? She wondered if Dante had told him. She asked him with a look, but Dante shook his head. He hadn't said a word.

"I know things," was all Iggy said as a way of explanation. He stretched his arms overhead and yawned before he slapped his hand down on the table. "One of you is going to have to explain to me what's going on or I can't help you."

Chapter Twenty

Harper and Jackson finished reading all of the articles and cross-checked the information again. Harper had a nice timeline of the murders and some biographic details of the victims. From what was in front of her, Harper couldn't see any ties among the victims – other than they were all from New Orleans and found shot with a voodoo doll next to them. There seemed to be no rhyme or reason to the victim selection. They gathered up their things and headed back to Rick's office.

Jackson knocked and pushed the door open when Rick told them to enter. They sat down on the couch and waited for Rick to finish typing. Finally, he picked his head up. "Did you solve the case?"

Harper laughed. "Hardly, but it was more information than we had. I appreciate you giving us the insight. We were hoping to discuss the cases with you."

Rick nodded and gave Harper a wink. "I bet you were."

His comment had a sly tone to it, but Harper didn't know the meaning behind his words. She and Jackson shared a look. "Am I missing something?"

Rick got up from his chair and came around to sit on the edge of his desk. "Full disclosure, I called Maggie and asked more about you. She told me a wild tale and asked me not to tell you that she spilled the secret. I can't help it though. It's fascinating."

CHAPTER TWENTY

Relief washed over Harper because she genuinely liked Rick and didn't like having to keep information back. "Maggie told you everything?"

"Everything from your family background to her great uncle's immortality curse and the connection to your aunt." Rick laughed. "This is far more than an article for *Rock City Life*. I'm in!"

"You're in?" Jackson asked confused.

Rick waved his hand as he talked. "You know I'm down to help, whatever you need. The case was interesting before when I thought it was a serial killer terrorizing the city, but now with voodoo curses and immortality, it's even more interesting."

"And dangerous..." Jackson said, letting the words hang in the air.

Rick pointed at him. "I looked you up, too, Colonel. Impressive military record. You don't seem like someone who would get all mixed up in this kind of thing."

Jackson reached for Harper's hand and closed his fingers around hers. "I've found an adventure of a lifetime. Believe it or not, my sister is a medium who can speak to the dead so it's something I grew up with as well. Meeting Hattie and Harper was serendipitous."

"I like you...open minds are good." Rick hopped off his desk. "Where do we get started?"

"What can you tell us off the record about these cases? I know what we read is not everything you know. I'm sure you have sources you spoke to who were off the record or even information you dug up you didn't print." Harper pulled out the notepad she had been writing in earlier.

Rick dug around a drawer in his desk until he came up with a notepad similar to Harper's. He held his up. "Are we ancient for still writing in these?"

Harper laughed. She had felt the same every time she brought hers out. "I think we are, but it works much better than trying to type notes on my phone or an iPad. Plus, I'm never going to accidentally delete this."

Rick flipped through a few pages. "Det. David Joya is the primary detective on the case. He's a seasoned detective with close to twenty years of investigative experience so they didn't put a rookie on this. He's been a source for me for a long time, but even he is stumped. There are no similarities among the victim type and hardly any evidence besides the voodoo doll left at the scene."

"Nothing?" Jackson asked with concern in his voice. "How can the killer leave no clues to their identity behind but leave actual items at the scene?"

Rick shook his head. "No idea. Maybe they wore gloves, but so far, there's been nothing. There haven't even been signs of a struggle. None of the victims fought back. There were no defensive wounds."

Harper didn't understand how that could happen. "The victims just let someone shoot them in the head?"

"It seems like that, and they were definitely shot up close. There were burn marks on each of the victims' foreheads."

"Every victim was shot? It's for sure?" Jackson asked.

"Yes, all of them, up close with the same antique gun from the ballistics reports. The same ballistics and the dolls were how they were able to connect the cases." Rick grabbed his phone off his desk and typed. When he was done, he held the phone out for Harper and Jackson to see. "This is the kind of gun the killer used. It's an antique gun from right around the time of the Civil War. Given the age of the gun, it's not going to be all that accurate firing far off."

Harper sighed. "What position were the victims in when they were shot?"

"The shot came at a downward angle so the killer was above them. They were possibly on the ground, but the cops don't believe they were shot where they were found. Each of the victims had a significant blood

CHAPTER TWENTY

loss. Not all of it gone but enough to seem strange."

"I don't think I'm following," Harper said. "You think the victims were shot someplace else and that accounts for the missing blood at the scene?"

"No," Rick said, sudden tension in his voice. "The coroner believes they were shot someplace else, but someone took blood from them before they died. It was hard to see, the coroner said, but each victim had a tiny puncture on their arm as if they had recently had blood drawn."

Jackson looked to Harper but she was stunned into confused silence. After a moment, she asked, "What do you think it means?"

"The coroner and cops have no idea." Rick flipped a few pages in his notebook. "It did remind Det. Joya of a case before his time as a detective. About twenty-five years ago, when he was still a beat cop, there was a string of murders – three I think in all – where the victims were found in the Garden District of the city. They had been suffocated, but before death, they had been drained of their blood. Back then, a reporter called it the vampire killings. They never caught the guy."

"Does Det. Joya think those cases are related to these?" Jackson asked, pulling out his phone to search for past news stories. Harper glanced at the screen as he pulled up a few articles.

"No, Det. Joya doesn't think they are connected. There was a different method of death. Those victims were completely drained of their blood. Not a drop left and they were found in their own homes, not on the streets."

"Where was the blood?" Harper asked, but didn't wait for a response. Her head started to spin and she spoke a bit frantically. "If they were found at home, does that mean they were killed at home or moved and killed someplace else? I would think if they were killed at home there would be a mess."

Rick smiled at her. "Slow down. I can explain it. They were killed someplace else and their blood was taken. They were then returned home and placed on their couches like they were sleeping. I only brought up the case because it was the only other one Det. Joya knew where blood had been taken. This time, it wasn't all their blood, just like two to three liters."

"That's more than half," Jackson countered. "Are you sure there are no similarities?"

"None." Rick sat back down on the edge of his desk. "What's your instinct on these current cases?"

Jackson turned to Harper. "You should just tell him everything."

"I thought Maggie told me everything," Rick countered. "There's more?"

"There's more Maggie didn't know. Dante knows the man who cursed him," Harper started. "His name is Pierre Lacourt—"

Rick stopped her. "The Pierre Lacourt, the one whose family practically founded the city?"

"Yes," Harper said slowly. "You know of him?"

Rick typed something into his phone and then handed it to Harper. She glanced down and it was a website for the Lacourt Family Foundation. She read a few pages and then skimmed through the family history back to the 1700s and Pierre Lacourt. Clicking on his name brought Harper to a page with a very regal painting of the man. Harper shivered as she looked into the man's eyes. Harper didn't have Hattie's power, but there was pure evil behind his eyes even though outwardly he might have been doing good. Dante was right. Pierre was the man from her vision.

"As you can read, the Lacourt Foundation funnels hundreds of thousands of dollars a year into nonprofit organizations here in New Orleans. Across the state, it's millions. They have a hand in everything and are very powerful." Rick narrowed his eyes at Harper. "What are you saying exactly?"

CHAPTER TWENTY

This was a major complication. Harper said seriously, "We are saying their ancestor – the founder of this family – is a very evil man who cursed two people we know of and now might be committing these murders."

Rick's eyes grew wide. "You think Pierre Lacourt is back from the dead and killing people?"

Harper shook her head. "No, I'm saying it's possible Pierre didn't die. I think whatever immortality curse he put on Dante he might have used on himself and is now out there killing people."

Jackson exhaled. "It might be the blood is part of whatever spell or ritual he's doing to keep himself alive. You said you were in, Rick. Is that still true?"

Rick whispered to himself with disbelief and fear in his voice. "You want us to go up against the most powerful family in New Orleans to take down their immortal family founder who now might be a serial killer."

"Sounds about right," Harper said. "We need to get started."

Chapter Twenty-One

Dante had knocked back half his glass of bourbon in one gulp and set the glass down. He had locked eyes with Iggy and told his long sad tale from start to finish. The priest barely moved. At times, it didn't even look to Hattie like he was breathing. His stillness, the fear in his eyes, the sorrow for Dante. It was all there – the very same range of emotion Hattie had gone through hearing Dante's experiences.

Dante explained to the priest about his relationship with Celeste, reincarnating over and over again to only find and fall in love with him each time. He expressed how hard it was to lose her again and again and again. When Dante was done with his tale, he explained the connection to the recent murders and the voodoo placed in Hattie's yard. Iggy took it all in without uttering a word.

After hearing the tale, the priest paced around the downstairs of his house with a new glass of bourbon in his hand, muttering to himself. Hattie wasn't sure exactly how many glasses he had consumed while they were there. She had stopped counting at four, and it didn't account for how many he had before they arrived. How the man wasn't passed out drunk was beyond her, but it didn't seem to have much effect on him at all.

Finally, Iggy stopped pacing and leaned against the kitchen counter. He pointed at Dante. "I always knew there was something a little off

CHAPTER TWENTY-ONE

about you, but I wasn't sure what. It occurred to me you never aged. I had wondered about your secret – good genetics, eating healthy, exercise. I didn't know."

Dante said sadly, "I've known your family for generations – all good people. I don't know why it didn't occur to me until now to seek your help. I didn't know how you could if even the strongest voodoo didn't help. I've tried everything to break this curse to no avail." He stressed, "And I mean I tried everything – voodoo, hoodoo, witchcraft. I've tried every magical potion and spell under the sun. I've sought out shamans and practitioners on every continent. Nothing breaks it. The same for Celeste. She keeps coming back and the pattern keeps repeating. Now with this killer on the loose, it has to be stopped. Is there anything you can do?"

Iggy set his glass down on the table with a thunk. "It's not possession I can tell you that much. Possession would be easier. No, this is something much more diabolical. I've seen it before."

"You have?" Hattie asked surprised. She had researched and hadn't come across it at all.

"Once in Budapest," Iggy said, sighing. "It was a messy situation. The man had been cursed like you, Dante, but the only way to break the curse was to kill the host. I have no idea what kind of magic was used on him though so I have no idea if the same situation applies to you."

Hattie raised her hand as if she were in school. "One question. If Pierre is the one committing these crimes now then he must have the same sort of immortality. How do you kill an immortal man?"

Before Iggy could respond, Dante said, "Iggy, I can't die. Trust me, I've tried in various ways over the years to kill myself. I even fought in the Civil War where I was shot, stabbed, and blown up with cannon fire. I feel pain, but my wounds never stay. I was shot in the head at the battle of Shiloh only to wake later in a field of dead men." Dante shook his head. "Try having to explain why you're not dead to your commander."

"It's not about killing you," Iggy said like they were clueless, which they were. "You can't die because someone has cursed you. Pierre can't curse himself, but he can cast a spell on himself. It means, though, that there is something he has to do to keep feeding the spell over time. We need to figure out what that is and stop him from doing it. Once Pierre dies, his power over you stops or at least lessens enough we can reverse the curse on you, Dante." Iggy paused and shrugged. "At least that's how I think it might work."

"Do you think Pierre has to kill people to feed the spell he's done on himself? Taking a life to feed his own?" Hattie asked. She shuddered at the gruesome thought of it.

"It's possible," Iggy said. "There is only one person I trust enough with something like this." Again, Iggy left the room without explanation. He was gone longer than before.

Hattie and Dante stayed at the table talking to each other. Hattie still wasn't convinced Iggy would be of help to them. Dante reassured Hattie, saying he felt like he was finally getting more answers than he had in several lifetimes.

"Call it a gut feeling if you like, but I think we might finally be on the right track." Dante patted Hattie's hand. "You're just feeling a little weird since Iggy isn't like any priest you've ever met. But what do you expect? The man has been hunting demons his whole life. It's bound to have impacted him."

"True," Hattie agreed. She knew she probably wasn't being fair. After all, who was she to judge? Iggy just seemed too...well *Iggy*. "Where did he go?"

"No idea, but every time he leaves and comes back, he has a good idea."

A few minutes later Iggy came back into the kitchen. "She's on her way, and she's very excited to meet you, Dante."

CHAPTER TWENTY-ONE

Dante looked at the priest with confusion blanketed on his face. "Who are you talking about? I didn't want to tell many people about this. I've been trying to keep a low profile."

Iggy waved him off. "It's Lucinda Bell – demon huntress." He paused for dramatic effect, but neither Hattie nor Dante said a word. Iggy giggled like a child. "Lucinda is my right-hand woman. I don't know what I'd do without her. Every spiritual warrior needs backup, and Lucinda is more backup than any man needs." Iggy whistled.

Hattie wasn't sure what Iggy's innuendo meant until she turned her head and caught sight of the woman walking down the hall. Hattie's mouth hung open in shock as she took in all five-foot-ten, curves for miles Lucinda Bell. As if the woman wasn't tall enough, Lucinda perched herself on three-inch heeled black boots, black leather pants hugged her hips, and a midriff-baring black sweater left little to the imagination on her top half. A silver chain belted her tiny waist. The mane of dark curls around her gorgeous face only accented her high cheekbones, pouty lips, and dark eyes. Hattie wasn't sure if the woman leaped from a comic book or straight out of the underworld.

Lucinda popped a hip out with every step she took and her eyes meant all business. She strutted into the kitchen, bent down to the priest, and smacked her lips against his cheek. She stole the glass of bourbon right out of his hands. "You're not supposed to be drinking, Iggy," Lucinda scolded. She swished the bourbon around in the glass twice and drank it down in one gulp.

Lucinda set the glass down on the table across from Hattie. "I'm Lucinda. You are?"

Hattie swallowed hard and fumbled over her name. Finally, she regained a smidge of normalcy and told Lucinda who she was but not why she was there. Dante, whose eyes had practically bulged out of his head, also introduced himself. Hattie might have slapped him, but she too was mesmerized by Lucinda.

Pointing to Dante, Iggy said, "He's the one with the curse."

Lucinda grabbed a chair and spun it, straddling the seat and leaning her arms on the back of the chair. "Tell me your sad tale." It wasn't a question but rather a command, and Dante quickly complied. Lucinda showed nearly no emotion – no shock like most people had. No sadness for Dante – nothing.

When Dante was done, she asked, "You want this curse broken?"

"Of course," Dante said. "Trust me, there is no joy in living forever."

Lucinda nodded but said nothing.

Hattie took that moment to ask, "What is it you do?"

It was the first time Lucinda smiled. "I'm a demon huntress. Demons are supposed to be punishing evil, but sometimes they go rogue and try to bring souls to the dark side. I make sure they don't. There is a balance of good and evil in the world. I make sure that balance is maintained."

Hattie nodded like she understood, but she had no idea. "You think you can help Dante? He's not possessed by a demon."

"Is that what you think?" Lucinda laughed. "Just because the devil himself hasn't cursed this man, don't believe that spell work of this kind isn't controlled by the very underworld below. If I can't help him, no one can."

Hattie liked the woman's confidence. She also hadn't given any thought to how the curse had come about. Hattie thought more in terms of positive and negative and light and dark than in good and evil. But it was probably all the same.

"What is your plan?" Dante asked, looking between Lucinda and Iggy.

Without missing a beat, Lucinda explained, "We must catch the man who cursed you, extract all the negative, and break his spell. Then we kill him, of course."

Hattie sat back. "I can't kill anyone."

CHAPTER TWENTY-ONE

Lucinda waved her off. She reached around her back and pulled out a shiny silver dagger. "This is what I shall use to kill him. It's the only thing that will work on a soul that old and dark."

Chapter Twenty-Two

Harper and Jackson spent the rest of the morning and early afternoon with Rick calling victim's families asking questions about the victims and the days leading up to the murders. Jackson and Harper even visited a few people to ask questions in person, but there were no clues to be found. The absence of connections among the victims and other suspects led them right back to the Lacourt family.

On Harper's insistence, Rick had given them the address to the Lacourt Family Foundation in the Garden District. Harper wanted to visit and snoop around. She would say she was writing a story and wanted historical information about Pierre. Jackson wasn't necessarily on board.

"Aren't we showing our hand a little too soon?" Jackson asked as they walked to the corner of Canal and Carondelet Streets to catch the St. Charles streetcar to Magazine Street where the foundation's office was located.

Harper's eyes remained on an article on her phone. "Possibly. I want to assess whether the family has any idea about their ancestors. For all we know, they believe Pierre is long-since dead."

"But what if they know? What if they are in on it? You know how these powerful families work."

Harper did. She had a powerful family of her own back in New York

CHAPTER TWENTY-TWO

City. Her father, Maxwell, was a force to be reckoned with. The Ryans went back generations on Manhattan's upper eastside. They protected their own, but Harper had trouble believing any family would protect a monster like Pierre. She told Jackson as much.

Jackson sucked in a breath. "I hope you're right."

Luckily, the streetcar pulled up mere minutes after they arrived at the corner. It wasn't very crowded either so it was a pleasant trip across town. Harper had never ridden in a streetcar in New Orleans so she spent the time taking in the sights. The city had such beautiful architecture it was hard not to enjoy being a tourist even if their mission for being there was grim.

Jackson took her hand. "I don't know if we will get the vacation we planned, but this is nice."

"I was just thinking the same thing. I feel bad enjoying it while people out there are dying." Harper turned her head and watched the houses go by. "It's hard not to enjoy it though. This isn't a city I could ever live in, but it's nice to explore while we are here."

They rode in silence for a few more minutes. Jackson's cellphone chimed and he pulled it out of his pocket. He glanced down at the screen, clicked open a text message, and cursed softly under his breath.

"Everything okay?" Harper asked worried it might have something to do with one of Jackson's consulting projects.

Jackson put his phone away but hesitated about telling Harper who had contacted him. She let it go, having learned over the last year that Jackson wasn't a man to be pushed to talk when he wasn't ready. Harper went back to looking at the houses and shops as the streetcar turned onto Magazine Street.

"It was my ex," Jackson said finally. "She's asking for money again." Jackson had been married before to a woman who had cheated on him and financially used him. Part of the reason he had moved to Little Rock was to have a fresh start after his divorce.

115

"I thought Cora had stopped bothering you?" Harper asked, not sure how much she wanted to wade into this conversation.

"She had stopped. She had even stopped calling my family after Sarah told them to stop answering her calls." Jackson looked over at Harper. "I'm ignoring her text."

Harper smiled at Jackson, happy he wasn't falling for his ex's drama. "You don't have time right now anyway. We're here. How are we going to approach this?"

Jackson gave her a sideways glance and laughed. "I thought you had a plan?"

"I do, but every time we do something like this, we end up winging it. It never goes as planned."

Jackson shrugged. "We wing it then."

Harper and Jackson stepped off the streetcar onto Magazine Street. They walked a block and easily found the Lacourt Family Foundation. The office wasn't in an office building but rather a home. The Greek Revival architecture was typical for New Orleans. The house sat behind a wrought iron fence and had two wide porches on the first and second floors. Four ground-to-roof columns ran across the front and green shutters accented each window. A tall weeping willow shaded most of the front yard.

"You ready?" Jackson asked, opening the gate.

Harper and Jackson walked across the stone walkway that split the front yard in two and up the porch steps. Jackson was about to knock when a woman opened the door. The petite woman, who looked to be in her mid-thirties, had short, straight dark hair cut in a blunt bob at her chin. Her bright red lipstick matched the color of her earrings.

"Welcome to Lacourt House," she said sweetly. "I'm Alexandria Lacourt."

Harper and Jackson introduced themselves. Harper explained she was writing an article about New Orleans for *Rock City Life* magazine

CHAPTER TWENTY-TWO

and asked if she could speak with someone about the Lacourt family and the wonderful work of the foundation. Alexandria smiled broadly, showing off a perfect row of white teeth, and welcomed them in.

"I'm the only one here at the moment, but I run the foundation. I'd be happy to answer any questions you have and give you a tour." Alexandria stepped out of the way and let Harper and Jackson into the home, which looked as grand on the inside as it did from the street. The entire entrance hall had beautiful dark wainscoting and floors so shiny Harper was sure she could see her reflection.

"The house is beautiful," Harper said, following Alexandria into a front parlor.

"It was my great-granddad's home originally and passed down through the family line." Before she explained more, Alexandria offered them something to drink, which they declined. As they sat, she said, "Excuse me for saying so but you look very familiar to me. Are you by any chance associated with *Charlotte*? It's a lifestyle magazine in New York City."

Although a bit caught off guard, Harper smiled. "Yes, that's my family's magazine. I was the editor-in-chief for years."

Alexandria raised her eyebrows. "You no longer work there?"

"No, I wanted time outside of the hustle and bustle of the city. I have family in Little Rock."

Alexandria smiled stiffly. Harper could tell the woman thought she was a moron for leaving *Charlotte*. Harper only hoped she didn't know the real story of how her father fired her.

Harper raised her eyebrows. "I wouldn't have thought you'd read *Charlotte* down here?"

Alexandria nodded enthusiastically. "My mother has been a reader of the magazine for years. I used to flip through and look at all the pretty houses when she was done. I've seen your face countless times on the masthead." Alexandria crossed her legs. "Now what would you like to know about the Lacourt Family Foundation?"

Harper paused as if thinking of the best approach. She had it planned but wanted her questions to come across as spontaneous. "I think it would be helpful if you told me about the foundation and its activities first, and then we can go into the history of your family. Our readers love history."

Alexandria detailed for Harper and Jackson all of the good works of the Lacourt Family Foundation, including all the nonprofits around the globe that had benefited from their philanthropy work. Alexandria was quite proud of the work they were doing. Harper sat listening, asking questions as they went. Harper didn't have much of an interest in the foundation, but she feigned interest long enough to make the interview appear legit.

When Alexandria was done, she offered them a tour. Harper was surprised to see the home wasn't an office at all, it was where Alexandria lived. As they stood in the newly remodeled kitchen, Alexandria explained, "It might seem strange that I live here, but I opened the front two rooms of the house for foundation work and live in the rest. My parents still live in the French Quarter. We had a bigger office once, but it's just easier this way. Our employees work from home. It's why we can funnel so much of the foundation money directly into the programs."

"That's a really smart way of doing it," Harper commented. "I mentioned before I'd love to learn more about your family history. Can you tell me how your family got its start? The research I did before coming today indicated your family is one of the oldest here in New Orleans. Is that true?"

"It is." Alexandria sat back proudly. "This house was one of the first built back in the 1830s when the area was little more than woods. It was passed down my father's family until now." Alexandria spent about twenty minutes detailing some family history but only went back a few generations. She didn't mention Pierre at all.

At a lull in the conversation, Harper asked, "I read your family founder is Pierre Lacourt. Did he build this house?"

Alexandria paused longer than Harper thought she should have. "No," she finally said. "That would be his son who built the house. Let's go upstairs. I'll show you the rest of it."

Harper followed but kept questioning about their history. "I read on the website Pierre was a businessman who traveled the world before coming back to New Orleans and settling. Where did he live originally?"

"In the French Quarter," Alexandria responded. "Pierre was an astute businessman. He was involved in shipping and had a large fleet of ships. He traveled all over the place. His one son, who is the line we are descended from, built this house and kept up the family business here in New Orleans. His other son left the area and never returned."

"It seems like there might be a story there," Jackson said.

As they went into a guest bedroom, Alexandria laughed. "Nothing too scandalous. Pierre's son didn't follow the family business and wanted to strike out on his own. He didn't keep much in contact with his brother and father after he moved."

Where Alexandria had been forthcoming about the foundation and general family history, she had completely clammed up about Pierre. As they got to the end of a long hall, there was a doorway. Harper thought it might be to an attic. The home clearly had one. Harper had seen the windows from the outside. "What's behind there?" Harper asked, pointing.

"Nothing to see up there," Alexandria said quickly, ushering them back down the hallway in the opposite direction. When she saw the look on Harper's face, she smiled. "It's just a messy attic."

Harper caught it and so did Jackson. He raised his eyebrows at her. The attic was off-limits, but by her tone and the look on her face, Alexandria was lying about something. Harper had the feeling there was more than storage above their heads.

Chapter Twenty-Three

Harper and Jackson followed Alexandria back down to the first floor. "I appreciate the tour and all the information about the foundation and your family history, I just have a few more questions if you don't mind." Harper noted the look of annoyance on Alexandria's face. "It will only take a moment," she assured.

"Sure," the young woman said stiffly. "Let's sit back down in the office."

As they took their seats, Harper geared up the courage to ask what she most wanted to know. Harper wasn't sure about the politest way to ask so she just went for it. "Alexandria, this might be an odd question, but it's something I've heard about quite frequently when exploring New Orleans. It's a topic our readers are fascinated by. In the history of your family are there any voodoo practitioners?"

Alexandria sucked in a sharp breath. "Why would you ask that?"

"I've had the chance to read some journals from people who were among the first families here in New Orleans and one of them mentioned Pierre and his love for a woman named Celeste. There is a rumor he might have cursed Celeste and her husband Dante. The story was fascinating to me. I just wondered if it was something of folklore or if you knew of any truth to it."

"Of course, there is no truth to it," Alexandria said, her voice nearly screeching and her eyes shifting away. "Pierre was happily married to his wife Marie. They were married at St. Louis Cathedral. The entire city came out for their celebration. I don't recall any mention of the name Celeste in any of our family's history. He certainly wasn't a voodoo practitioner. That's just silly."

Harper smiled. "Right, of course. I would assume that any suggestion that Pierre might have placed a spell on himself to be immortal might be just as ludicrous?"

"Good heavens, that's just downright silly. I can assure you Pierre is not among the living."

Jackson winked at her. "But is he among the undead?"

Alexandria finally broke into a grin. "Pierre is not a vampire, zombie, or immortal. I think people watch too much television."

"It was just a fascinating story when we came across it." Harper gathered up her things. "Thank you so much for your time. I'd be happy to send you the magazine when the article is published."

"I can't wait to read it." Alexandria walked them to the door and said goodbye.

As Harper opened the door to leave, she gripped the doorknob, hoping for an impression. Flashes of information came to her until she was forced to let go.

"Are you okay?" Alexandria asked.

"I think just a little hungry, probably some low blood sugar." As Harper stepped out onto the porch, she turned back. "I hope you and your family are safe. We heard this morning about the terrible murders happening in the city."

Once they were safely on the sidewalk, Jackson looked back at the house. "What do you think? Do you think Alexandria knows?"

"She gave herself away when I first asked the question. She didn't laugh casually and say no. She asked why I'd ask the question. If it wasn't true, Alexandria would have denied it immediately. Her first

CHAPTER TWENTY-THREE

instinct was to ask how I knew." Harper headed toward the street and away from the house. She crossed Magazine Street and stopped at a small deli with outdoor seating. The temperature had warmed considerably from the cool evening before.

"I guess we are eating," Jackson said, sitting down next to her at an outdoor table and grabbing a menu held in a holder on the tabletop.

"Less eating and more spying. You're always hungry so I figured you'd be good with this."

Jackson peered down at the menu. "I'm always good with food."

The server came over a few minutes later and took their order. The young man, who introduced himself as Zak, engaged them in conversation about the city and their visit. Harper mentioned her magazine article and told him they had just visited the Lacourt Family Foundation.

His eyes grew wide. "At least you made it out alive." He laughed.

Jackson glanced up at him. "What do you mean?"

"You haven't heard?"

Harper and Jackson both acted like they didn't know what he was talking about.

Zak crouched low and said quietly, "Everyone knows about the Lacourt family. Someone is living in the attic. My girlfriend thinks they are vampires. I think it's just haunted by Pierre Lacourt. The creepy stories about that guy could fill a horror book."

Harper tried to look shocked. "I read a little history about him on the foundation's website and then found a few odd articles about him, but when I asked Alexandria, she denied anything strange about Pierre."

"She would," Zak said dramatically. "Let me get your drinks and order, and I'll tell you the gossip if you're interested."

"We are interested. I love a good scandal." When Zak walked away, Harper leaned on the table. "Good thing we stopped here. I knew there was something more going on in that attic. That's why I wanted to hang around."

Jackson turned his head to look across the street. "I didn't want to say anything, but twice now, I thought I saw someone up there."

They talked for a few minutes until Zak returned. When he set down their drinks, Jackson said, "I'm surprised such a prominent family would have so much gossip about them."

"It's not something talked about in the open," Zak explained. "It's more an underground current of speculation about them. It's certainly not something the family has ever addressed. It may not even be true, but the rumors, at least here in the Garden District, have persisted for years."

Harper looked at him eagerly. "Is the family bad or something? It seems like they do a lot of good with the foundation."

"It's all a front. I mean they donate money and help nonprofits, but it's so the family looks good from the outside. Behind closed doors, it's a different story. It's part of the reason they got rid of their office. They say they have staff, and they did for a while, but too many started asking questions. At first, people thought maybe the foundation was a front for the mob or money laundering, but people started realizing it's to keep the family in power."

Harper wasn't sure she understood. "Why do they need power?"

Zak smiled. "If the cops and mayor and even the governor are in their pocket, they can do whatever they want. If people are taken in by their good deeds, no one is looking at their bad."

"What is bad?" Jackson took a sip of his drink.

"It's all speculation. You get some people here who think vampires are real. I'm not one of them, but there have been rumors Pierre Lacourt has been feeding off humans for centuries. Dark voodoo is what the others say. Others, like me, believe he's a ghost. No matter what the particular rumor is, no one believes Pierre Lacourt has stopped running the family."

CHAPTER TWENTY-THREE

Jackson traced a droplet of water down his glass. "If Pierre is feeding off humans, aren't there missing or dead people to account for?"

"Why do you think it's so important for the Lacourt family to have the cops and people in power on their side?" Zak asked. "People go missing all the time in this city and are never found. Every few years or so there is a rash of murders right in a row that always go unsolved."

Harper asked, "Is there any speculation Pierre has been responsible for the recent murders that happened in the French Quarter?"

Zak's mouth was set in a firm line. "That's all everyone in this neighborhood is talking about. If you watch the house at night, you'll see someone leave and come back before daylight. That's the other reason people think he's a vampire. I'm not sure what's true. For all we know, it's a family member roaming around town keeping the mystery alive about them. The more interest people take in them, it seems the more power, wealth, and mystique they have."

"Have you ever seen him?"

"No, I have better things to do. I grew up here in the Garden District so my mother believes there's some dark magic keeping him alive. We've heard he's cursed all his enemies. Some even believe he had Marie Laveau herself casting dark magic for him."

"Marie Laveau?" Harper asked. She knew she had heard the name before but had trouble placing it.

"She's the most famous voodoo priestess who ever walked the streets of New Orleans. You should visit her grave before you leave." Zak finished telling them more about Marie Laveau and then left them to finish their lunch in quiet.

After the food was served and their bellies full, Harper pulled out her phone. "We should check in with Hattie and make a plan."

Chapter Twenty-Four

Hattie had sat mesmerized by the knife in Lucinda's hands. She had never seen anything quite so striking. The handle had an intricate design, and Hattie couldn't identify the writing on it. She wasn't even sure about the language. When Hattie asked what it said, Lucinda explained it was Sumerian and translated to *Back to the underworld ye shall be cast.*

Hattie had no idea people like Lucinda even existed. She didn't know demon huntress was a thing, a whole occupation that one based their life work on. But looking at Lucinda, Hattie couldn't imagine her as anything else. The four of them – Hattie, Lucinda, Dante, and Iggy – sat there waiting for Harper and Jackson to join them. Hattie worried Harper and Jackson might get lost and be unable to find Iggy's place since it was tucked away down an alley, but soon, there was a knock on the door and there they stood.

Hattie immediately got up and wrapped her arms around Harper. "Keep an open mind," she whispered to her niece. Hattie struggled to get on board with Iggy and Lucinda so the last thing she needed was Harper to be, well...*Harper.*

Harper pulled back from her aunt and searched her face. "I always keep an open mind," she said smirking. As they walked down the hall past the living room and into the kitchen, Harper and Jackson both stepped back when they saw Lucinda, who leaned against the counter seductively, one hip popped out.

Jackson sucked in his belly and Harper's eyes, much like Hattie's, couldn't seem to land on one spot.

"You've been making friends." Jackson let out a short burst of nervous laughter.

Harper slapped his side but nervously laughed when Lucinda walked over and traced a finger down Jackson's chest to the top of his pants and back up again.

"You look like you can hold your own in a fight," Lucinda purred. "Handsome, too."

Jackson swallowed visibly and coughed. "I'm retired military."

"I like that in a man...a willingness to kill." Lucinda ran her hand across his collarbone and over to his shoulder, squeezing and feeling him as she went. Lucinda kept her hand on Jackson as she strutted around his body to his back. She didn't let go. He seemed too mesmerized to move or stop it.

Hattie was sure the woman was going to grab Jackson's backside, and if that happened, she wasn't sure what Harper would do. Hattie didn't want to find out. Before any of it could play out, Hattie pulled Jackson away from her. "Come on let's sit down and discuss what we've found so far."

Jackson allowed himself to be pulled to the table. "What is going on here?" he whispered to Hattie as they sat down.

Harper didn't budge even as Lucinda got toe to toe with her. Lucinda raised a hand to run a finger under Harper's chin, but Harper gripped the woman's wrist before she had the chance to make contact. In a low voice, Harper growled, "I wouldn't do that if I were you."

Lucinda laughed and looked back at the priest. "I like this one – quick reflexes and feisty. She's protective of what's hers, too." Lucinda stepped back, took yet another glass of bourbon out of the priest's hands, and chugged it back. "I can work with this."

Harper took steps into the kitchen. "Someone needs to explain what's happening here."

"Come sit, Harper. We will catch you up," Dante said, patting the seat next to him.

"I'm fine standing." Harper didn't move.

Lucinda glanced in her direction. "See, I told you I liked her."

As Dante went to speak, Hattie interrupted and explained Father Ignatius Cormier's lifelong work of fighting evil. Hattie tried her best to explain Lucinda, even though she wasn't sure that what the woman had said about herself was true. It didn't matter, Hattie was happy Lucinda was on their side because she couldn't imagine anyone going up against her.

When Hattie was done, Harper said calmly, "We met Alexandria Lacourt today when we visited their house and checked out the Lacourt Family Foundation."

Lucinda raised her dark eyebrows in shock. "The Lacourts in the Garden District?"

"The same," Harper responded. "Why?"

Lucinda bore her eyes into Iggy. "You didn't tell me this had anything to do with the Lacourts."

"If I had, would you have come?" Iggy returned the look.

Hattie looked up toward the heavens and then gave an exasperated sigh. "Can you explain what's happening here?"

Lucinda leaned against the kitchen counter. "Dante only told me his name was Pierre. That's a common name in the history of this city. I had no idea you were discussing going after Pierre Lacourt and his family. He's an extremely dangerous man who has his power from the underworld."

"Explain," Hattie said again, feeling like she had stepped into a movie at the midway point.

Lucinda, who had been a force of confidence, suddenly grew quiet.

CHAPTER TWENTY-FOUR

"Tell them," Iggy encouraged. "We don't have a choice if they want our help. If they don't accept you, they can go it alone. I've told you this before – never be ashamed, Lucinda."

Lucinda pushed herself away from the counter. "There are families who have made deals with the underworld. They are given wealth and power and abilities beyond most humans. The Lacourt family is one of those families. Pierre made a deal with a demon for his vast powers. He practices one of the darkest forms of voodoo known to man. Even at that, it's been enhanced."

"What does that even mean?" Dante asked.

"Think of it as a little spiritual boost but from below instead of above." Lucinda pointed between the underworld and the heavens.

"What did Pierre have to give in exchange?" Iggy asked.

"One of his children. At the time, Pierre didn't have children, but he would later. When the time came, he had to sacrifice one of them and give him to the underworld."

"Was it a son?" Harper asked, looking at Jackson.

"How did you know that?" Lucinda asked suspiciously.

"Alexandria Lacourt told us today one of Pierre's sons severed ties with the family." Harper stopped and narrowed her eyes at Lucinda. "How do you know what the deal was?"

"The demon was my father." Lucinda looked away. "I'm not fully human. More like human adjacent."

"I'm still not following," Hattie said, looking between Lucinda and Iggy. "How can you be human adjacent? What does that even mean?"

Lucinda finally looked up and caught Hattie's eye. "It means my father was a demon who had a relationship with a mortal woman. I'm the product of that relationship. Not quite demon but not quite human either." Lucinda looked at each of them and when no one said a word, she went on. "My mother was killed by my father shortly after I was born. He raised me. I spent more time than I care to remember torturing souls and wreaking havoc on Earth. I never fit in that world though. As he would tell it, my light always shined too bright. I had too many questions in the face of his evil, and I wasn't good at following orders. I was cast out. I roamed the earth for longer than I care to remember looking for a home. I finally found it here. Centuries later, I found Iggy."

Iggy raised his glass to her. "Lucinda's been fighting evil ever since, and I'm darn proud of her."

Hattie was stunned into silence. Jackson and Dante sat there looking like they could no longer speak.

It was finally Harper who broke the silence. "And here I thought I had daddy issues. Not quite the same, Lucinda, but my father kicked me out of the family business, too."

Hattie couldn't help but laugh. Here she was worried about how Harper would handle the news about Lucinda, and she was doing a better job than all of them.

Harper asked for a glass and poured herself some bourbon. As she finished a sip, she asked, "Lucinda, how do we stop Pierre Lacourt?"

"It's not going to be as easy as I thought. Pierre won't be the only one in the family with his power." Lucinda stopped for a moment collecting her thoughts. "Any idea where he is?"

"If I had to guess," Harper said, "I'd put money on the attic of the Lacourt house in the Garden District. We need to see what's going on up there."

"I'll go with you," Lucinda said.

"Hold up," Jackson interrupted. "I don't think it's safe for Harper to go. Plus, what if this serial killer isn't Pierre? Call me crazy, but I feel like we are putting all our eggs in one evil basket."

Hattie didn't disagree. "What did you find this morning at the newspaper office?"

Jackson leaned forward on the table. "We ran down some potential

CHAPTER TWENTY-FOUR

leads but all roads bring us back to the Lacourts. Even still, I think we need to keep an open mind."

Harper added, "Rick, at the newspaper, told us the victims had lost blood but not from the murder. It happened before they were killed."

Dante nodded in agreement. "They are being held someplace then. It's probably like when Pierre first cursed me. He drugged us and we were held in his house. To this day, I don't even know what ritual he used to give us our curse."

"I think Harper and Jackson should continue with gathering information from the newspaper and connect with the cops," Hattie said. "The more we know about these murders, the more we will know to either use against Pierre or find the real killer. I think Jackson is right. We can't assume it's Pierre."

Harper poured some more bourbon. "I still want to see what's in the attic. Besides, it might be helpful given my ability. I might be able to pick up some useful information."

"Your ability?" Iggy asked. The priest had remained fairly quiet until that point. Hattie noticed he seemed to defer to Lucinda.

Harper explained her gift of psychometry, and how when she touched an object, she would get an imprint. "Mostly, I can see the past. I've never been able to use my gift to see the future. I have on occasion been able to read someone's current thoughts though."

"You're definitely coming with me to that house," Lucinda said.

"Alexandria lives there. It's a home as well as an office. How are we getting in undetected?"

Lucinda smiled. "Leave that to me. Let's do it tonight."

Chapter Twenty-Five

"Are you attracted to her?" Harper asked Jackson as soon as they were out of the priest's house and back on the street.

"What?" Jackson asked, stumbling over his words. He wouldn't look Harper in the eye.

"I'm not going to care if you are. Lucinda is just very different from me. You seemed to have a strange reaction to her."

Jackson grabbed Harper's hand. "Yeah, she's part demon. Don't you think I had enough drama with my ex-wife? I'm not looking to be with an actual demon."

Harper shrugged. "She's nice for a demon. Is it weird I relate to her daddy issues?"

Jackson stopped walking and turned to her. "This whole thing is weird, but I'm trying for Hattie's sake to keep an open mind. I was serious though. We don't know for sure this is all connected to Pierre so if we are going to do this, we should try to run down every lead. As long as we are here, we are all in danger, but particularly Hattie."

"I agree so let's go back and talk to Rick. Maybe he has a lead in with the cops." Harper and Jackson walked back to the newspaper office. They both noted a couple of shops and restaurants they wanted to visit before they left the city.

Harper texted Rick on the way back just to confirm he was still in the office. He responded quickly, letting Harper know he had a surprise waiting for her. Harper had had enough surprises for one day. She had told the truth earlier. Lucinda did seem nice, but she was a demon and it didn't sit well with Harper. She also wasn't the jealous type, and the feeling that overwhelmed her when she saw Lucinda touching Jackson wasn't something she ever wanted to feel again. It was a mix of possessiveness and anger. As they walked, Harper tried to shake it off, but Jackson noticed her mood as he usually did.

Before they walked into the newspaper office, Jackson stopped her. "What's wrong? You're too quiet." Harper reached for the door, but Jackson stopped her. "Seriously, tell me what's wrong. If I did something, tell me. Don't let it fester."

"I'm not angry with you," Harper reassured. "I didn't like how I felt when Lucinda touched you and your reaction to it. I've never been the jealous type before. I didn't like how it made me feel."

Jackson wrapped Harper in his arms. "It's normal to feel that way. I wish I hadn't reacted to her either, and I can't explain why I did. Yes, I think she's attractive, but I see attractive women all the time and don't react. It doesn't mean anything though. Can we just chalk this up to the fact she's a demon?"

"You think that's what it is?"

"I have no idea, but it was an odd reaction on my part. That's all." Jackson kissed her and they dropped the subject. On the way to Rick's office, Jackson added, "I don't like the idea of you going with her to break into the Lacourt house, but I know you're going to do it anyway, so I'm not going to argue." Jackson knew her too well.

Harper knocked on Rick's door and then realized he wasn't alone. As Rick waved them in, his guest stood and greeted them. "I'm Det. David Joya. Rick said you had an interest in our voodoo case." He shook Harper's hand. "Full disclosure - I also had a conversation with Det. Granger in Little Rock. He said you'd be coming down here, and even if I tried to keep you out of my case, you wouldn't listen."

Harper smirked. "You're here to scold me before I even get started?"

"No, nothing of the sort. We use civilian consultants all the time. Det. Granger said you were excellent, if not mildly irritating." He smiled, showing off a row of straight, white teeth. Det. Joya held his hand out to Jackson. "Pleasure to meet you, Colonel. I'd be happy to have your thoughts on the case so far."

"Jackson is fine," he corrected. "I'll let Harper take the lead. I don't know that we have found anything verifiable yet to offer."

Harper caught Jackson's meaning without having to say anything else. He didn't think it was a good idea to share anything about demons and curses right now since nothing was solid evidence. Harper sat down on the couch. "We haven't dug into the information yet. Just what was in the newspapers and the little Rick was kind enough to tell us. We made a few calls and talked to a couple of people, but I didn't see any similarities in victim type. Is that correct?"

Det. Joya nodded. "We haven't had much to go on. There are no similarities among the victims. It's a mix of male and female victims who range in age from twenty to forty-five. None have criminal records. Two were simply coming home from work."

Harper shifted in her seat. "They were all young though so that's somewhat similar."

"What do you mean?"

"All were in the prime of their lives," Harper explained. "You don't have anyone in their teens and no one even into their late forties. I'd say that might be a pattern if it holds. Rick said there was blood loss, the age and health of the victim might come into play there."

"I hadn't thought of it that way," Det. Joya said. "We can look into the prior health of the victims to find out more."

Jackson said, "It also seemed to me if blood was taken, then they had to be held someplace before they were killed."

"We believe they are being held."

CHAPTER TWENTY-FIVE

"How does this person abduct them?" Jackson asked, looking between Det. Joya and Harper. "You have fully grown people taken on the streets. How does that happen without anyone indicating they heard or saw a struggle?"

Det. Joya exhaled a breath. "We don't know. No street surveillance has captured them. We don't have any leads. It's like they just vanished off the streets and are found dead with a gunshot wound sometime later."

"What's the timing?" Harper asked. Det. Joya gave her a puzzled look so she explained, "Timing is important. How long from when they went missing to when their bodies were found? Are they gone for hours or days?"

Det. Joya understood now. "It's hours but not very many at that. One man was speaking to a friend on the phone and said he'd call him right back, that he needed to help someone. Three hours later, he was found dead in an alleyway."

"Was the victim found close to where he was last speaking to his friend?" Jackson asked.

"No, it was several blocks away. It's similar for other cases, too."

Harper bit at her bottom lip. "Whoever is taking them isn't going far then."

"Correct. We believe the killer must live close, maybe right in the French Quarter."

Jackson looked at Harper. She was sure he was thinking the same thing. She asked, "Is there any way the killer might live as far as the Garden District?"

Det. Joya shrugged. "It's possible but that would entail a lot of transport. Based on what I know I think it's someone much closer to where the victims are taken and found. The person is hunting in their neighborhood. I think it's the only way they can pull it off."

"You said one victim was on the phone. Did the person on the other end of the call hear anyone else speaking?" Jackson asked.

"No," Det. Joya responded. "It's what you found earlier talking to people. We have nothing to go on."

Rick leaned back in his chair. "I know we've talked about this before, but do you think the voodoo dolls at the scene are staged, or do you think they have something to do with an actual ritual being performed?"

"We don't believe the dolls are anything more than a signature. But from talking to a few people far more knowledgeable about voodoo than I am, they believe there was a ritual performed based on the markings on the body and the blood loss."

"I saw mention of the markings near the body in the newspaper," Harper said. "What were the markings?"

Det. Joya hesitated for a moment. "We aren't releasing this information to the public, but the bodies and crime scenes have strange voodoo symbols that experts on the subject tell me are for power and longevity."

Harper needed to find a way to tell Det. Joya what she knew about Dante without coming across as crazy. She still didn't see a way though. "Did the voodoo experts give any clue as to what kind of ritual was performed? Its purpose, I mean."

Det. Joya scrunched up his face and then ran a hand through his hair. He looked at them skeptically. "You're probably not going to believe this, but they think the person performing the ritual is stealing the victim's lifeforce for their own or trying to, that is."

"That means what?" Rick asked, glancing between Det. Joya and Harper.

Det. Joya explained, "I'm not saying I believe this, but the experts I spoke to say there is some very dark magic where you can steal the lifeforce of another to live longer. One even suggested immortality."

Rick went to speak, but Det. Joya held up his hand to stop him. "I'm saying what they believe. I don't believe in all that nonsense. I think

CHAPTER TWENTY-FIVE

we have a very theatrical serial killer whose signature is this elaborate ritual."

Harper's hopes were dashed. She couldn't share what she knew about Dante with Det. Joya. He wasn't a believer, and Harper didn't think right now, at least, was the time to push the issue. "I thought I heard someplace there were murders like this before here in New Orleans. Is that true?"

"Yes, ma'am. Not just here in New Orleans. I've been talking to some of my colleagues and every ten to twenty years or so, there has been a rash of murders with blood loss like we are seeing now. But those victims weren't all shot and no voodoo dolls left at the scene."

Jackson locked eyes with the detective. "Is there any chance you're dealing with the same killer who changed how they operate?"

"I doubt it. I found similar cases going back more than eighty years. That's certainly not the same killer. He'd need to be immortal or something."

Jackson, Rick, and Harper all shared a look that Det. Joya was oblivious to.

Chapter Twenty-Six

"What did you think of Iggy?" Dante asked as they walked back to his house.

Hattie didn't like speaking ill of anyone, and she was sure all those years fighting evil had to have taken a toll. Still enough, her opinion wasn't one she wanted to share. She thought he was a drunk, but Hattie wouldn't tell Dante that. "I think he's a man who has faced evil much in his life and probably doesn't always have the best coping mechanisms."

Dante peered down at her. "You think he's a drunk?"

"I was trying not to say that." Hattie laughed. "Are you sure he will be able to help you?"

"He's the Vatican's best exorcist. If there is anyone on Earth who knows about fighting dark energy, it's him. Lucinda was right when she said we are kidding ourselves if we don't believe Pierre is in some way or another demonic. I hadn't even given any thought to that until she said it, but it makes perfect sense."

Angels and demons weren't something Hattie pondered too often. As a child, her mother always cautioned her about the devil making her do bad things. As soon as Hattie was school-aged, she believed that was ridiculous. People did bad things because they wanted to. Maybe her frame of reference needed to change.

"Help me understand if you can, Dante, are you saying you think

CHAPTER TWENTY-SIX

Pierre is possessed?"

"No, not at all," Dante said emphatically. "It's free will. Pierre is freely choosing to do what he's doing, but he has help. It's the only thing that makes sense to me now. I don't know why I didn't see it before. It's why nothing I tried broke the curse. He has unlimited power beyond any human capability. I think that's why we were sent to Iggy."

Hattie stayed quiet for several more moments and then said, "I think you might be right. I'm not sure what we are supposed to be doing in the meantime."

Just as the words left Hattie's mouth, a woman came out of a side street and ran towards them. She had a streak of mascara under her eye running down her cheek and her lipstick was smudged. Her hair looked like it hadn't been brushed in a few days. "Are you Dante?" the woman asked frantically, reaching out and gripping his arms.

Startled, both Dante and Hattie took a step back. "I am," he said. "Who are you?"

"I was told to deliver you a message, and if I did, my husband would be returned to me."

Hattie looked around suspiciously, assuming they were being watched. "Who took your husband?"

"I don't know," the woman cried. "They took him this morning." The woman fumbled in her pocket and pulled out her phone. She pulled up a video and showed it to Hattie. "Here, look at this."

Hattie took the phone from her and Dante peered over her shoulder to watch the video. The clip was grainy and not in focus. A person stood in the shadows, but there wasn't enough light to see them. Hattie couldn't even tell if it was a man or a woman. Their voice was also distorted, coming out more electronic than human. *Dante, we have Celeste. She's ours now.*

"I don't understand," Dante said looking down at Hattie. His face grew paler than normal. "What do they mean they have Celeste? No one has seen her in years. Even when I tried to find her recently, I just hit dead ends."

Hattie didn't understand either. To the woman, she said, "Where is your husband now?"

"They said if I showed you this video, he'd be at home waiting for me."

"How would they know if you found Dante and showed him the video?" Hattie asked.

"I don't know, but I wasn't taking any chances."

Hattie looked up at Dante and back at her. "We are going back to your house with you."

Dante barely moved. It was like his feet were cemented in place. Hattie tugged at his arm. "Come on, we have to go." Dante's blank expression gave away his shock, but Hattie wasn't going with this woman alone. It could be a trap. "Dante," she said shaking him.

Dante finally looked down at her. "They have Celeste."

Hattie reached out and grabbed his hand. "Let's go and speak to her husband, Dante. He might have seen or heard something that will help us find Celeste. If they have her, that's the most important thing right now."

"I'm Sandy," the woman said as they started to follow. "I only live a few blocks away on Rampart Street. My husband was taken this morning. He went to get us some coffee from a shop down the road. He never came back. Soon after, I got this video."

"How did you find Dante?" Hattie asked.

Sandy glanced back at her as they walked. "I was given a photo of Dante along with his address. When he wasn't at the house, I set out to search. I've been walking the streets for hours. I was so relieved when I saw you."

Hattie was nervous for the woman. She didn't know if Sandy's husband would be there when they arrived or if he'd be the next body

CHAPTER TWENTY-SIX

found. "Sandy, you said they contacted you with Dante's information and the instructions. How did they contact you?"

"There was a note slipped under my door," Sandy said. "It was so strange. It happened about an hour after my husband left. I was expecting him home when there was a knock at the door. I went to look out and there was the note, half under the door and half outside of it."

"Did you see anyone?" Dante asked, his voice shaky and skin still pale.

"I looked up and down the street and no one was there," Sandy explained. "I stepped back into the house and opened the envelope. There was the message with Dante's details and a photo of him, along with a web address for the video I shared."

Dante nudged Hattie's arm, and she assumed they were both thinking the same thing. Dante asked, "Do you still have the envelope and materials inside?"

Sandy nodded. "It's home on my kitchen table. I'll give it to you once we get there." She walked in silence but then looked up at Dante. "Who took my husband and how are you involved?"

"I'm not involved," Dante responded angrily. He stopped walking, but Hattie bumped into him and pushed him along. He softened his tone. "I'm sorry, I don't know who exactly took your husband, but this may be connected to something in my past. If it is, I'm very sorry you were involved."

Sandy didn't say anything, but she quickened her pace. It was hard to keep up with her, but Hattie understood her urgency. She wanted to tell Dante to go ahead with Sandy and she'd catch up, but Hattie worried what Dante would do alone.

They finally reached Sandy's house. She fished in her pocket, pulling out her keys. When the door was unlocked, Dante turned the door handle and opened it. He looked down at Sandy. "I think I should go in first."

Sandy protested, and Hattie reached for her arm. "It's better this way. Let's hope your husband is in there, but if something goes wrong, better to let Dante face it first."

Sandy nodded once, but it was clear she wasn't happy about the decision. Dante opened the door and stepped inside. He closed the door behind him. Hattie was left standing outside of the house with Sandy.

"I can't lose my husband," she said, holding back sobs. "He's my entire world. He only went out for coffee."

"I never asked his name." Hattie realized she was so focused on Dante and Celeste that she hadn't even tried to comfort Sandy.

"Max. We've been together since high school, married twenty years last month." Sandy watched the house, on edge waiting for Dante to return.

They didn't have to wait long. A few minutes later, Dante pulled open the door and stepped outside with them. "There's no one here. Did the instructions tell you to call or text someone once you found me?"

"No," Sandy said nearly in a whine. "Where is he? I did exactly what they asked."

Dante looked to Hattie for an answer, but she didn't have any. All she could do was help ease the woman's pain. She took Sandy by the arm. "Let's go inside and call the police. I'm sure they can help find Max."

They stepped inside the house, which was a stark contrast to Hattie's mood. The home had a warm inviting feel. The energy was one that radiated love and peace. Hattie knew without even having to ask that Sandy and Max had a happy life together. She hoped it wasn't over.

Hattie guided Sandy over to a chair in the living room. "Do you have any tea in the kitchen? Sometimes it's best to just breathe and have a cup of tea. This situation will sort itself out."

"It's in the cabinet by the stove." Sandy sat in the chair, tears in her eyes, staring off into space.

CHAPTER TWENTY-SIX

Hattie hitched her head toward the kitchen for Dante to follow. "I'm going to call Harper and then the police. You do another search of the house. I don't feel like this guy is dead."

Dante peered down at her. "You can tell that?"

Hattie didn't respond because she couldn't. She didn't have a reason why she felt that way, she just did. While Dante stood there in shock about the whole situation, Hattie put some water on to boil, fixed the cup with the tea, and called Harper. She quickly explained the situation and gave Harper the address. Thankfully, Harper was still with Det. Joya and they were all on their way to Sandy's house.

Turning to Dante, Hattie said, "Harper will be here in a few minutes with a detective. You better think fast about what you want to tell him about Celeste. There's no way we can explain this situation without bringing Celeste into it."

Before Dante could respond, Sandy let out a high-pitched wail that sent Hattie and Dante scrambling to the front of the house. They didn't even make it to the living room. Once in the hall, they saw Sandy sitting on the floor in the open doorway with a man's head on her lap.

Chapter Twenty-Seven

Sandy raised her head and looked down the hall at Hattie and Dante. "It's Max, he's alive but barely. I thought I heard a knock on the door and when I opened it, there he was just lying on the stoop. Help me, please. I don't know what's wrong with him. He's barely breathing."

Dante and Hattie rushed down the hall. Hattie checked his pulse while Dante looked Max over for any obvious signs of trauma. As Hattie turned the man's wrist to hold it in her hands, she saw the small puncture wound on his arm. His coloring told the same tale. Max had lost a considerable amount of blood. Hattie reached for her cellphone and called 911, explaining the situation and begging for an ambulance.

Sandy sat cradling her husband's head looking up at Hattie in confusion and terror. "I don't understand," she said when Hattie ended the call. "How could he be missing blood? Why would someone do this?"

Hattie wasn't sure what to say. She certainly wasn't going to explain the connection to the rash of murders in the city. It would send poor Sandy over the edge. All Hattie could do was lie. "I don't know, but the paramedics and the police are on their way. I'm sure they are going to get a blood transfusion going and he'll be okay. Let's just keep him comfortable and think positively."

Hattie looked at Dante and whispered, "They must have just dumped

CHAPTER TWENTY-SEVEN

Max's body so they can't be too far off. Go outside and see if you can find them."

Dante agreed there was nothing more he could do for Max so he set off on foot. Hattie would handle it from there. It wasn't long before they heard the sirens and a little hope returned to Sandy's face. Hattie stepped outside to ensure they stopped at the right house, and as soon as she saw the paramedics, she waved.

Soon the house filled with medical personnel who made quick work of getting Max on a gurney, taking his vitals, and treating him. They started the blood transfusion right there on the spot.

As Sandy followed her husband to the ambulance, she looked back at Hattie. "My keys are on the coffee table. Please lock up before you leave or wait here. I don't care. I just need to go. My phone with the video is on the table, too."

"I'll handle everything, don't worry," Hattie assured her. As soon as they were gone, Hattie went to get the keys and the phone and sat waiting for Harper to arrive. She was taking longer than expected so Hattie texted her. Harper assured her they were just a few minutes away.

Hattie exhaled, feeling the tension rise in her shoulders. She went to the mantel over the fireplace and looked at the photos of Sandy and Max and their family. It didn't look like the couple had any children, but it appeared they had a loving group of family and friends. Hattie heard the turn of the front door handle and rushed to the hallway to see who it was.

"I couldn't find anyone," Dante said as he stepped through the doorway. "Did Max make it?"

"He's off to the hospital. The paramedics started a transfusion so I hope so. Harper is on her way." As soon as the words left her mouth, Harper appeared right behind Dante with Jackson and two men she didn't recognize.

Hattie waved them in. "Let's all go to the living room to speak." She explained that the paramedics had taken Max to the hospital and Sandy went with them. Looking at the man with the badge around his neck, who Hattie assumed was Det. Joya, she said, "You'll have to go to the hospital to interview them, but we can fill you in with what we know."

"I can wait to do that," he said. "Let the hospital do what they have to do."

Harper made quick introductions and rushed to hug her aunt. "I can't imagine how scary that was."

Hattie patted her back. "I think Max will be okay. That's all that matters."

All of them sat down in the living room. Rick asked, "We've been covering this case in the newspaper from the start. I wonder why they didn't kill him."

Hattie shook her head. "I don't think killing was their purpose this time." Hattie explained the video and that they told Sandy to find Dante specifically. She handed the phone over to Det. Joya who played it once and then passed it to Rick and finally to Harper. She and Jackson watched it together.

Jackson looked up from the video when it was finished. "How did Sandy find you?"

"We were walking back to Dante's house, and from a photo they gave her, Sandy recognized Dante. She said she had gone to his house and then started wandering the streets when he wasn't at home. She played us the video and we came back here with her."

Det. Joya looked at Hattie. "Who is Celeste?"

Dante cleared his throat. His expression showed the uncertainty of what he was about to say, but Hattie was surprised once he spoke. Dante turned to the mantel and didn't look at them as he spoke, but his voice was clear and strong. "I'm going to tell you a tale you won't believe, Det. Joya, but it's the key to solving these heinous crimes. All I'm asking is

CHAPTER TWENTY-SEVEN

for you to hear me out with an open mind."

Dante spent the next twenty minutes telling the tale that Hattie had now heard several times about meeting Pierre and the curse that followed for him and Celeste. Dante even explained his last life with Celeste and the way she ended it. When he was done, Dante turned around and looked at Det. Joya, who at that point was sitting back on the couch with his mouth open too shocked for words. "You see, Detective, it wasn't until recently that I even learned Celeste is alive. The voodoo markings on the dolls you are finding next to the bodies are a signature Celeste used in her voodoo. I cannot believe she would do this on her own. Pierre must be making her do this. I think she added the signature as a way to send me a message. That's the only explanation I have. I think Pierre is telling me he has Celeste and is trying to draw me out for some reason, goading me maybe."

Det. Joya didn't say anything for several moments. He just watched each one of them, assessing for credibility and wondering if they were crazy, or worse, the killers – Hattie wasn't sure.

"I know this is hard to believe," Hattie said sympathetically. "It was a lot for me the first time I heard Dante's story, and I've known him for a long time. I even have my own metaphysical shop in Little Rock where I give psychic readings, do spells, and can speak to the dead. If it's hard for me to understand, I can't even imagine what you are feeling right now."

"It's a lot to process," Det. Joya said slowly. He turned to Rick. "Did you know about this?"

"I learned earlier today. You know me, Det. Joya, I'm a skeptic, but what they say adds up."

Jackson locked eyes with Det. Joya. "I wouldn't be involved in anything like this unless I believed Dante's story one hundred percent. I know men like us want facts and concrete evidence. Harper is that way, too. But sometimes we just have to accept there are things we don't understand."

Det. Joya exhaled. Hattie was sure he was going to storm out of the place or arrest them all. He didn't do either. He simply looked up at Dante and asked, "Why is he taking the victims' blood?"

"I think he needs it for whatever voodoo ritual he's doing to keep himself alive. That's the only thing I can figure. I'm cursed. No matter how many times I've tried to end my life – and trust me, there's been more than a few attempts – I can't die. I don't think it's the same for Pierre. He's using some very dark forms of magic to keep himself alive, and I think he needs blood to do that."

"That's the same response I received from the voodoo experts I asked." Det. Joya moved back on the couch and kept silent for a few minutes. No one else said a word. Hattie wasn't sure if the man was in shock or feeling the enormity of the challenge in front of him.

Finally, after a few minutes, he said, "As I told Harper, there have been cases like this with blood loss in the past. Is there any chance it's been Pierre all along?"

"It could be," Dante said seriously, walking over and sitting down near Det. Joya. "I don't understand everything that's happening. I had no idea until a few days ago Pierre was even still alive."

"Do you have proof that he is?" Det. Joya asked.

"If today isn't proof, I don't know what is."

"Right, I know what you're saying, but it's not definitive," Det. Joya argued. "It could be some sicko who knows the story and is now playing it out like some twisted fantasy he has of being immortal. It might not be real."

Hattie hadn't thought of that. She was so focused on Dante's story and swept up in everything Iggy and Lucinda had told them, she never even stopped to consider an alternative. "Det. Joya, if it's not Pierre, then who could it be?"

"I think only Dante would know that." Det. Joya looked over at Dante.

CHAPTER TWENTY-SEVEN

"Any ideas?"

Dante didn't say anything.

It was Harper who seemed to have worked out an alternative theory. She looked at Dante first. "Please, don't be angry with what I say. Celeste was presumed dead this whole time, killed in a fire, but I know from a vision she wasn't killed. She set the fire and left. Then voodoo showed up in Hattie's yard with Celeste's signature and now again with these murders. I understand the gun used in these killings was an antique gun similar to one Dante had. Who more likely to have the gun than his wife?"

Harper had connected so many pieces all Det. Joya could do was rake a hand down his face and look to Dante. He stood and motioned for Dante to follow. "You need to come down to the station with me to talk."

Hattie stood as well. "I'm going with you."

Chapter Twenty-Eight

"What fire?" Rick asked Harper as they left Sandy's house. Hattie had locked up the house to go with Dante and Det. Joya. Harper, Jackson, and Rick were headed back to the newspaper office.

Harper glanced up at Rick. "Several years ago, when Celeste disappeared, she set fire to her house. Dante and everyone else assumed it was Celeste who died because a woman's body was found burned in the home. They weren't able to match DNA so it was more an assumption it was Celeste than hard proof."

"Where was the fire?" Rick asked, his eyes lighting up with some recognition.

"Here in the French Quarter," Jackson said. "Do you know anything about it?"

Rick nodded, smiling. "I think I covered the story when it happened. Let's go back and look at the archives. There might be something in them that gives us more clues."

They were almost to the newspaper office when Jackson asked, "Are either of you feeling as overwhelmed as I am?"

Harper exhaled, releasing some tension she had been holding since leaving Sandy's house. "Definitely. I thought I was the only one. Dante and Hattie seem to take all of this in stride, but I hate when I can't make heads or tails of something."

CHAPTER TWENTY-EIGHT

Rick nodded along. "It's going to take one good lead and then the case will start to unravel. Once we know more Det. Joya can hopefully stop them."

Jackson looked to Harper with eyebrows raised. "What if they can't be stopped by conventional means, Rick? What if it's going to take some spiritual warfare to stop this killer?"

Rick let out a nervous laugh as he pulled open the door to the building. "That's on you guys then."

The three rode the elevator to Rick's office. Once Harper and Jackson took a seat on the couch, Rick sat down at his desk and typed away until he found the archived articles he was searching for. "Right here, Celeste Grand. She died in a house fire. It was a significant enough blaze that the fire investigator knew it was arson." He looked up at Harper. "You're telling me it was Celeste who set the fire?"

"Grand must be her maiden name," Harper explained. "But yes, I saw Celeste set the fire in a vision. Are there witnesses we can speak to, anyone who might have known her back then?"

Rick scanned articles and then pointed to one section. "Gabriel Taver is quoted several times in these articles. She was a friend of Celeste's and one of the last people to speak to her before the fire." Rick raised his head. "What do you say we go have a chat with Gabriel?"

Harper stood and went to Rick's desk to read an article. He spun his laptop around and she scanned the information he had just read. "Are you sure you don't have other work to do? I feel bad we are taking up so much of your time."

Rick smiled. "I haven't had this much excitement in years. I'm all in unless you think you should go alone."

Jackson shook his head. "You should come with us. You interviewed her before. It gives us some credibility."

"It's settled then. Let me just search a current address for her." Rick zeroed in on his laptop and searched. A few minutes later, they had an address. Luckily, Gabriel still lived in the French Quarter so it was only a few minutes away.

As they were leaving the building, Rick said, "I can walk you by where Celeste used to live if you'd like. Someone bought the land and built a new house."

Harper didn't know if anything would connect to the vision she had, but she figured it wouldn't hurt. "Sure, that might be helpful."

Harper was grateful for his help. As they hit the corner of Dauphine and Toulouse Streets, Rick pointed to a small two-story home. It wasn't fancy by any means, but from their vantage point, they could see the house had far more depth than width.

"There is a courtyard in the back," Rick said.

Harper wondered if the courtyard had remained intact from when Celeste lived there. There was a high wrought-iron fence around the property and a good deal of vegetation to offer some privacy, but Harper wanted to check it out. She crossed the street and went directly toward the back of the home. Rick and Jackson followed.

"What is it, Harper?" Jackson asked, walking in step with her.

"I remember a courtyard from my vision. I could see out to it from the door Celeste left through. I only saw it from the interior of the home." Harper got right up to the fence and peered through. Through the vines and shrubs, she could see the courtyard. It wasn't so much that the furniture looked the same, but everything else did – the red brick patio flooring was similar and the door to the home was positioned in a short, enclosed area off from the rest of the patio. Harper was sure this is what she had seen Celeste walk out into in her vision.

Harper took in the area. There was a short alleyway right behind the house. Celeste could have easily gotten into a car or left on foot. The back of the home offered privacy so she wouldn't have been seen by anyone passing by on the street. What Harper wanted to know most was if it was even possible for Celeste to sneak away after starting the fire. Now, Harper knew it was. She explained to Jackson and Rick. "As I said, I only saw out that back door so I didn't realize there was an alleyway back here. At the time, I didn't know how plausible her escape might be. I'm seeing now it would have been easy for her."

When she was done, they followed Rick down two more blocks and stopped on Orleans Street. He stepped up on the short stoop in front of a house and knocked on the red door. A few minutes later, a woman with short dark hair and large hoop earrings stepped out. She had red and blue paint all over her hands, arms, and shirt. There was a streak of blue under her eye.

"Can I help you?" she asked, squinting at them.

Rick asked if she was Gabriel and when she said she was, he introduced the three of them. "I covered the story about Celeste Grand years ago, and you gave me a statement. I had a few more questions."

Gabriel blinked rapidly and wrinkled her forehead. "I'll tell you what I remember. I'd shake your hand, but I'm covered in paint." She stepped out of the way and let them into her house. "Have a seat in the living room while I wash up. I've been in my studio painting all morning."

Harper was about to ask Gabriel what she painted but that became abundantly clear as they stepped into the living room off the foyer. Large prints of brightly colored scenes of New Orleans and people's portraits hung all over the space. Gabriel had signed each one at the bottom. They were all so beautiful Harper wasn't sure where to look first. The contrast of color, the brush strokes, the scenes – the woman had serious talent. Harper could easily imagine these paintings as a collection at a gallery in New York City. She told Gabriel as much when she returned.

Drying her hands on a rag, Gabriel laughed. "I had a showing once or twice up there. It's not my scene, but I make a good living showing my work across the south. I set up shop sometimes down by Jackson Square. I make a good enough living."

She sat down on the edge of an ottoman. "Now, what do you want to know about Celeste?"

Harper had no idea how she wanted to start the conversation. She wasn't sure if she wanted to draw out what Gabriel might know slowly or get right to the point. Harper looked down at Gabriel and shot straight. "I have reason to believe Celeste is still alive and didn't die in that fire. That means someone else's body was found. I'm looking for any information that might tell me where Celeste is now and who the dead woman might be."

Gabriel never took her eyes off Harper. She barely blinked and didn't react. After a moment, she asked, "How do you know that?"

"I have the gift of psychometry. Before Celeste left, she returned earrings to Dante. I've held those earrings and was given a vision. Celeste set the fire and walked out of that house alive."

"I see," Gabriel said evenly. "What was Celeste wearing when she left?"

Harper was taken aback by the question, but she scanned her memory for the answer. "When Celeste left the house that night, she had on a red flowing peasant skirt and a white shirt. She had several beaded bracelets on her left wrist."

Gabriel dropped her head and took several deep breaths. "I assume you know about the baby, too."

"What baby?" Harper asked sharply. She glanced at Jackson who shrugged. Rick didn't say anything either.

Gabriel snapped her head up. "I hope you have some time. This could take a while."

Chapter Twenty-Nine

Hattie and Dante had been sitting in a small conference room at the New Orleans police department for the last hour. Det. Joya assured Dante he wasn't under arrest and wasn't even a suspect. He simply wanted to gather more information from Dante. After Det. Joya asked Dante some biographical information, he left the room.

"It's going to be okay," Hattie said, patting his hand.

Gruffly, Dante said, "I need to be out there searching for Celeste. This is a waste of time. I've completely exposed myself so it better be for a good reason. I've done a good job of hiding my immortality for more than two centuries."

"I have a good feeling about Det. Joya. Let's give him a chance." Hattie and Dante sat talking for a few more minutes until Det. Joya came into the room.

He set a file down on the table and tapped his finger on it. "This doesn't prove you're immortal, but it's close." Det. Joya opened the file and pulled out several records including old photographs printed off the internet, a birth certificate, and several other documents. After laying all the documents on the table, he said, "The birth certificate, land records, and marriage certificates match up. I had four people searching and no one can find a death certificate for you here or anywhere. Is there any way you can prove you're immortal and don't just look eerily similar to a deceased relative?"

"What about fingerprints?" Hattie suggested.

"They don't go that far back," Det. Joya said. "Do you have any definite proof to your claim, Dante?"

Dante leaned forward, resting his arms on the table. He didn't say much, but what he said was effective. "You can shoot me."

"What will happen if I do?" Det. Joya asked seriously.

Hattie couldn't believe the man was considering it. She was about to argue when Dante responded.

"I'll bleed, probably pass out, and in about twenty minutes be good as new again. I'm not offering this lightly, Detective. Being shot is painful. I still feel all the pain you'd feel, but my body regenerates. I don't know how else to prove my immortality. You've looked at all the documents. I've never changed my name or birthday or anything. I've been in plain sight for all of these years. I haven't moved around much. New Orleans is my home, and it's where I'm most comfortable. But outside of trying to kill me yourself, I don't have any way to prove it."

Det. Joya exhaled a breath and considered what Dante said. He picked up a photo that looked like it was from the late 1800s and studied it. Then he looked across the table at Dante. "How did you get away with it all of these years?"

"People are focused on their own lives. They aren't paying attention to others too often. When anyone became suspicious, I'd disappear for a few years. I mostly stayed to myself though, solely focused on breaking the curse. It wasn't that hard getting away with it. That's what you have to understand, I'm taking a huge risk telling you. But I have to find Celeste, and Pierre has to be stopped."

Det. Joya dug through his files until he came upon a photo of a gun. He slid it across to Dante. "Is that yours?"

Dante picked up the photo and carefully examined it. While still holding it, he said, "I think so. The initials certainly are mine. There

CHAPTER TWENTY-NINE

were many guns around at that time similar to this. I can't say for sure but probably. It was stolen from my home at the turn of the century."

Det. Joy's face registered surprise. "Stolen? What happened?"

Dante looked to the ceiling as if trying to remember the details. Hattie wasn't sure how he did it. She could barely remember the details of last week.

After a moment, Dante recounted the break-in. It was around 1889, but Dante couldn't remember the exact date. It was a weekend he had traveled out of town. "I came home to find the doors unlocked and the house trashed," Dante explained. "Several things were missing, the gun among them."

"Did you make a police report?"

"I did, Detective. Normally, I wouldn't have, but the gun was important to me along with some jewelry that belonged to my wife."

"Do you keep records that far back?" Hattie asked, hoping they did. She didn't know where Det. Joya's line of questioning was heading so she wasn't sure whether or not to be impatient with him. The feeling Dante had earlier was starting to set in. She wanted out of this room so they could do something more constructive.

Det. Joya didn't respond to Hattie. Instead, he asked Dante for some details about the break-in, including double-checking his home address and the approximate date it happened. When he had what he needed, Det. Joya pulled out his phone and texted a message to someone. When he was done, he looked back at Dante. "Let's say for the sake of time, you're immortal and everything you've told me is true. You're telling me the man who cursed you is now running around the city killing people. How do we catch him?"

"If it's him and I believe it is, you have to find him first," Dante said. "I know where he used to live in the French Quarter, and I know the family has a home in the Garden District. Otherwise, I have no idea."

Det. Joya pulled another sheet of paper from the file folder and slid it across the table. Both Hattie and Dante peered down at it. It was Pierre Lacourt's death certificate. Dante looked up. "I can't explain this."

Det. Joya sat back and folded his arms. "I can't explain it either. But the person you're telling me kidnapped your wife and is committing murder is long dead. He is buried in Saint Louis Cemetery. He can't both be dead and running around killing people."

"I have no explanation," Dante said again. He leaned forward on the table. "Are you arresting me for anything?"

"Have you done something wrong?"

"No," Dante said definitively. "But it's clear you don't believe me so I'm going to find Celeste on my own. Every moment I sit here is precious time wasted."

Det. Joya and Dante sat with their eyes locked for several moments, neither one of them moving. It was finally Hattie who broke the stalemate. "Listen, I think we can all agree nothing is going to be solved just sitting here. Detective, you have a serial killer to catch. Dante, you have Celeste to find. If you don't want to help each other, at least let's go our own way and see what we find."

Det. Joya's cellphone pinged and he read the message. He bit the inside of his cheek, making a popping sound when he let it go. "You're correct, Dante. There was a police report made at that address back in 1889. Funny enough, your name is listed along with the gun and jewelry like you said. You're one step closer to me believing you."

Det. Joya looked between Hattie and Dante. "I have leads to run down. I expect you not to get in the way. But I assume you'd like to go with me when I question Sandy and Max."

Hattie couldn't believe he was letting them go with him, but she wasn't going to argue. Dante didn't respond so Hattie did. "We'd like to go with you. I'm hoping Max remembers something he can share that might give a hint where he was being held."

Det. Joya nodded and got up to leave. Dante and Hattie followed. As

CHAPTER TWENTY-NINE

they made their way down the hall, Dante reached for Hattie's arm and pulled her back. "I need to go to the cemetery and see who is in Pierre's tomb. I don't believe he's dead."

"Neither do I, but I think since Det. Joya is trusting us to go with him to the hospital, we shouldn't back out. We can go to the cemetery later, and we might want to bring Lucinda with us. In fact, why don't you get a hold of Iggy who can track down Pierre's burial plot so we aren't running all over the cemetery searching?"

"He's not buried. He'd be in a tomb," Dante reminded her. As they stepped outside and into Det. Joya's car, Dante pulled out his cellphone and whispered, "I'll text him."

Hattie had forgotten that in New Orleans most people were laid to rest in above-ground tombs, which even for all her ghostly encounters kind of creeped her out. Hattie had already decided when she passed, she was going to be cremated and turned into a tree. She'd have a bench with her name and Beau's on it.

Hattie was so lost in thought about her demise that before she realized it they had pulled up in front of the hospital. They followed Det. Joya inside and through the halls until they found Max resting comfortably with Sandy sitting in a chair at his side.

When Sandy saw them, she stood and walked toward them preventing them from coming too far into the room. "Max is sleeping. He'll make it thankfully, but they had to give him something to calm him down. The nurse said he'd probably sleep for the next few hours."

Det. Joya nodded. "Was he agitated?"

Sandy exhaled and looked back at her husband. When she turned back around, she had tears in her eyes. "Max was rambling incoherently. I tried to find out who took him or where he was being held. All he had was bits and pieces. He said he got coffee, but as he was standing in line to pay, he thought he felt a prick on his arm like a bug bite. He swatted it away but nothing was there. He remembered walking out of the shop and then nothing until he woke up in a dark room. He felt really weak and there was blood on his arm. He figured right away someone took blood from him. He tried to stand to find a way out, but he was too weak."

"Did he hear anything?" Hattie asked.

"He said he heard a man and woman talking, but that was it. Max said he couldn't make out what they were saying. He said he was in and out of consciousness but felt like he was in a house. He was on a bed and the windows had shutters that weren't open."

"Does he know how he got home?" Dante asked.

"He doesn't remember. One minute he was in that house and the next I was there with him on the stoop. The doctor thinks he also might have been drugged so they are giving him some fluids and watching him closely. When Max wakes up and if he knows more, I'll call you."

"Do that please," Det. Joya said. "I hope Max fully recovers. If you need anything, call me."

Hattie handed Sandy back her house keys and phone since the cops had the video now, and hugged her. She gave Sandy her cellphone number. "Let me know how I can help."

The three of them stepped back into the hall. Det. Joya said he'd drive them back to the station, but Dante said they had a ride. Det. Joya promised he'd let them know if Max called and said anything useful later on.

When he left, Hattie asked, "Dante, what are we doing?"

"I want to check something out. I texted Lucinda on the drive over. She's coming to get us."

Chapter Thirty

"Who had a baby?" Harper asked again, unsure she had heard correctly.

Gabriel sighed. "It's a long story, but Celeste was pregnant with Dante's child when she left."

Harper was completely floored by the revelation. "Dante has no idea. In fact, he said they had never been able to conceive a child."

Gabriel seemed on the brink of saying something but then pulled back. "I don't know how to tell you this story. It's going to sound unbelievable to you."

Harper held her hand up. "We know about the curse."

Gabriel's eyes grew wide. "You know?"

"We know," Jackson reassured. "What we don't know is what happened to Celeste around the time of the fire. It's important we know because we need to find her."

"You're not going to find her." Gabriel smiled and when Harper tried to interrupt, she asked her to wait. "I'm glad you know. It makes this easier. As you know Celeste broke up with Dante about six months before the fire. What you don't know is why. She had just found out she was pregnant and worried she wasn't going to be able to keep her baby safe in New Orleans. She knew if she told Dante, he'd want to raise the child, which would only put them more at risk. No, Celeste wouldn't have it. She tried to come up with every conceivable plan under the sun.

Even if Dante ran away with her, someone would know. Celeste was sure they'd look for them. She thought the only way to keep her child safe was to leave and not tell Dante."

Jackson shook his head. "That's cruel, isn't it? Keeping Dante's child away from him, especially after how long they tried to have a baby?"

"I agree with you wholeheartedly, if the circumstances were normal. Which as you know, they weren't." Gabriel's eyes pleaded with them to understand. "Celeste isn't a bad person. She's one of the most amazing women I've ever known, but she suffered literally throughout centuries. There was no way she was going to allow their child to have the same fate so she left, but she waited too long."

Harper started to put it together. "Someone found out?"

Gabriel nodded. "At the time of the fire, Celeste was heading into her eighth month of pregnancy. Celeste always wore long skirts and flowing shirts so it was somewhat easy to hide. Most people thought she put on weight. I didn't even know at first. I joked with her that we both needed to get back to working out. It wasn't until late into her seventh month when she told me the whole story."

Gabriel looked to the ceiling. "You can imagine I was flabbergasted. How could it be true? But Celeste showed me photos of her and Dante from generations upon generations ago. I had no other explanation. If you knew Celeste, you'd know she didn't lie."

"Celeste planned to make everyone think she was dead," Harper said, not a question but a statement.

"That's right. Celeste wasn't sure how she was going to do it if no one found a body, but she figured if she was gone long enough, everyone, including Dante, would assume she had died."

Rick started to speak but the words didn't come out right. Even for a newsman, he seemed unsure of what to ask, but he gathered his thoughts. "There was a body found though. Who was it?"

"Marie Lacourt." Gabriel watched each of their faces, letting them

CHAPTER THIRTY

register surprise before she explained, "The same curse the Lacourts put on Dante, they put on themselves. I know most people only blame Pierre, but it was equally Marie. Celeste found that out later. While Dante and Celeste were having dinner, who do you think was preparing the spell work? It was Marie."

Harper inched forward on her seat, anticipating the next part of the story. "Did Marie find out about the baby?"

Gabriel frowned, a worry line creasing along her forehead. "Marie was always jealous of Celeste because she was the second choice for her husband. Pierre wanted to marry Celeste and had to settle for Marie. She knew that every day of her life. Of the two, Celeste was beautiful and graceful. Marie was a hag in comparison. Celeste was filled with positivity and light. Marie was bogged down with negativity and bitterness. Even with immortality, Marie wore the years on her face. It was like her negativity ate her alive."

Gabriel locked eyes with Harper. "The first time Marie came to Celeste she begged to know why Pierre didn't love her in the same way. Celeste didn't know what to say. She wanted nothing to do with Marie. She was, after all, the one who cursed her. Celeste tried to broker a deal for her and Dante's freedom, but Marie wouldn't relent. It was when she was leaving Celeste's home that Marie

noticed her belly. Marie told her she'd never keep her baby. That the child would be hers if she had to rip it out of Celeste's body herself. That set the plan in motion."

"Wasn't there any way to go to the police and ask for protection?" Rick asked.

Harper glanced over at him. "I wouldn't think so under the circumstances."

"That's right," Gabriel said. "It's a bit of a complicated story. Besides the obvious, it was just a threat. All Marie had to do was say she never said it. Celeste came to me, but I had no idea how to help her. She said the only way out would be to kill Marie. But how do you kill an immortal? Celeste didn't know. She had to find help quickly."

Jackson raised his eyebrows. "I'm guessing she found help?"

"A woman," Gabriel said. "I never knew much about her. Celeste told me I was better off not knowing. She said this woman knew how to kill an immortal. I don't know how Celeste found her or if she paid her. I just know this woman helped. Celeste knew Marie would come back, and she did about two weeks later. Celeste set a trap. She let it slip that she was leaving town. Celeste knew that would draw Marie to her house to stop her. I guess Celeste and the woman waited a few nights and finally, Marie showed up."

"Do you know what happened?" Rick asked, his face registering the same kind of shock and surprise Harper felt.

"I don't know the ins and outs of it all, but from what I know, Celeste lured Marie there and then doused her with holy water, which weakened her power. Celeste quickly put a salt ring around her and enclosed her in the circle. It prevented Marie from moving. Then the woman who was helping Celeste stabbed Marie with a special kind of blade. It killed her on the spot. Celeste said it did more than that though - it caused Marie's body to completely shrivel up like she was in a tomb for two hundred years. Celeste left the body in the living room where she had been killed. She gathered her things, set the fire, and left."

Harper's mind was spinning. What Gabriel explained answered so many questions for Harper and lent credibility to Dante's story. "It's why no one was ever able to tell who the dead woman was."

"What do you mean, Harper?" Jackson glanced over at her.

Harper explained, "Marie wouldn't have had fingerprints or dental records on file anywhere. They didn't have that kind of technology back in the 1700s before Marie and Pierre did the immortality spell on themselves. They'd just find the body and assume it was Celeste and never be able to tell otherwise. It's why no one was able to identify the body properly."

"That's exactly right," Gabriel said. "Celeste left that night with the help of the woman. She's never returned to New Orleans, and I've never seen her since."

Harper pinched the bridge of her nose, hoping they hadn't just hit another brick wall. "You don't know where she is?"

"I didn't say that, but I can't tell you where she is." Gabriel sat back defiantly.

"You don't understand. There was a man who was attacked this morning and held until his wife brought a message to Dante. Whoever took this man said they have Celeste."

Gabriel's hand flew to her mouth. "That can't be."

"It is," Harper insisted. "Celeste placed a special signature on all the voodoo work she did. Celeste's mark was found on spell work recently found in my aunt's yard in Little Rock and found on dolls left at the recent crime scenes of the horrific murders in the French Quarter."

"No, no, Celeste would never harm someone like that. I know she and the woman killed Marie, but that was different. Celeste didn't have a choice."

Jackson held up his hand. "It's okay. We don't think Celeste did anything wrong. We are trying to find her to see if she was taken or if this person, who we believe is Pierre, is bluffing. Did Pierre know Celeste killed Marie?"

"Celeste never knew. She never saw Pierre. In fact, until this last life, she never remembered seeing Marie before. It was a complete shock when Marie came asking about Pierre. Celeste and I spoke about whether Marie and Pierre were even still together. We never knew, but I'm sure he found out that Marie was gone. Given how jealous Marie was I don't know if she'd tell Pierre about the baby."

Harper wasn't sure either. She didn't have a good read on the situation, and it wasn't like there was anything around she could touch and tap into a vision to find out the truth. Harper spoke directly to Gabriel. "Is there a way you can call Celeste and make sure she's safe? We need to be sure. I'm concerned about her wellbeing. We have to know if she was taken or if it's all a ruse."

Gabriel nodded and stood. "Let me try to call her."

When Gabriel left the room, Rick looked to Harper. "What do you think?"

"I think she's telling the truth. What we know from Dante, the story makes sense. It also lines up with the vision I had. I never saw the living room. Before my vision, I had never seen more than Celeste's face in a photo. She was heavier than I thought she'd be, but it didn't even occur to me she might be pregnant. It makes sense now."

Gabriel shrieked from the other room, and the three of them stood abruptly. Gabriel came back into the room holding her phone in her shaking hand. "Celeste is gone. Her daughter is safe, but Celeste went to bed one night and was gone by morning. No one has seen her in several months."

Chapter Thirty-One

"Dante, where are we going?" Hattie asked as they stood outside of the hospital waiting for Lucinda. They had been waiting for more than an hour and Hattie had grown tired and impatient. Her right knee smarted with each passing minute. She was too old and too mortal to be standing around for no reason.

"I don't know why I didn't think of it before, but we should have checked Pierre's old house. When Sandy explained Max had said there were shutters on the windows it reminded me of the room Celeste and I were in." Dante shifted his eyes toward Hattie. "I've been to the house over the years to see if Pierre had come back, but no one was ever home. I waited a couple of times to see who was coming and going from the house, but I never saw Pierre."

"You really think Pierre went back to his old house?" Hattie asked skeptically.

"No, not back," Dante corrected. "If he's still alive, then there's a good chance he never left. Pierre was a creature of habit if nothing else. I don't think Pierre ever gave up his original home. I think if he's hiding anywhere, it's in there. I think that's where he took Max."

Hattie couldn't debate the logic, but she didn't think it was a very good idea to go there alone, even with Lucinda. "Dante, if Pierre took Max to that house, he had help. There is no way Max was drugged and then carted off the street by one person."

"You don't know that for sure. Sandy said Max felt something like a bug bite in the coffee shop. I assume someone injected him with something, and a few minutes later, it took hold. Kind of like the dinner we had with Pierre." Dante glanced toward Hattie. "If Max stumbled out onto the street, anyone could have taken him. Max doesn't know what happened until he woke up in the room."

"Let's see what Lucinda thinks about going there." Hattie didn't think taking this direct approach was wise. They had no idea what they were walking into.

"She's already agreed, which is why she is coming to get us."

It seemed Hattie was outnumbered. A few minutes later, a large black SUV with Lucinda behind the wheel pulled to a stop right in front of them. Dante opened the back door and helped Hattie inside. He climbed into the passenger seat. On the drive, Dante and Lucinda discussed details, but Hattie didn't say a word. She wasn't even sure why she was feeling so grumpy, but after leaving the hospital, a dark mood came over her. Her bones and joints ached, too.

Beau had promised to be there to help and keep an eye on her, but she hadn't seen him once since they had arrived. Hattie wondered if that was the growing discomfort she felt. Maybe it was just that she was being driven around by a half-demon. That probably would put a kink in anyone's day.

Hattie sat back and closed her eyes. She took a few deep cleansing breaths trying to clear her mind and improve her mood. Hattie sat like that for the rest of the car ride. When the car pulled to a stop, Hattie popped her eyes open and looked around. They weren't at a house.

"Where are we?" she asked.

Lucinda craned her head around to look at Hattie. "We are in the alleyway behind Iggy's house. I'll leave the car here. There aren't many places to park in the French Quarter. We can walk."

As they got out of the SUV, Hattie struggled with the height of it, but

CHAPTER THIRTY-ONE

Dante made sure she was back on solid ground. Hattie had no idea where they were going, but they walked a few blocks until they reached a corner lot and a house Hattie had trouble believing from the outside was just one family home. It spanned the width of at least three and wrapped clear around the block. The upstairs porch had a beautiful iron railing.

"Why is it so big?" Hattie asked, tipping her head back and looking up at the home.

Dante smiled at her. "It was one of the first homes built on this street. Similar to mine. The rest of the city was built around it."

Lucinda took in the expanse of the house. "Do you want me to lay low for now or come to the door with you?"

"We should all go together," Hattie said, the fear rising in her stomach. She pointed to the house. "Dante, if you believe Pierre is in there, then I'm sure whoever might answer the door will at least know who you are. We can't risk it. If someone else lives there, we can just act like we're lost and no one will be the wiser."

Dante didn't argue. He didn't say anything at all, but his face constricted and his eyes remained laser-focused on the door. He walked up to it without any hesitation and used the brass doorknocker, rapping it three times in a row. He stepped back with Lucinda and Hattie behind him and waited.

A few seconds later, an older woman with pleasant soft features and white short hair, not unlike Hattie's, answered the door. She wore navy blue pants and a soft pink blouse. "Can I help you?"

"I'm looking for the owner of the home," Dante said confidently.

"I'm Ann. My husband and I own the home, but he's not here right now. May I ask what this is about?"

Dante didn't immediately respond so Lucinda covered for him. "Do you know when he will be back?"

Ann smiled. "We do a bit of charity work. James is meeting with some donors right now. You might have heard of the Lacourt Family Foundation. It's run mostly by my daughter Alexandria now, but we actively fundraise."

Dante offered a stiff smile. "I had thought maybe the Lacourt family still owned this home, but I wasn't sure. That's in part what I was hoping to speak to the owner about."

"We've been the only owners, well my husband's family that is. We moved in after his parents passed away. Do you know my husband?"

Dante shook his head. "No, I don't know him. My family and your husband's go back hundreds of years in this neighborhood. I had ancestors who knew Pierre Lacourt – at least that's how the family stories go."

Ann laughed and smiled more broadly this time. "What is your name?"

"Dante La Croix, I was named after my great-grandfather, the one who knew Pierre," he lied with ease. "Is it just you and your husband in the house now?"

"We are," Ann said. "It's such a big house, we don't even use the upstairs anymore."

Dante and Ann spoke for a few more minutes about the house and their families. Hattie eventually interrupted. "I don't mean to be a bother, but is there any chance I can use your powder room?"

Ann's face faltered for only the briefest of seconds, but she forced a smile and said tightly, "Sure. There is one right at the end of the hallway here." She stepped out of the way to let Hattie pass into the house. Hattie had no idea what she was doing or looking for, but they weren't getting anywhere standing outside and chatting. If she was going to be forced into these situations, she was at least going to take some action.

As she stood in the foyer, right in front of her was a winding staircase that went to the second floor. Hattie glanced up as she walked farther

CHAPTER THIRTY-ONE

into the home. The hallway walls were brick which she imagined was original to the home, and lined with family photographs and one large painting of two people sitting side by side. Given how they were dressed Hattie assumed it was Pierre and Marie. Pierre looked exactly how he had appeared in the drawing from Harper's vision. There was a hardness around his eyes and soullessness when you peered into them. His mouth turned up in almost a cruel smirk. Marie, on the other hand, appeared as if she'd never seen a moment's happiness. Hattie shivered. If these were her relatives, she was sure she wouldn't have kept them on display.

Hattie made her way to the powder room and closed the door behind her. She didn't need to use the facilities, but she was stalling for time. Hattie caught her reflection in the ornate gold-trimmed mirror and frowned. She leaned in and pinched her cheeks to add color to her dreadfully pale face. She pulled the skin on her forehead and eyes back, remembering a time when the skin didn't sag like a basset hound. She looked as tired as she felt.

Hattie stepped away from the mirror and stood still, hoping to hear movement overhead. She glanced up at the ceiling but didn't hear anything. As she looked back at the door, a woman suddenly appeared in front of her. Hattie jumped but managed not to scream.

"Who are you?" Hattie asked, looking over the young woman. She was dressed in a long black skirt that went to the top of her black boots, a white high-collar blouse, and black apron over it.

"I'm Elsie. I was a maid here for the Lacourts." Elsie turned her head to the door and then back to Hattie. In a whisper, she said, "They killed me. You're not safe here. You need to go."

"Is there anyone else in this house?" Hattie asked. She knew she had to be quick.

"No one else living. They had a man here upstairs earlier, but he's gone now."

"Who had the man?"

"Ann and James, her husband," Elsie said, turning her head back toward the door.

"Is Pierre Lacourt here?" Hattie asked.

Elsie searched Hattie's face. "You know their secret?"

"I know Pierre's secret. Where is he?"

"I'm not sure. I can't remember the last time I saw Pierre."

"Have Ann and James had anyone else here recently?"

Elsie sighed. "There was a woman they called Celeste."

Hattie reached for the woman, but her hands slid right through her. "Is Celeste okay? Please, tell me that Celeste is okay."

"For now, she is, but I don't think for long. She didn't come here willingly. I heard James talking about killing her, but Ann told them he couldn't. They had to find out about the baby."

"What baby?" Hattie asked confused.

"I don't know, but I'm afraid for her." Elsie's expression turned sad.

"Where are they keeping her?" Hattie asked, taking a deep breath.

"There is a house in the Garden District and a warehouse, but I don't know where that is."

Hattie nodded and reached for the door. Elsie called her back though. "You have to be careful. James is more ruthless than Pierre. He learned well from his father. Ann and Alexandria, too. They will keep you and feed off your soul if they get a chance."

"Father? What do you mean?" Hattie asked, confused. She knew Pierre and James were related, but she had thought distantly.

"James is Pierre's son," Elsie explained. "The spell Pierre did on himself, he did on James, Ann, and Alexandria, too. You must be very careful."

Hattie swallowed hard. It meant the woman out there talking to Dante knew exactly who he was. They were all in danger, even if Lucinda was there with them. "Elsie, do you know why they are taking blood?"

CHAPTER THIRTY-ONE

"It's for the spell to keep them alive. The more lives they take, the more lifeforce they each have. It's how they have been doing it for years. They have to be stopped." Elsie raised her eyes up toward the ceiling. "All the souls they have taken reside in this house. We've tried to stop them, but they are too powerful."

"It's okay," Hattie reassured. "It's all going to be okay."

Chapter Thirty-Two

Hattie opened the powder room door and stepped out into the hallway. Hattie turned her head to peek down the rest of the hall and debated for a moment taking a look, but she thought better of it. As Hattie turned to walk back toward the front door, she collided right into Ann.

"I was just looking for you," Ann said. "Everything okay? I thought I heard you speaking to someone."

Hattie pulled her phone from her pocket. "I'm so sorry I took so long. My niece called me, and then I got a bit turned around coming out of there. Thank you again for allowing me to use your bathroom." Hattie brushed past her and didn't stop moving until she was outside and standing at Dante's side. She smiled at him like everything was fine. "Dante, we have to go. Harper is waiting for us. We've taken enough of Ann's time today."

"I don't mind," Ann said, narrowing her eyes at Hattie. "Are you sure you're okay? You seem a bit flustered."

Hattie laughed. "I just hate to be late. Harper has been waiting for us. I don't want to keep her. We have dinner plans tonight."

Dante looked down at Hattie with a curious expression on his face, but he let Hattie pull him away. He thanked Ann as they left. Lucinda followed them.

As soon as they were out of earshot, Lucinda said, "She's a demon,

CHAPTER THIRTY-TWO

isn't she? They have a smell about them."

"What is wrong with both of you? I'm trying to get some information, and you're both behaving strangely," Dante scolded.

Hattie sighed, exasperated with him. "You're clueless, you know that. No wonder you were so easy to kidnap and curse." As soon as the words were out of her mouth, Hattie's hand flew to her mouth in regret. "I didn't mean that, Dante. I'm sorry."

Dante stopped walking. "If you're behaving this strangely, Hattie, then something must be wrong. Tell me, please."

"Not here. At your house." Hattie grabbed his arm and pulled. She wasn't going to have this conversation in the middle of the street when Dante's house was only a mere three blocks away. Lucinda agreed with her. Hattie could tell by the way Lucinda kept looking around as if waiting for someone to attack at any moment. They needed to get inside and sit down and hash this out. Hattie needed Harper in on the conversation as well.

Dante was much stronger than Hattie so even when she pulled him to move it along, he didn't budge. "Dante, please," she begged. "We can't have this conversation out in the open. We need to get Jackson and Harper and all sit down to talk. You know I see ghosts and I spoke to one while inside the house. I found out information about Celeste, but we need to regroup right now."

Dante started to argue but caught the look on Hattie's face and gave in to her demands. The three of them walked quickly back to Dante's house. Hattie saw more spirits who tried to get her attention, but she kept her head down, ignored everyone in her path, and remained singularly focused on the safety that Dante's house would bring them.

They walked in the back way through the small patio and found Harper and Jackson waiting for them. Harper stood when she saw them. "We didn't have a key," she explained, "so we've been waiting. Dante, we have something we need to tell you."

Hattie rushed over to her and put her arms around Harper. "I'm glad you're here. There's something I need to share as well."

Harper whispered, "It can't possibly be bigger than my news."

Hattie pulled back and searched Harper's face and all at once what Elsie said about a baby clicked in her mind. It was something in Harper's eyes and tone that gave it away. This happened with the Ryan women. It was the bond they shared.

Hattie patted Harper's arm. "My news first, trust me on that."

Harper nodded. "Sounds like you've had a productive day as well."

Dante opened the back door to his house and let them all in. As Hattie stepped through the kitchen door, she said, "Why don't you all sit at the dining room table and I'll fix us a little snack and some tea. Then we can discuss."

They did as they were told. Hattie asked Dante where she could find teacups, tea, and some sort of snack. When he showed her around his kitchen, Hattie put water to boil on the stovetop, wishing she was back in her shop where she felt safe and comfortable. Not to mention, Hattie would kill for a chocolate cupcake right about now. Maybe her doctor had been right and she was a stress eater. The crackers, cheese, and assorted fruit Dante had would have to do.

Dante carried the tray for Hattie into the dining room, and he sat down with Jackson, Harper, and Lucinda. Hattie went back into the kitchen to grab the teapot.

When everyone had tea in front of them, Hattie sat back in her chair and clasped her hands in her lap. She first explained to Jackson and Harper about their meeting with Det. Joya and then visiting the Lacourt house. "When I was in the bathroom, a spirit appeared to me. Her name was Elsie and she had been a maid for the Lacourts. She was murdered by them as were many others. She told me that James, Ann, and Alexandria are all immortal."

"I don't..." Dante started, but Lucinda told him to keep quiet.

CHAPTER THIRTY-TWO

Hattie nodded a thank you. "As I was saying, James is Pierre's son, and according to Elsie, worse than his father. Ann is his wife and Alexandria his daughter. They have been immortal, lying about who they are and their family history to keep their secret under wraps. I can't say for sure there is no other family, but it doesn't appear so. It's just the four of them. As we suspected, the blood is used in spells. It's how they are keeping themselves alive."

Lucinda slapped her hand down on the table. "We have to take out the whole family."

Dante seemed to quickly digest the information. "What about Marie, Pierre's wife?"

Harper raised her hand and gave a little wave. "I know what happened to Marie. That's what we wanted to tell all of you. Celeste killed her. Rather," she amended, "Celeste got help to kill her." Harper looked across the table at Lucinda. "Is there any chance it was you who helped? This would be about fifteen years ago."

"I've killed so many. It's hard to keep track." Lucinda shrugged. "Where did this take place?"

"The corner of Dauphine and Toulouse Streets," Jackson said. It looked to Hattie like he wanted to say more, but he didn't.

Lucinda pursed her lips for several moments and scrunched up her face. "Pregnant woman?" she asked.

Harper bit her lip and looked to Dante. "Yes, Celeste was nearly eight months pregnant."

Dante's eyes widened. "It can't be..." was all he said, no other words came out of his mouth. Hattie reached for his hand, but he didn't even seem to register it.

Harper started to speak, but Jackson interrupted. "Dante, man to man, I understand how you're feeling. But Celeste was only trying to protect your daughter. She had no idea what would happen to your child given her curse and yours. She wanted to go far away from here and protect the baby. Celeste knew if you found out, you'd do everything in your power to protect them, even leaving New Orleans, but that would only draw more suspicion. Celeste didn't feel like she had much of a choice so she left to raise your child in safety. Marie found out though. Celeste didn't have a choice but to kill her."

Hattie appreciated that Jackson had delivered the message. She didn't think either she or Harper could have said it better. Dante seemed to come out of his fog quickly hearing what Jackson said.

"I understand," Dante said slowly, his voice filled with emotion. "Celeste was right. I would have put them more at risk. It was good she left. I just wish I had known Celeste was in danger from Marie." Dante looked down at Lucinda. "You didn't think it was important to tell me you killed Marie Lacourt?"

Lucinda put her hands up in defeat. "I didn't know the woman's name that I killed at the time. A woman, who called herself Gabriel, came to me and said there was a dangerous woman after her and her baby and that the woman had placed a spell on them. When Gabriel explained her curse, I knew the woman was dangerous. I told her to lay a trap and I'd wait for her. When she came, I'd know right away if she was a demon or had the mark of a demon, which she did. These malevolent forces have a smell. It's nearly like rotting meat but not quite. It's pungent and sour. Some will try to mask it with thick perfumes. Sometimes humans can smell them. Sometimes not, but a demon can always tell their kind."

Dante rested his hands on the table. "You wouldn't have connected it then. Gabriel was Celeste's best friend. It seems Celeste didn't use her own name." Turning to Harper, he asked, "Is that who you spoke to?"

"We went to see Gabriel. When the fire happened, she had given statements to the newspaper about how distraught she was to lose her friend. It was all part of the cover. Gabriel knew what was happening all along." Harper took a deep breath. "There's more, Dante. Gabriel

CHAPTER THIRTY-TWO

tried to reach Celeste while we were there and found out she's been missing for several months."

Hattie brushed her hand against Dante's arm. "Elsie said that James and Ann have her. Maybe at the house in the Garden District or maybe at a warehouse. She wasn't sure where that was located."

Dante turned to look at Hattie, but his eyes weren't focused. "What about Pierre? How does he fit into all of this?"

"I don't know," Hattie said honestly. "Elsie didn't say anything about him other than she hasn't seen him in a long time. He could be dead."

Dante pushed his chair back from the table and stood. "I have to go to the cemetery and check the tombs."

"We can't go now, Dante. I told you," Lucinda stressed to him, "tonight, in the dark we can go."

"What are we going to do about sneaking into the Lacourt house in the Garden District?" Harper asked.

"No, absolutely not," Hattie said. "Harper, this is far more dangerous now."

Harper started to argue, but Lucinda spoke up. "Hattie's right. Before you go into that house, we have to make sure they are gone. Let me work on a plan and get back to you." Standing with Dante, she said, "We need to wait to go to the cemetery until tomorrow night. Iggy is still trying to find Pierre's tomb."

Dante pounded his fist into his hand. "I can't just sit here and do nothing while they have Celeste."

Lucinda said, "You must rest for battle. In the meantime, let me handle a few things."

Dante took a deep breath. "As you wish."

Chapter Thirty-Three

It had been a sleepless night for Harper and Jackson. After Lucinda left, Dante had retired to his room, and Hattie, Harper, and Jackson had found a nice restaurant close by to have dinner. The traditional Cajun fare had been excellent, but they were all tired and a bit cranky from the day. Hattie had been uncharacteristically quiet. Even when pressed, she didn't offer up more than an assurance that she was fine.

Later, when they returned to the house and went up to their bedrooms, Harper checked in with her aunt again. This time, Hattie offered a sad smile and told Harper they should be happy for their simple lives and admitted to being a bit overwhelmed. Hattie, who normally could read her cards and get glimpses into the future, wasn't able to tap into the outcome of this situation, even though she had tried several times. She also didn't have the power to whip up a spell to make everything all better.

For the first time, in as long as Hattie could remember, she was completely powerless to affect any sort of change over her life or those she cared about. It had broken Harper's heart to hear how downtrodden Hattie felt. Harper had offered her aunt words of encouragement even though the words felt hollow as she said them. It bothered Harper that she couldn't seem to help Hattie more, especially with how much her aunt had positively impacted her life.

CHAPTER THIRTY-THREE

Harper told Jackson as much before they tried to go to sleep. He reassured Harper as best he could, but even he sensed Hattie wasn't herself. They both tossed and turned for most of the night but by morning Jackson had finally dozed off. Harper sat with her laptop on the bed pouring through property records in New Orleans, the surrounding parishes, and then nationally. She had called Det. Granger in Little Rock to ask for help. He balked at first, but finally relented when she explained what had been happening.

Harper sat in front of her laptop, trying different searches to trace the lineage of the Lacourts through public records. What she found astounded her. Unlike Dante who had been simply hiding in plain sight, keeping his family home and other records in his name, there was no record of Pierre Lacourt after his death. As per the rest of the family, to an outsider, it looked simply like a normal family tree ending with James, his wife, and daughter. Except that's what it always was through the generations – husband, a wife, and daughter. They all had the Lacourt last name but changing first names and birthdates. There were death certificates for all of the aliases. The Lacourts had worked hard to hide their identities.

Harper kept digging. Years of being editor-in-chief at her family's magazine had given her stellar research skills. Harper knew the ins and outs of public records and all the tricks to try. It didn't surprise her when she came across a photo from the 1920s. Their names were George, Ruth, and Margaret then. There was no denying it though. Margaret in the photo was clearly Alexandria who Harper had met at the Lacourt Family Foundation. Sure, her hair was styled differently and she wore clothes fitting with the time, but there was no doubt it was her. At least the family kept the same last name.

Initially, Harper didn't find any warehouse records for James, Ann, and Alexandria, but Harper tried these new identities, and sure enough, a warehouse down near the port of New Orleans came back to a George

Lacourt. With a little more searching, it seemed he bought the building back in 1918. Harper sat back. They would need to check it out.

Harper got up from bed and threw on her robe. She made her way downstairs, expecting to run into Dante or Hattie, but there wasn't a soul in sight. She made some coffee, and when it was ready, she carried two cups upstairs. By the time she made it back to the room, Jackson had roused himself from sleep.

"Have you been up long?" he asked groggily as he wiped the sleep from his eyes.

Harper waited for him to sit up to hand him the coffee cup. "I figured we both could use a little caffeine this morning. I know you didn't sleep much more than I did." Harper went around to her side of the bed and got in. She sank in with her back against the headboard and told Jackson everything she had found that morning about the Lacourts. Harper put her coffee cup on the bedside table and even pulled up the photo of Alexandria Lacourt.

"She went by Margaret then," Harper said pointing to the photo.

Jackson pulled the laptop closer to him and peered down at the photo. "It looks like her."

"More than just an ancestor you're related to, right?"

Jackson squinted at the photo. "Definitely. That's her. I don't think there's any question about that." Jackson sighed. "What's the plan for today?"

Harper reached for her phone and coffee cup. She took a sip and then checked her phone. There was one message from Lucinda. Harper had been waiting for this. She read it over and then explained it to Jackson. "Lucinda and Iggy are going to ask Alexandria for a meeting to discuss a rather sizable donation. They will insist they pick her up and take her to lunch. While in the house, they will make sure the coast is clear. Lucinda will also go and unlock the back door while Alexandria isn't looking. She will text me if all goes according to plan and then when

CHAPTER THIRTY-THREE

they leave, we can sneak in."

Harper looked down at him, arching an eyebrow. "Does that sound like a solid plan?"

"What if the others are there? It's not like we can fight them off."

"I don't know, we will have to figure it out."

"What time does she want us there?"

"Lucinda wants me to confirm the plan works for us and then she will confirm a time for this afternoon with Alexandria." Harper typed a response back to Lucinda and then set her phone back on the table. "You know, I didn't say this last night, but you were really good with Dante yesterday. I don't think I could have given him the news about his child in quite the way you did."

Jackson didn't say anything for a moment. Then he shrugged like it was no big deal. "I think being in the Army all those years you learn how to deliver bad news directly and gently enough."

"Maybe," Harper said, "but you handled it well. I appreciate that you're here with me."

Jackson turned to her smiling. "I wouldn't be anywhere else. I'm not all that happy we are going after the undead and dealing with a half-demon, but at this point, nothing surprises me."

Harper chuckled. "They aren't undead. I think only zombies are undead. No one said anything about the Lacourts eating people."

Jackson scrunched up his face. "They need blood to survive. What if they are half-undead, half-vampire? I liked it better when we were just dealing with ghosts."

"See, this trip has given you an appreciation for spirits. Remember last year when you were avoiding the whole topic at all costs? Now, you miss those days. It's growth."

Jackson sank in the bed until his head was resting back on his pillow. "I think you took that the wrong way. I'm saying in comparison I'd rather deal with ghosts. In reality, I don't want to deal with any of it."

Harper reached her cold hand under the blanket and pinched Jackson's side. He yelped at her touch and rolled over to tickle her. She squealed in delight, pushing his hands away because she was afraid that she'd spill her coffee. She dropped her cup back on the nightstand and put her laptop on the floor and snuggled in next to him. "Can we skip the world and just stay like this all day?"

"Fine by me." Jackson ran a hand over her back and kissed her forehead. He breathed her in and let out a sigh of contentment.

Just as Harper got comfortable, her cellphone chimed. She groaned. "It's probably Lucinda. I need to check." She didn't sit up but rather rolled over and slapped at the table until she had the phone in her hand. Harper swiped the screen and navigated to her texts. It was Lucinda and she needed them to be ready and over to the Garden District for ten that morning. Alexandria already had a lunch date planned, but she could meet earlier in the morning. Harper didn't know if that would give them more time or not, but she'd take it.

She sat up and typed Lucinda a message that they'd be there. Looking down at Jackson who had closed his eyes, she said, "You can't go back to sleep. We only have ninety minutes to get ready and be there in time for Lucinda's meeting with Alexandria."

Jackson groaned but he struggled out of bed. Harper showered before he did in their ensuite bathroom so she'd have time to fix her hair. His bald head didn't need much tending to. Harper had never seen a man get ready as quickly as Jackson did each morning.

Forty minutes later, Harper joined Jackson and Hattie in the kitchen. "Where's Dante?" she asked, sitting down at the table.

"He said he needed some air so he took a walk," Hattie explained, pushing around scrambled eggs on her plate. "I told him not to do anything crazy."

Harper explained to Hattie what she had discovered about the Lacourts. "I'm hesitant to give Dante the warehouse address because I

CHAPTER THIRTY-THREE

don't want him going over there. We need to loop in Det. Joya. I was going to call him when I was done checking out the Lacourt house in the Garden District."

"Maybe you should just call him now," Hattie suggested. "Dante was keyed up last night, and I'm afraid he's going to do something stupid. He's angrier about Celeste and his child than he let on in front of everyone."

"Of course, he is," Harper said sadly. "I'm sure he feels betrayed. But he has to get his head right. He has a chance to get Celeste back. If the Lacourts are defeated, Dante might have an opportunity to still be a father."

Jackson rubbed his eyes. "What happens to Dante if you kill Pierre Lacourt? I know Lucinda said that would break the spell, but will it also kill Dante?"

Hattie set the fork down. "To be honest, I have no idea. Maybe I'll do a little research on that today." She looked at both Harper and Jackson lovingly. "Please, be careful today. I don't know what I'd do without both of you."

Harper reached for her aunt's hand. "Nothing is going to happen to us. Be safe today."

Chapter Thirty-Four

The question Jackson asked gnawed at Hattie. She had no idea what happened to an immortal man once the spell was broken. Hattie went upstairs to her bedroom and got herself ready for the day. She barely slept the night before. It came in starts and stops. She showered, dried her hair, and was applying makeup in the hopes she could disguise how tired she looked when Beau appeared to her. He waved her out of the small bathroom.

"I didn't think I'd see you," Hattie said, relieved to see him. She sat down in the chair in the bedroom to speak with him.

"I've been around." Beau shook his head. "Back in Little Rock, I see the occasional spirit or two, but here it's like no one wants to stay dead."

Hattie rubbed her hands down her thighs. "That might be why I feel so tired and sore here. Everything aches and I'm drained of energy. I'm not even trying to see spirits. For the most part, I think I've been doing a good job of blocking them, but my whole body feels heavy and sore like I just finished running a marathon."

"That's why," Beau confirmed. "They are constantly feeding off the energy of the living. Most people might not even notice, but with your ability, it's going to affect you. Is there any spell you can do to protect your energy?"

Hattie exhaled. "I've tried, but it doesn't seem powerful enough. I'm

CHAPTER THIRTY-FOUR

going to talk to some voodoo practitioners today and maybe they can suggest something. I even had all of us carry tiger's eye, but that hasn't had any effect."

"Are you okay otherwise?" Beau's expression changed to one of concern as he looked down at Hattie.

"I'm scared for everyone. We are dealing with some powerful spiritual forces that I'm barely equipped to deal with. Harper and Jackson are completely out of their element."

Beau nodded and said reassuringly, "Harper's smart. She'll figure it out. Don't worry about her but stay protected, especially if your spells aren't working."

"Will you stay close?" Hattie asked, pleading with her eyes.

Beau reached his hand out, but Hattie could only merge her energy with his. "I'll be here. It was hard finding you with so much going on over on this side. With so many spirits feeding off the energy, it was hard to tap into you. But now that I know where to find you, I won't be far."

After Beau's spirit faded, Hattie finished getting ready. She wasn't up for too much action today, but she could seek out some voodoo experts and see what they could tell her. Her first stop was to find Beatrix's mother Deidre. Hattie's assistant, Beatrix, had been working at the shop for more than a year now and had been a great help to Hattie. Deidre also was a voodoo expert skilled in darker magic.

Hattie went to the closet and pulled out her small suitcase. Tucked inside a front zipper was a small sticky note with Deidre's address. She ran a voodoo shop not too far from Dante's house. Hattie had planned to stop by and say hello anyway, but now, Hattie was on a mission for information. Hattie went downstairs, but Dante still wasn't home. She left him a note on the table and left out the back door, closing and locking it behind her. At least Dante had given her a key so she could come and go as she needed. She hoped wherever Dante was or whatever he was doing, he was okay. She had grown quite attached to him since he barged back into her life.

It was a shorter walk to Deidre's shop than Hattie had anticipated. The shop had a lovely storefront with double French doors and open shutters to let the light fall breeze blow through. Hattie stepped through just as another customer left. For a woman who practiced darker magic, the shop certainly had a warm vibe about it.

"Can I help you?" a woman said from behind a large counter at the very back of the shop. She had her head of short dark hair bent down focused on a paper in front of her. Glasses rode low on her nose. Even as Hattie approached, she remained focused on the writing on the page.

Finally, as Hattie stood there for a moment quietly, the woman snapped her head up. "I'm so sorry. I didn't mean to be rude. I've tried to read this at least ten times today, and I keep getting interrupted. I'm Deidre. What can I do for you today?"

Hattie smiled, understanding exactly how Deidre felt. She had done the same a few times to customers when she was the only one available in her shop. "I'm Hattie. Your daughter, Beatrix, works with me."

"Oh, of course," Deidre said, moving around the counter and wrapping her arms around Hattie, who hadn't been expecting such a warm embrace. The hug wasn't unwanted as much as unexpected. Deidre let Hattie go and stepped back. "Beatrix said you might stop in. She shared a little about your trip here. How is everything going?"

"Not as good as I had hoped. Do you have a moment to speak with me?" Hattie asked, turning back toward the door, worried about customers interrupting them.

Deidre waved her off. "My sister is in the back. Let me call her out to watch the shop."

Hattie watched as Deidre went back behind the curtain at the side of the shop down from the counter. Deidre was about Hattie's height but narrow hipped and thin. Her features were far more angular than

CHAPTER THIRTY-FOUR

Beatrix's, but they had the same quirky earthy style of dress. Deidre had a blue tee-shirt, several beaded necklaces hanging down the front and a skirt Hattie guessed was made of hemp. She also sported black thick-soled boots. Hattie laughed. Deidre and Beatrix looked nothing alike, but their energy was the same.

A few minutes later, Deidre reemerged with another woman who looked just like her. "My sister Colleen," Deidre said. Colleen gave Hattie a wave but remained otherwise quiet. "Come on back." Deidre held the curtain aside for Hattie.

There were only two rooms in the back, an office, and a large workspace lined with shelves from floor to ceiling filled with magical supplies. Hattie wasn't sure where to look first. It was like a witch's Christmas morning.

Deidre noticed the look on Hattie's face. "I have everything you can think of back here. You would not believe some of the requests I get from tourists." Deidre laughed, clearly thinking back on some of those requests. She took a seat at a small worktable and pushed out a chair for Hattie. "Beatrix loves working at your shop. I admit I was jealous at first. We have everything here she needed to learn, but she wanted college, which I understand now. It wasn't easy to have her go so far away at first. Besides, she listens to you. She never listens to a word I say."

Hattie smiled. "That's only because I'm her boss. I don't have kids, but I hear from many mothers, they can tell their kid something one hundred times, but it takes a stranger telling them the same thing before it finally sinks in."

"Too true," Deidre said. "So, what can I help you with?"

Hattie took a deep breath. "My spells don't seem to be working here. I've done a protection spell, but I can tell the energy isn't strong. I'm also a medium so I can see the dead. I've been exhausted since I arrived. I'm normally excellent at protecting my energy, but here, I don't know.

I'm weak and I need to fix that."

Deidre nodded along. "I hear that often from those who practice other forms of magic. This city can be dangerous if you're sensitive. I think it can be dangerous for those who aren't sensitive, too. Tourists come here and make bad decisions all the time they wouldn't make anywhere else. They also seem to get drunk faster. I don't think it's just vacation bad decisions if you know what I mean. I believe the spirits here feed off the living and it weakens them. That's what's happening to you, and you're feeling the effects."

"What can I do about it? I need to be strong right now."

Deidre stood. "I know what will help. This won't even take long." She went over to her bench and pulled out a cloth doll with no face. She gathered some red, purple, and black thread and brought it over to the table. Deidre went back to the shelves and came back again with small bottles of different kinds of oils. She looked at Hattie. "I need a few strands of your hair for this to be most effective."

"Just pull out a few?" Hattie asked and Deidre nodded. Hattie reached up and yanked a few out of her head, wincing as she pulled. She placed them on the table next to everything else.

Deidre was quick with pulling the items together. She chanted something Hattie didn't understand as she rubbed the oils over the doll. Then she threaded the colors around it. Black for banishing energy vampires, purple for a boost of spirituality and red for power. In the threads, she also wound Hattie's hair.

When she finished, Deidre gave the doll to Hattie. "Carry this with you at all times. Have it on you while you do your protection spells for those you love, and you should have your power back."

Hattie gripped the doll in her hand. At first, it felt a bit awkward holding the strange-looking doll, but almost immediately Hattie began to feel the energy surge through her body. She held the doll up. "Your magic is quite strong."

CHAPTER THIRTY-FOUR

"Years of practice. Is there something else you need?"

Hattie explained in detail what they were up against with the Lacourts and even explained the help they were receiving from Lucinda and Iggy. When Hattie mentioned them, Deidre chuckled. "You know them?" Hattie asked.

"I know a Father Ignatius Cormier if that's who you mean."

"It is. He is a character."

Deidre smiled broadly. "That's an understatement, but he's the real deal. No one fights off demons like he does. If he's on your side, you can't fail."

That made Hattie feel better. It wasn't like they had vetted demon hunters before. "I'm counting on him being successful again," Hattie started. "My concern is those the Lacourts have cursed. For instance, if we succeed in killing Pierre what will happen to Dante who he cursed with immortality?"

"The curse should be lifted," Deidre explained.

"Right, but will Dante die on the spot?"

"He shouldn't. Dante should live out the rest of his natural life. If he was destined to live to eighty, that's what he'll do."

Relieved and feeling more energy than she had in days, Hattie and Deidre chatted for a while longer, and then she got up to leave. Before Hattie could go, Deidre thought of something else. She asked Hattie to wait and then came back with her mother's grimoire.

"You can't kill a demon," Deidre explained, "but I'm going to give you something to use only in an emergency." Deidre sat there and explained the details to a very old but dangerous spell. Deidre wasn't positive it would work, but it was back-up Hattie was glad she had. Deidre refused payment, but Hattie promised she'd return the favor someday.

Chapter Thirty-Five

Harper and Jackson sat across the street from the Lacourt Family Foundation, having coffee and waiting for Lucinda and Iggy to arrive. They had the same waiter who remembered them from the day before but thankfully didn't question them about the Lacourts.

At a little after ten, Lucinda and Iggy pulled up in a large black SUV. As planned, Lucinda texted Harper to let her know they had arrived. Lucinda, her hair wild, wore skin-tight black leather pants, boots, and a bright red sweater that clung to her curves and came barely to the top of her pants.

Harper glanced over. "She's hardly dressed for a donor meeting."

Jackson turned casually and then snapped his head right back to Harper. He cleared his throat. "I don't think the Lacourts are going to care about anything more than the money she's claiming to donate."

"Do you think the Lacourts will know who they are? Iggy is fairly famous. At least, that's the way they told it."

Jackson shrugged. "The Lacourts are as well-known around here. Even if they know he's a demon hunter, it doesn't mean they know he's after them. They are both prominent members of the community."

"Let's hope you're right," Harper said dismissively as she watched Lucinda, Iggy and Alexandria walk out of the house and to the SUV. As Lucinda came around to the driver's side, she caught sight of Harper

CHAPTER THIRTY-FIVE

across the street and nodded her head once, giving the all-clear.

"Let's go," Harper said. They had prepaid their check as soon as they ordered to be ready to go at a moment's notice. That was paying off now. They got up from the table as soon as the SUV pulled away and was out of sight. They crossed the street and did their best not to look too conspicuous as they entered the property. They cut around to the back of the house.

"I hope Lucinda unlocked the door as planned," Jackson said.

"I'm sure she did. She would have texted and told me if she hadn't." Harper made it to the backyard first. Jackson was right behind her. The yard wasn't much bigger than a postage stamp of grass and patio. The porch though was as grand as the rest of the house. Harper bounded up the steps and reached for the doorknob. As she turned it and pushed the door open, she had a flash of a vision of Lucinda unlocking the door.

The back door led directly into the kitchen and a set of stairs. Harper tried to remember if she had seen an extra staircase from the upstairs on their tour, but she couldn't remember. It didn't matter, she took the stairs quickly but as quietly as she could.

"Do you know where you're going?" Jackson whispered from behind her.

"Not any more than you do." Harper reached the landing and was completely turned around. The stairs dumped them out into a large sitting room with a bathroom off to the right. "I think this might have been like a servant's quarters or something. Let's keep going."

Harper and Jackson walked out of the room and down a narrow hall until they were finally standing where they had stood the day before. Down the hall and to the left was the door Alexandria refused to open. Harper headed directly there. She pressed her ear to the door in the hopes she'd hear anyone up there, but all was quiet. Jackson pulled open the door. The look on his face when it opened matched Harper's. Neither had thought it would be unlocked.

Jackson turned back to look at her. "I'm not letting you walk into danger first. At least let me check it out, and if all is clear, you can come up."

Harper shook her head. "You're not more equipped than I am to fight them off. We go together."

Jackson led the way as they climbed the narrow set of stairs to the attic. They had only made it a few steps when the smell knocked them back. Jackson covered his mouth and nose with his hand. "It smells like rotting garbage or death or worse."

Harper's eyes watered. If finding out what was in the attic wasn't so important, she might have turned back. Jackson continued up the steps until he reached the landing. Harper stayed right behind him. Dust coated the hardwoods, making them look like they hadn't been mopped or swept in years. The ceiling slanted on each side, giving the room a tight and small feel. Harper hunched over not to hit her head on the exposed wood, but there was no reason to. She had more than enough standing room. While Jackson moved toward the back of the house, Harper turned to face the front.

That's when she saw it. She let out a high-pitched scream so loud that she was sure she had woken the dead. Jackson rushed to her side and asked what was wrong. All Harper could do was point. Jackson followed her finger with his eyes until he saw it too. A man – or rather what was left of a man – sat propped up in a chair with his skeletal hands in his lap.

"Is that real or a freakishly real Halloween decoration?" Harper asked, barely getting out the words.

Jackson took a few tentative steps toward it but stopped a few feet back. He assessed. Threadbare clothing covered most of the skeleton. Jackson didn't want to look at its face but he had to. The skin had mummified enough that you could tell it once had been a man. The hands were the same. Jackson turned back to Harper, reaching a hand out to her. "Don't scream, but he's real. What do we do?"

Harper could barely move her feet let alone think rationally at that moment. She swallowed hard, trying not to look at the dead man. "We need to search the rest of this attic and then call Det. Joya."

Jackson nodded. "I don't think he's causing the smell though."

"Let's search and get out of here." Harper couldn't think about anything else other than getting the heck out of that house. Jackson went to a stack of boxes on the front end of the house and Harper took the back. They worked in silence like that for nearly thirty minutes. Harper knew they were running out of time, but they weren't finding much.

Most of what Harper found was old bills and financial records for the Lacourt Family Foundation. Harper didn't have time to read through every document, but on a cursory glance, nothing stood out to her as strange. She dropped the files back into one box and moved to another.

Harper opened the flaps of the box and peered inside. This time, she hit a goldmine. Harper pulled out an old photo album and under it found stacks and stacks of photographs. Harper grabbed a pile and tore through them. The images spanned decades, all featuring the same faces in varying styles of dress. Harper dropped the pile back in the box and grabbed the album next.

Harper stared down and couldn't believe her eyes. The first photograph was of Alexandria and an unknown man on their wedding day. They stood side by side, happily smiling at the camera. Harper flipped through and found more photos of the happy occasion.

"Jackson," Harper called, still mesmerized by the photos, "come look at this."

"What did you find?" Jackson asked, getting up from his crouched position across the room.

"It's Alexandria's wedding album. I think based on how they are dressed it's got to be the 1920s or 1930s. I'm not really sure."

Jackson stood behind Harper, looking down at the photos as she flipped through more pages. "It's definitely that era." He got quiet for several moments. "Harper," he said again slowly, "do you think the guy over there could be Alexandria's husband?"

Harper's eyes got wide as she turned and looked up at Jackson. "No one has ever mentioned she had a husband before so maybe." Just then Harper's phone chimed. She dropped the photo album and reached into her pocket. She read the message and cursed under her breath. "We have about five minutes to get out of here. Lucinda said they are nearly back."

Jackson moved swiftly to the other side of the room, put files back in boxes while Harper did the same. When he was done, Jackson took out his phone and snapped a few photos of the dead man. He stopped and turned to Harper, who was closing the last box. She slipped something into her pocket as she stood and faced him.

"Let's go," he said quickly. "I hear a car out front."

Harper's heart beat faster. They couldn't get caught, especially now. She dashed down the steps and Jackson followed. They hit the second floor as Lucinda and Alexandria talked out front. It sounded like Lucinda was stalling for time. Alexandria wasn't having any of it though. Harper reached for Jackson's hand and pulled him down the hall and back into the sitting room where the stairs to the kitchen were. Harper didn't even think about the noise they were making as they bounded down the stairs. She reached for the doorknob just as Alexandria opened the front door.

Once outside, Harper tucked low on the porch as Jackson closed the door. They both had to crabwalk off the porch and onto the grass. Harper scooted around toward the side of the house and spotted an opening in the neighbor's fence. She squeezed through, hoping the space was wide enough for Jackson. He made it but barely.

Once they were on the neighbor's property, Harper breathed a

CHAPTER THIRTY-FIVE

momentary sigh of relief. Jackson pointed to a back gate and they walked towards it. As they did, Harper felt eyes watching her. She didn't want to turn around and look, not yet anyway. Jackson pulled open the gate and stepped out into an alleyway. Right before Harper did the same, she turned slowly. Alexandria stood in a second-floor window with her eyes glued on them. Harper locked eyes with her and a moment later, Alexandria was gone.

Harper grabbed Jackson's hand. "Run and don't stop!" she shouted. They sprinted toward the end of the alleyway. As they ran, Harper turned again. This time Alexandria stood in the alley watching them. "Keep running!" Harper yelled.

"What is going on?" Jackson asked out of breath but still running.

"Alexandria knows we were in the house." Harper thought the woman might give chase, but she didn't. They kept running until a few moments later Lucinda pulled down a crossroad a few blocks up, her tires screeching to a stop. Even then Harper didn't stop running until they reached the safety of the waiting SUV.

Chapter Thirty-Six

"Where are we headed?" Lucinda asked from the driver's seat.

Iggy, who sat in the passenger seat, turned around when Harper and Jackson climbed in the back, both trying desperately to catch their breath. Before they could answer Lucinda, Iggy squinted at them. "What happened to you two?"

Both Harper and Jackson started to speak at once. Jackson stopped and let Harper go first. "Take us back to Iggy's place if that's okay. We have to make some decisions about what we're going to do. I need a quiet place to tap into my gift."

Lucinda responded by taking off like a shot down the narrow road. Iggy asked his question again, and Jackson explained, "Father, there was a man in the attic who's been dead for a long time. He's partially mummified. I've never seen anything like it."

"I said just call me Iggy," the priest scolded. "You calling the cops?"

"We are going to have to, but I want to tap into a vision first and see what I can find out." Harper pulled a bent photograph from her pocket. At the last minute, she had decided taking it would be a good idea. She might be able to read an imprint from it, and it was proof that Alexandria was immortal. It might also give the cops a good idea about who the dead man might be.

Jackson looked over at her and then down at the photo. "I wondered

CHAPTER THIRTY-SIX

what you had stolen."

Harper explained her reasoning, which Jackson agreed with. "I didn't see anything else up there though. No signs of other people or even that anyone had been up there in a long time. I'm sure if Alexandria goes up there, she will know immediately. The floor was covered in dust, which we disturbed. It's not going to take much to put two and two together." Harper reached around and touched Lucinda on the side. "How was lunch with her?"

"She was all about the money, but otherwise nothing out of the ordinary. Iggy even told her what he has been doing for the church and shared some of his more colorful tales. Alexandria didn't even flinch. She smelled terrible though so I know she's been touched by dark magic and a demon or two."

Harper rubbed her nose remembering the attic. "The attic smelled awful, too, but the dead guy has been up there for so long I don't know that it's him."

"He might have been a sacrifice." Lucinda pulled the SUV to a stop in front of Iggy's house and let them out, promising to be right back after she parked.

Jackson slid out and helped Harper down to the ground. "I could use a drink," she whispered. "You think Iggy has any bourbon left?"

As he unlocked the door, Iggy glanced over his shoulder at Harper and smiled. "I have bourbon and whatever else you may need inside."

"Thanks," Harper said, slightly embarrassed he heard. As she crossed the threshold into Iggy's house, Harper asked, "Is there a place where I can sit quietly?"

As they made their way down the narrow hall, Iggy stepped into the living room and flipped on a light. "Have a seat in here. It should be comfortable and quiet enough for you. We didn't have anything to eat at the meeting with Alexandria so let me fix us all some lunch."

Harper thanked him as she and Jackson sat down on the couch. She took the photo and placed it on her lap. Harper wasn't sure what kind of images she'd pick up in her vision. For the first time since she discovered her gift, Harper was apprehensive about using it. She was afraid of what horrific thing she'd see.

"You okay?" Jackson asked, sensing her mood.

"Once I see whatever vision this photo holds, I can't unsee it. What if it's something terrible?"

Jackson reached over and took her hand, comforting her. "You've seen terrible things before, haven't you?" he asked softly.

"We are dealing with real evil now. An evil that nightmares are made of. Things I didn't even believe last week were real."

"Don't do it then. No one will think less of you."

"I will," Lucinda said, standing in the doorway to the living room. She sauntered in and dropped down on the chair across from them. "I haven't known you very long, but you're tougher than this, Harper. I told you I was a half-demon, and you didn't even flinch." Lucinda raised her eyebrows and winked at Jackson. "And you look like you want to rip my face off every time I flirt with your boyfriend. No mere mortal woman would fight a demon for her man, but I think you would. You have to face evil to fight evil. I know that better than anyone."

Jackson squeezed Harper's hand harder, but her eyes were pinned on Lucinda. She barely registered Jackson's touch. "I would fight you for him if I had to."

Lucinda threw her head back and laughed. "It's a fight you'd lose, but I like your guts." She hitched her jaw at Harper. "Now, do your thing. We are both here to protect you."

Harper let go of Jackson's hand. She sank back farther into the couch and placed one hand under the photo and the other palm down right on top of it. Harper took a deep cleansing breath and closed her eyes. Immediately, a black veil tried to prevent Harper from seeing, but she pushed through it in her mind. This was the hardest vision to tap into

CHAPTER THIRTY-SIX

she had ever experienced. It was almost like it was fighting back to keep her blind to the truth. Harper fought harder mentally and then surrendered to the darkness, allowing her breathing to even out.

In a flash, Harper tore through the blockage and her vision became crystal clear. Harper stood on the edge of a vast green lawn surrounded by perfect landscaping. A large home was off in the distance. Harper wasn't sure where she was exactly, but she knew instantly she wasn't in the city of New Orleans. She watched as Alexandria stood with her groom for the very photo she held. Harper moved closer to the people standing in small groups watching them.

As she moved through the crowd, she caught bits of conversation. Among the many well-wishers, some comments jumped out to Harper. *"Henry is such a lucky young man." "Margaret is fortunate to marry into such a wealthy family. You know the Jacobsen's are old money." "I can't believe Henry is willing to move back to New Orleans. You'd think this home would have been good enough for her." "Poor Henry. I can't believe he lost both his parents two months before his wedding."*

Harper stayed in the vision longer, waiting to see if anything else would reveal itself, but there was nothing. She held on and focused her thoughts on the corpse she and Jackson had seen in the attic. Her next vision didn't take her all the way there. Instead, Harper stood inside the house in the Garden District in the middle of a fight between Alexandria and Henry. From what Harper could tell Alexandria told Henry the truth about her family and his face registered shock and then disgust. They screamed at each other. Alexandria begged him to accept them, but Henry moved her out of his way, screaming at her that he was leaving and never returning.

Henry ran up the front stairs of the house with Alexandria chasing right after him. Harper slowly made her way up the stairs, knowing she couldn't be seen or heard but nervous still. Henry stood in their bedroom pulling a suitcase from the closet. He threw clothes in haphazardly not even looking at Alexandria. She cried and tried to convince him she could make him just like her, and they could be together forever.

Alexandria reached for him, and Henry pulled back in disgust. "Don't touch me," he shouted. "Don't ever touch me again, you vile creature. You and your family will never have my family's money." He continued to pack, but he stopped and finally looked at her. "Did you kill my parents to get them out of the way?" When Alexandria said nothing, he demanded, "Tell me. Did you kill them?"

Alexandria stepped back like she had been slapped, and in a sense, she had been. It was clear Henry had been a pawn in some scheme the Lacourts had cooked up. Alexandria stopped begging. Her expression turned cold. "We did what we had to do. Your parents would never have understood."

"I'm going to the police," Henry said, throwing the last of his items in the suitcase.

Alexandria let out a dismissive laugh. "They will never believe you."

"We'll see about that." Henry yanked the suitcase off the bed and headed for the door. Before he even made it to the hall, Alexandria pulled a thin silver blade from her dress pocket and stabbed him once in the side of the neck. The suitcase dropped to the floor with a thud. He gripped his neck as blood covered his hand. He looked to Alexandria, but she just watched him die. As Henry sank to the floor, she stepped over him.

"We could have had a beautiful life together if you hadn't had to ruin it." She walked out of the room as Henry died on the floor, his eyes searching the ceiling for help that wouldn't come.

Harper came out of the vision and slumped forward, feeling more nauseated than she had ever felt in her life. She rested her head on her knees and took slow breaths. It wasn't so much witnessing the murder that made her sick as it was being in the presence of such evil. She reached for Jackson's hand for reassurance, and he was right there with her. He rubbed the back of her head and said soothing words until she felt better.

"What did you see?" Lucinda asked.

"Give her a minute," Jackson responded sharply. "It takes a lot of energy. Harper has to recover."

"I'm okay," Harper said softly, her voice unsteady. She sat up and adjusted her eyes to the room. She was surprised to see Iggy standing next to her with a chocolate bar and a glass, the contents of which Harper couldn't discern.

Iggy handed it to her. "The sugar helps and so does the bourbon and ginger ale. I know it sounds like a gross combination, but try it. I've fought evil for a long time. It's the only thing that works."

Harper took both willingly. She unwrapped the chocolate and broke off a piece. She popped it in her mouth and chewed slowly. She wasn't ready for the bourbon yet and would have preferred just the ginger ale. As Harper started to tell them about her vision, Iggy interrupted.

"We have bigger fish to fry right now." He clicked on the television that sat in the corner of the room. There on the screen was a news conference with Det. Joya, who announced that he had caught the New Orleans serial killer. The television flashed to a man in handcuffs being led from a cop car into the police station. The man was young, had a terrified expression on his face, and visibly shook.

Iggy pointed to Det. Joya. "That dummy has the wrong guy."

Chapter Thirty-Seven

Sitting in Dante's living room, Hattie read the text from Harper about Det. Joya arresting the wrong man. She let out a sharp breath. "They never learn," she said aloud to no one in particular. Hattie reached for the television remote and stared at it, trying to figure out the many buttons. She was sure a man had to have made television remotes because no woman would have made anything so complicated.

"You need some help with that?" Dante asked from the hallway.

"Dante, you're back. I'm so relieved and glad you're okay." She shook the remote at him. "Yes, I need your help. This thing is ridiculous."

Dante smiled down at her and took it from her hands. Within seconds, he brought the screen to life. Dante handed the remote back to Hattie, pointing to the button to change the channel.

He laughed. "Do you know how long I lived without television? We've only talked about the bad things that have happened as a result of my curse. Watching the technological advancements has been astounding. What's on that you want to see?" Dante sat next to her.

Hattie found the news and set the remote down, glad to be rid of it. "Harper texted me that Det. Joya made an arrest, but we both know he didn't get the right guy."

Dante shook his head. "That certainly complicates things. I wonder what evidence he has on him."

CHAPTER THIRTY-SEVEN

"I don't know, but it must be something. I wonder if the Lacourts planted evidence on someone." Hattie looked straight ahead and watched the news. Twenty-seven-year-old Rory Gleeson had been arrested for all of the recent voodoo murders in New Orleans. Neither the police nor the media could offer any connection the suspect had to voodoo or any of the victims. They found Rory unconscious in an abandoned house in the French Quarter with the gun suspected to be the murder weapon. Next to him were several unused voodoo dolls and the materials used to dress them.

The police said they received an anonymous tip that the man responsible for the murders could be found in the home. When police arrived, he was unconscious, required unspecified medical care, and released to police custody.

"That's it?" Dante said with his eyebrows raised and a skeptical look on his face. "That's all they have on him? A planted gun and some voodoo materials? They are desperate for an arrest."

"Do you think there will be more murders?" Hattie asked, still with her eyes glued to the television.

"I doubt it. They ditched the murder weapon. I don't think they will do anything now to raise suspicion it might be anyone other than poor Rory Gleeson."

Hattie looked over at him. "Where did you go? You were gone all day, and I was worried about you."

"I went to the cemetery."

Hattie grew concerned. "Please tell me not to Pierre's tomb."

"No." Dante sighed and ran a hand through his hair and then folded his hands in his lap. With emotion in his voice, he explained, "A long time ago, I bought a tomb and have been keeping Celeste's remains in there throughout the ages. I don't know why, but sometimes I go and sit on the bench in front of the tomb and talk to her. I know she's not there, but it makes me feel better, particularly if I'm trying to work through a problem." He wiped a tear from the corner of his eye. "Do you know how many times I've laid her to rest?"

Hattie didn't know, but hearing it broke her heart. She didn't even have words of comfort for him. All she could do was sit with him in his pain. "I can't even imagine what you've been through. We will get her back, Dante. I know you don't believe me, but I feel it in my bones. Maybe then you'll have a chance to be a family."

"I hope so." Dante sat there quietly, neither of them speaking. Another news report came on the television and they watched it for a few minutes. When it was over, he turned to Hattie. "We have to do something."

Hattie opened her mouth to speak but her cellphone rang, drawing her attention. She pulled it from her pocket. "I don't recognize the number." She held the phone out for Dante.

"It's a local number. You should answer it."

Hattie said hello and recognized the woman's voice even before she said her name. It was Sandy calling from Max's hospital room. "You have to help me," she pleaded. "Det. Joya has arrested the wrong man. We know Rory Gleeson. He is our neighbor's son. He didn't kidnap my husband."

"Did you call Det. Joya?" Hattie asked, fearing the worst now.

"I did, but he said he was sure he had the right man and Max must be mistaken. He also suggested that maybe there were others involved and Rory was the ringleader. Hattie, I've known Rory for years. He isn't the ringleader of anything. He's a good kid. I fear he was kidnapped just like my husband and is being framed."

Hattie felt the same. "Dante and I don't believe it either. What do you want to do?"

"I want everyone to know he's got the wrong guy, but I don't know how to go about it. Max is livid, but he's still recovering and I'm trying to keep him calm. Is there anything you can do to help?"

CHAPTER THIRTY-SEVEN

"Let me talk to my niece. She has spoken to Det. Joya a few times. She might be able to talk some sense into him." Hattie knew she was temporarily appeasing Sandy. She had no idea if Harper would be able to help or not, but Hattie didn't see too many other options.

"At least that will be something," Sandy said dryly. Hattie thought she was going to hang up, but before she did, Sandy added, "If Det. Joya doesn't do the right thing, I'm going to call the news because Max wants to do an interview and tell everyone the detective got it wrong."

"Hold off on that for now," Hattie cautioned. "I think that will only make Det. Joya more uncooperative."

"Well then, he better make this right," Sandy said before ending the call.

Hattie started explaining the call to Dante when Harper's voice echoed down the hall from the kitchen. Harper called Hattie's name and then followed her aunt's voice to the living room.

Hattie was taken aback by Harper's appearance. Her hair was blown around her face and a stain trailed down the front of her shirt. It wasn't like Harper at all. "Are you okay?" Hattie asked concerned.

Harper pointed to the TV. "I spilled bourbon and ginger ale down the front of my shirt when I saw the news report. I had just come out of a vision and was nauseated. Then Iggy showed us that Det. Joya arrested the wrong man. We have to stop him."

"We both agree with that," Dante said seriously. He waved them to take a seat.

"I just got off the phone with Sandy," Hattie started. "Max doesn't believe it was Rory Gleeson. They know him and Max is sure it wasn't Rory who kidnapped him."

Dante asked, "How do you propose we get Det. Joya to believe us?"

"I'm not sure," Harper said, sitting down. "It's more complicated now. After I saw the news report, I called in an anonymous tip that there is a body in the attic of the Lacourt house in the Garden District."

"What?" both Dante and Hattie said in unison.

"Are you being serious?" Hattie asked.

Harper nodded. "I'm deadly serious. Jackson and I were able to search the attic when Lucinda and Iggy took Alexandria to lunch. There was a body of a man sitting in a chair in the attic." Harper pulled the crumpled photo from her pocket and waved it toward them. "I took this photo. When I got to Iggy's house, I tapped into a vision of a wedding and then a murder. I think the dead guy is Henry Jacobsen, Alexandria's husband from the 1920s or 30s. I'm not sure about the exact date. But she murdered him. I saw that with my own eyes."

"Is there any chance the dead man is Pierre?" Dante asked.

"I don't know," Jackson said, sitting in a straight-back chair with his legs crossed at his ankles. He looked as worn out and stressed as Harper. The few wrinkles in his forehead creased more than usual. "The body wasn't in good enough shape to identify. I have a few photos if you'd like to see." He pulled out his phone and carried it over to Dante.

Hattie didn't want to look, but Dante took Jackson's phone and scrolled through them. He looked up at Jackson when he was done. "It's hard to tell. I don't think this is Pierre though. I wonder if there's been some family discord and they killed Pierre. No one seems to have seen him lately."

"Could be," Jackson said, "but I'm inclined to think the dead guy is Henry. I'm not sure why Alexandria kept his body. Maybe to avoid a police inquiry."

"Harper, did the police take your call seriously?"

"I don't know, but I made the call. I'll tell Det. Joya more if I see him, but I didn't want to get caught up in all of this now. I want to do some research first and see what I can find about Henry Jacobsen. I wanted to alert the police though so Alexandria didn't move the body. She saw us near the house. I'm sure she can connect the dots and probably suspects we were in her house."

CHAPTER THIRTY-SEVEN

That worried Hattie. "You two better watch yourselves."

"For once, I'm not even going to fight you on that." Harper looked at Jackson and then stood. "I'm going to change and do a little research. Rick is trying to get me another meeting with Det. Joya so we can convince him he's wrong." As Harper headed for the stairs, she turned back. "Dante, Lucinda said tonight we can all go to the cemetery and prove Pierre's body is not in the tomb. Iggy found the tomb."

Chapter Thirty-Eight

Harper couldn't believe she had made such a mess of herself today. Instead of just changing, she jumped in the shower. Jackson called from the bed that he would be in to join her, but as the minutes passed, he was nowhere to be found. Just as well. Harper wasn't in the mood for romance at the moment. She couldn't wait to dig into some research about Henry Jacobsen. Harper was also curious about when the police would get to the Lacourts and what exactly they'd do when they found a rotting corpse. Harper didn't believe it would stop them, but she was hoping it would slow them down. She had no idea how she was going to find Celeste and hoped it would be in time.

Harper stepped out of the shower and wrapped one towel around her middle and another around her hair. She wiped the steam off the mirror and brushed her teeth. When she was done, Harper tipped her head over and shook her hair free, combing it out so it wouldn't tangle. As she opened the bathroom door, Jackson's snores filled the room. He was sprawled out across the bed still fully dressed. His head wasn't even on the pillow. Harper stood there for a moment, wishing she could crawl into bed with him and take a nap, but that wasn't going to happen.

Harper swapped her towel for a light bathrobe, grabbed her laptop, and sat down in the chair, propping her feet up on the ottoman. She clicked to her favorite internet search engine, tapped a few keys, and

CHAPTER THIRTY-EIGHT

accessed public records. Harper started searching in the 1920s Census and almost immediately found Henry and his family. Her vision had been correct. His parents died months before his wedding, which was listed as June 1927. Harper pulled up their death certificates and additional public records. Their deaths were listed as accidental but no mention of anything more. Harper moved on to Henry's death certificate, which was issued in December 1935. There was no cause of death listed. Odd to say the least.

Harper switched to an archived newspaper website. It took her a few different tries with different dates, but eventually, Harper found Henry again. His wife, Margaret, reported him missing in October 1932. There were major newspaper write-ups at the time given his disappearance. Margaret said Henry had left to go hunting and never returned. There were searches of the area, but he was never found.

After exhaustive searches and no record of Henry Jacobsen ever being seen again, Margaret petitioned the court to have her husband declared dead. All of his assets were already hers, but this now made it official. Harper was sure now that the body they found was Henry.

Harper dug through more newspaper records in search of what happened to Henry's parents. Sure enough, there were two articles about their deaths. Henry's parents' bodies were found on their property in a pond behind the home. The speculation was Henry's mother had gone in for a swim and drowned and his father drowned trying to rescue her.

A few people interviewed thought the story was suspicious, but Henry, their only child, was distraught and there was no police inquiry. It was deemed an open and shut accidental drowning. Harper suspected, as Henry had in her vision, that the Lacourts played a hand in their deaths. With them out of the way, they stood to inherit the Jacobsens' fortune, which was valued near six million dollars at that time.

Harper picked her eyes up from her laptop and peered over at Jackson, who was still sleeping. They couldn't do anything until Rick called back with a meeting time confirmed for Det. Joya. They were planning to go to the cemetery later with Dante and Lucinda. With the research done, Harper could justify a nap.

Just as she tugged back the blanket and nudged Jackson out of the way, who curled up in a ball on his side as soon as Harper touched him, her phone rang. Harper exhaled and rolled her eyes and then moved across the room quickly to grab her phone off the chair where she had left it.

"Hello," Harper said unsure who was calling.

"Did you break into the Lacourt Family Foundation in the Garden District?" the voice barked at her. Harper knew it was Det. Joya. There was no mistaking his angry tone.

Harper had been outed. "I didn't break in. The door was unlocked but no one was there."

"Let me guess, you just took it upon yourself to have a look around." Harper didn't say anything so Det. Joya continued. "I'm assuming it was you who called 911. There's nobody in the attic, Harper. I don't know what you think you saw, but there was no body. Alexandria said she saw you and Jackson sneaking away from the property when she got home."

"We have proof," Harper responded evenly, glad now Jackson had taken the time to snap a few photos.

"What do you mean you have proof?"

"We have proof there was a dead body in that attic." Harper paused and then went all in. "I think I know who it was, too, but we need to meet in person. This is too much to go into on the phone."

"My office in twenty minutes," Det. Joya barked.

"No, Rick's office. We need some neutral space." Harper wasn't going to relent on that. She and Jackson technically committed a crime by going into the house to snoop around so there was no way she was

CHAPTER THIRTY-EIGHT

going to walk into the police station willingly. It didn't matter that this was all for a very good cause.

"Fine, don't be late." Det. Joya hung up, clanging what Harper assumed was his desk phone back into its cradle.

Harper nudged Jackson awake and explained the situation, feeling completely horrible that she had gotten him into trouble with her. She felt worse for waking him from a nap that he so desperately needed. Like the good soldier, Jackson put on a brave face and got himself ready to go. On the way out the door, Harper explained to Hattie that they were off to see Det. Joya, leaving out how much trouble she could be facing. There was no point in worrying Hattie.

Harper and Jackson made it to Rick's office in record time. After racing through the newsroom, Harper banged once on Rick's office door and then pushed it open. "He's not here yet, is he?"

Rick glanced up at her. "Nope. Sit and tell me exactly what you two did. He was angrier than I've ever heard him."

Jackson didn't respond to the question. Instead, he placed his phone with the photo of the corpse on Rick's desk. He jabbed his finger at it. "We're trying to prevent him from arresting the wrong guy while leaving these killers to keep terrorizing New Orleans."

Rick peered down at the photo and then took the phone in his hands to get a better look. "Is this what I think it is?"

"Dead guy in the Lacourts' attic," Harper said dryly, sitting down. "Det. Joya tells me they didn't find anything, but it was there earlier today. I admit I probably should have called 911 sooner, but it's not like we could have saved him."

"Shouldn't you have a lawyer with you?" Rick asked, giving the phone back to Jackson.

Harper pulled a thumb drive and the wedding photo out of her pocket. "I have all the evidence I need right here."

Rick shook his head, the corner of his mouth turning up in a smile.

"Maggie said you were crazy."

A few minutes later, Det. Joya marched into Rick's office full of anger and bluster. He slammed the door shut and then turned on Harper and Jackson, reading them the riot act. They both sat perfectly still watching and listening as he railed on them for a full ten minutes. When Det. Joya ran out of steam, Jackson handed him the phone and Harper turned over the thumb drive and photo. They didn't say a word otherwise.

Det. Joya looked down at the photo, his face contorting as soon as he saw it. When he looked at the wedding photo, Det. Joya stepped back, bumping into Rick's desk. Harper and Jackson had silenced the man without even speaking a word.

He held up the thumb drive. "I assume there is more evidence on here?"

"All public records," Harper explained. "I'm fairly certain the dead guy is Henry Jacobsen. There are newspaper accounts, too. He was a missing person before being declared dead in court. His body was never found, well that is until this morning. Information about his parents' untimely deaths is there as well."

Det. Joya looked over at Rick. "Did you see this?"

"Just the photo. I haven't seen what's on the drive, but if that's not proof then I don't know what is." Rick sat back, giving Harper a smile and nod that conveyed both respect and awe.

Det. Joya turned to Jackson. "Colonel, you truly believe the Lacourts are immortal and have killed people."

Jackson stood so he was looking the man right in the eyes. "I saw the corpse with my own eyes. I saw a wedding photo and met Alexandria. They are the same person and that's not possible in the world we know. Harper has a special gift. She can hold an object and tap into a vision. Now, you might not believe it. I had trouble believing it myself, but I've seen her in action. I've seen her be able to garner enough information law enforcement can use to solve a homicide and make an arrest. You

CHAPTER THIRTY-EIGHT

asked me if I believe it. It's not belief. It's cold hard facts. All I can do is hand you the evidence and hope you explore it enough until you see it, too."

Det. Joya didn't break eye contact. "I can't make an arrest based on Harper's vision."

Jackson smiled. "No, you can't. That's where you need to do a little creative police work."

Det. Joya stood for several agonizing moments. Harper wasn't sure if he was going to walk out, arrest them, or what he was going to do. At that moment though, she couldn't have been more in love with Jackson. Harper kept her eyes on the detective, anxiously waiting. A moment later, she breathed a sigh of relief.

Det. Joya pulled up a chair from Rick's desk and sat down. "Tell me everything you saw."

Chapter Thirty-Nine

Harper explained her vision from start to finish. Because Det. Joya hadn't looked at the evidence on the drive, she explained what she found in detail. His expression gave nothing away as she spoke to him.

As Harper finished, she added, "Hattie wanted me to tell you Sandy called her. Max does not believe Rory Gleeson had anything to do with his disappearance. Max and Sandy know Rory and know you have the wrong man. Has Rory confessed to anything?"

Det. Joya shook his head. "We had our best interrogator sit down with him. Rory told a nearly identical story to Max about being out in a shop. One minute he was fine and the next he woke up in an unfamiliar place. Next thing he knew, the cops were there arresting him."

Rick raised his eyebrows. "I don't think your master criminal getting away with all these murders for weeks is going to be so easily caught."

Det. Joya shrugged. "Serial killers have been caught on less. Son of Sam was snagged by a parking ticket. But regardless, you're right. I arrested the easiest and most obvious suspect. I'm waiting for calls back to confirm his alibis. Rory claims he wasn't even in town for two of the murders. As soon as I have that, I'll let him go and make a statement." He looked at Harper and Jackson. "I'm not sure how I'm going to use this information to bring in the Lacourts. I'll need to give it some thought."

CHAPTER THIRTY-NINE

Harper shook her head. "You don't have a lot of time. They have a woman named Celeste. Her life is in danger if she isn't already dead. You have to act now."

"We won't even be able to get a search warrant with this information. Alexandria let us willingly search the house and we found nothing. Not one shred of evidence of anything. I need something more concrete and current than this to prove it in court to get a warrant."

Jackson nodded and stood. "I understand. Harper and I need to go. If you can't find Celeste then we are going to have to do it on our own."

Det. Joya motioned for him to sit back down. Jackson remained standing. Det. Joya sighed. "I didn't say I wasn't going to look into this. I said I can't go arrest them right now. The Lacourts are among the most philanthropic families in New Orleans. Until I can prove something, I have to use a level of sensitivity here."

Harper looked around Jackson. "Would it help anything if we proved Pierre Lacourt isn't in his tomb?"

"How would you prove that?" Before Harper could answer, Det. Joya held up his hand. "I don't want to know, but yes, if his body isn't in the tomb, I might be able to do something. I'm not sure what, but at this point, any solid evidence can help." He pointed between Harper and Jackson. "No more breaking the law though or I will bring you in."

As Harper stood to leave, she pointed to the computer drive still in Det. Joya's hand. "I provided property records for the Lacourts on there, too, in case you want to search everything they own."

Det. Joya smiled. "You ever think of becoming a cop?"

"I get that a lot," Harper said. "But you have too many rules to follow."

Det. Joya stood and shook both of their hands. "I appreciate it. I know I don't seem like I'm going to do much, but I'm taking it seriously. I don't have a plan yet, but I'll let you know if I find anything of interest. Please don't do anything else illegal."

With that, Harper and Jackson left Rick's office and headed back through the newsroom. As they hit the street, Harper received a text from Rick. He congratulated her for a job well done and told her to let him know if Pierre's body wasn't in the tomb because it was a story he could run. Rick suggested a little public pressure on the Lacourts might not be a bad thing right now. Harper couldn't have agreed more.

"Where are we going now?" Jackson yawned.

"I want to go over and see the warehouse I found in the Lacourts' property records. I don't want to go in. I just want to see the area around it to know what we are working with."

"Okay," Jackson said, yawning again. "Why am I so tired?"

Harper used the app on her phone to track down a rideshare. Then she reached for Jackson's hand. "We've barely slept since we got into town. Hattie told me this city is a natural energy zap. I was going to ask you if you wanted to stay back tonight and keep an eye on Hattie when we go to the cemetery. I don't think Hattie should go. Given her mediumship ability, I'm not sure wandering around breaking into a tomb at night is the best thing for her, but I don't want to leave her home alone."

Jackson looked over at her. "Are you sure that's what you want? I don't doubt you'll be safe with Lucinda, but I don't want you to feel like I've bailed on you."

"Not at all," Harper said as the rideshare pulled up. Jackson opened the door for her and they slid in. "I need you to be there with Hattie."

Harper smiled as the relief washed over Jackson's face. She didn't need him to stay at home with Hattie. She had told a white lie, but Harper could see how exhausted he was, and she felt horrible for dragging him on yet another murder investigation. One night of Jackson laying low wasn't going to hurt anything. She'd be safe with Lucinda and didn't doubt that for a second.

Harper checked the address she had found earlier for the warehouse and told the driver where they were headed.

The young man turned around in the driver's seat with a grimace and one eyebrow raised. "Are you sure that's where you are headed? There's not much out there."

Harper leaned forward. "What do you mean?"

"That area of the port is closed. It's an abandoned section. For years, the city has been talking about tearing down those old warehouses and building up the area. It's wasted space, but you know how it goes with these things. Meeting after meeting and nothing gets done."

Harper checked the address again to be sure. "Just drive me out there and I'll see for myself. Then you can take us back. I shouldn't take long."

The driver shrugged. "It's your dime," he said as he pulled away from the curb.

"Are you sure you want to go out there?" Jackson asked, leaning his head back.

"It won't take long. Just a quick look around." Harper stared out the window as they drove farther away from the city center. Given how desolate the area was, according to the driver, it would be the perfect spot to be up to no good. That said, the longer they drove, Harper began to wonder if it was too far away from the French Quarter. It didn't seem like the murdered victims had been moved too far from where they were killed. Max had been nabbed on the street and returned hours later. He thought he'd been in a house, not a warehouse. Still, though, something about the spot intrigued Harper, and she wasn't sure why.

The driver pulled off the main road and turned down a side road. By his third turn, they were no longer on paved roads. It had given way to dirt tracks. Up in the distance sat a series of dilapidated warehouses with high fencing surrounding them.

"I told you. There's nothing out here."

"I see that," Harper said, leaning forward to get a better look out the front window. "Can you just stop for a moment? I want to get out and take a look. I'll be right back." Harper leaned into Jackson and said quietly, "Stay here. I don't want him to ditch us out here."

Jackson gave no argument. Harper got out of the car, not even bothering to shut the door and walked right up to the chain-link fencing. Dusk had started to settle so Harper assumed if someone was in any of the buildings, they would need light. She didn't see any, not even the glow of a flashlight. There was something about the building in the middle. It was calling to her like a beacon, and she wasn't sure why.

Harper closed her eyes and tried to settle her mind to see if anything came to her. There was nothing other than the overwhelming feeling that she had been in that building or she could be in the future. It was an unsettling feeling she couldn't quite shake. Harper snapped a few photos of the area with her phone and got back in the car.

As she shut the door, the driver said, "Are you like a real estate developer or something?"

Harper laughed. "Not quite, but I got what I needed." She gave him Dante's address and they left. As they drove out the way they came in, Harper turned and looked at the buildings one last time and wondered if maybe Celeste was being held in there. Something caused the feeling that sank deep in her gut. She couldn't pinpoint the cause.

Jackson reached for her hand. "You okay?"

Harper tried to explain, but the words didn't come out quite right. Finally, she said, "I think we are all feeling a bit off since we arrived. I'll be glad to get back home." Her cellphone chimed a moment later. Harper read the message from Hattie. She was leaving Dante's to go for a walk with Lucinda and Iggy. They wanted her to walk the French Quarter with them and stop at each place a body was found to see if she picked up any impressions. Hattie said they would be back and then they could go to the cemetery.

Harper wasn't sure her aunt should visit the crime scenes, but she

CHAPTER THIRTY-NINE

wasn't going to stop her. Hattie might pick up something useful. At least, there would be time before heading to the cemetery. Harper leaned back and rested her head against Jackson's, hoping this would be all over soon. She missed home. She missed Dan and even annoying Det. Granger.

Chapter Forty

"I'm not sure what you're hoping I pick up," Hattie said, leaving Dante's house with Lucinda and Iggy. "I'm willing to help if I can though."

Iggy walked between Lucinda and Hattie. "We understand you are a psychic medium. You might connect with the deceased or get an impression that might be useful to us. What I'm after most is who is killing them. They need to be our foremost target."

Hattie understood what they were asking. She had been seeing spirits all around her. The doll that Deidre had given her had been working. Hattie had more energy and could protect her energy better, too. She said cautiously, "I don't have much control over my mediumship. I'm learning to keep the spirits at bay, but I don't get much choice in who shows themselves to me. With my psychic abilities, I use my Celtic tarot deck most of the time. I am clairvoyant but have probably relied too much on my cards over the years. I've found it hard to trust the impressions I receive."

Iggy patted her on the arm. "You're exactly what we need. I don't trust psychics or mediums." He laughed, looking at the ground and shaking his head. "I don't trust much of anything. Do you know how many times I've sat in the front of the television and yelled at some of those ghost finder shows? Too many to count. I like the ones where they stop and ask if maybe it's just a tree branch scraping on the window. There's one..." Iggy tapped at his head with his finger. "Oh well, I can't put a name to it right now, but every ghost they find is evil and demonic. Good grief, you'd think the underworld was terrorizing suburban America. It's probably just some grouchy old guy who is annoyed he's still stuck hanging out. If they saw real demons, they'd need to change their pants."

Hattie laughed right along with him. She had no idea what television show he was talking about, but he was right. For all of the spirits she'd seen and years of doing this work, she hadn't come up against real evil until now. "Tell me about your work. It's both terrifying and fascinating to me."

"It's a calling. I don't know that I would have chosen this life for myself," Iggy started with a tinge of sadness in his voice. "I've always had an interest in the battle between good and evil. It's rare – demons, demonic possession. It's not what they show in the movies. When it comes to an exorcism, there's a lot of screening ahead of time – drugs, mental illness, and basic criminal behavior. For far too long anything that can't be explained is chalked up to demons. Sometimes there are biological reasons like mental illness, and we need to do a better job of making sure people get treatment. The same with drugs." Iggy paused and took a break. "Then, and people hate to hear this, sometimes there are just bad people. They do bad things and, no, the devil didn't make them do it. It's a cop-out instead of taking responsibility for their bad actions. No, real demonic possession isn't common, but when it happens, it's unlike anything you will ever see. It's the eating away of a soul."

"Aren't you afraid?" Hattie asked.

"Sometimes, but not often, especially not with Lucinda by my side." They stopped walking and were standing right in front of an alley between two houses.

"This is the place where a body was found," Lucinda said. "I'll walk us to the spot."

Hattie didn't know how Lucinda had these details and she didn't ask. She allowed Lucinda to guide her down the alley and they stopped midway. The ground was littered with debris, not from the crime but rather the everyday grit of a city. Hattie didn't feel anything particular about the spot, and there certainly weren't any spirits around. She had the voodoo doll in her pocket protecting her. Hattie closed her eyes and allowed her clairvoyant ability to take over. It was like exercising for the first time after a long break. The muscle didn't quite move the way she wanted it to. It was stiff and awkward. Eventually, though, Hattie settled into a vision.

A click of a heel, a scrape, and a man's voice. That's how the vision started. Hattie stood in the alleyway transported in her mind. She looked around to see where the sound came from. Night had fallen, but off in the distance she could hear the rattle and hum of people. Suddenly, at the end of the alley, there was the woman whose heels Hattie had first heard. She was with two men walking toward Hattie. As Hattie focused her vision, she realized she was wrong. On second look, the man and woman dragged the man in the middle as they walked, the toes of his shoes scraping along the pavement. To a casual observer, he appeared like a tourist being carried home after too much fun at night.

Hattie knew though that wasn't the case. The pair made it halfway down the alley and dumped the body close to where Hattie stood. She didn't want to look at the dead man, but she forced herself. Blood stained his dark hair and the back of his neck. His face was pale and his eyes closed. There was no question he was dead. Hattie focused on the two who had brought him there. The man stood as the lookout while the woman dropped shell casings, placed the voodoo doll next to him, and moved his body to her liking. Then the pair were gone as quickly as they had arrived.

As Hattie opened her eyes and grounded herself back to the present,

CHAPTER FORTY

she explained what she had witnessed. "He was already dead though. I never saw who killed him. I believe the woman is Alexandria Lacourt, but I didn't recognize the man."

Lucinda handed Hattie her phone. "Is the man in this photo the man you saw?"

Hattie looked down and then enlarged the photo. "Yes, that's him," Hattie said handing back the phone. "Who is he?"

"James Lacourt."

"This is good, Hattie. You did well. Let's move to the next spot," Iggy said, walking back down the alleyway. "Maybe you'll see more there."

"I'm not Harper. I don't normally tap into visions like this," Hattie explained. "I'm using my clairvoyant ability. I'm not sure we should trust it."

"You're doing great, kid." Iggy patted her arm.

The three went through the same process with four more places where bodies had been found around the French Quarter. It was clear to Hattie what they said in the news was true. The victims weren't being killed where they were found. The scenes were staged. Hattie started to believe the voodoo dolls didn't have anything to do with the ritual at all. But if that were true, why use Celeste's marker at all. Hattie still didn't understand.

When they came to the final spot, Hattie pulled up short. A man stood over a spot at the side of the road. He picked up his head and looked right at Hattie. "You can see me," he said, a tinge of excitement and awe in his voice. "Help me, please. They killed me. I can't find my way home."

"Do you know who killed you?" Hattie asked, stepping toward the man. Lucinda and Iggy stayed behind her offering words of encouragement.

"It was hazy at first, but I've seen them in the newspaper before. They run a local charity." The man stopped and put his hand to his head giving himself a moment to think things through. His face finally registered recognition. "The Lacourts, that's their name. I didn't understand at first what was happening. I left work and stopped in a store to pick up the anniversary gift I had ordered for my wife. As I was standing in line, a woman bumped into me. There was pain like I had been jabbed with something, but I couldn't figure out what had happened. She was very sweet and apologized several times. I didn't think anything of it."

The man stepped back and leaned his ghostly body against a wall. "I don't think I ever made it to the counter. I remember feeling nauseated and dizzy. This woman guided me outside, telling me maybe I needed some fresh air. There was nowhere to sit so I walked with her down the block. The next thing I remember I was in a house on the floor. I couldn't move. They were taking blood out of my arm and there were weird symbols drawn all around me."

Hattie could imagine the scene. It wasn't too unlike what Dante had told her about his experiences, minus the blood. "You said they. Was there more than one person?"

The man nodded slowly. "A man and a woman were talking, but the woman kept yelling that it wasn't working. I had no idea what they were talking about. I know at some point I turned my head to the left and there was a...I don't even have a word for it. A man, maybe, but he was old, shrunken down. The more I think about it, he didn't even look human. I was terrified. Another woman was standing in the back. The woman who had taken me was screaming at her. 'Make it work. Make it work.' She yelled over and over again. I had no idea what was happening."

Hattie tried to piece together what the man described. She wanted to ask him questions without leading him or implanting memories that didn't exist. She knew from others the time right after death is confusing and suggestive for spirits.

"Did anyone use any names that you recall?" Hattie asked.

The man closed his eyes and swayed a little. He ran through several names, saying them aloud and then shaking his head like it wasn't exactly right. Finally, the man said, "Celeste, I think. She was the woman in the back. She looked so scared and sad. Right before they killed me, I worried about what they were going to do to her."

Hattie stepped even closer, trying not to react to what the man had said. "This is very important. Who killed you?"

"The man. It was definitely a man. He stood over me and aimed the gun." The spirit of the man looked around where they were standing. "Next thing I knew I was standing here over my body, but even that's gone now. I don't know what to do."

Hattie waved Iggy over. "We need to help this man cross over."

Together, Hattie and Iggy said a few prayers and encouraged the man to cross over. The man looked past Hattie and Iggy as they prayed. "My mother and father are here."

Hattie turned around but didn't see anyone. "Go to them," she encouraged and he did.

When the spirit was gone, Hattie explained all that had happened. "It's James doing the kill. I think Pierre is hurt or near death. I think the ritual they are doing is to try to keep him alive."

Lucinda nodded. "His soul is breaking down. It's why you don't make deals with demons. It never lasts and eventually, you have to pay up." Lucinda looked at Iggy. "We have to kill James first. Then we can take on the others."

Chapter Forty-One

"Are you sure you don't mind staying home tonight?" Harper asked Jackson and Hattie as the server cleared dishes from the table. Dante had stayed back at the house preparing for tonight at the cemetery. Iggy and Lucinda were doing the same. Harper felt so bad about not having any time to relax with Jackson and Hattie she suggested they go down the street and have dinner.

As they relaxed at the table waiting for dessert, Harper wanted to ensure they were okay with the plan. Nothing in New Orleans had gone quite as Harper had hoped.

Hattie reached her hand across the table to Harper. "I'm happy for the night in. I've been exhausted as you know. Jackson and I always have fun together, don't we?" Hattie looked to Jackson who wasn't paying attention. He stared down at his phone, his brow tightly furrowing.

"Jackson, are you okay?" Hattie asked sharply.

"What?" Jackson asked and then lifted his head. "I'm sorry. Some drama back home."

Harper's eyes were on him. "What's going on?"

Jackson swallowed, looking like the words were caught in his throat. After a moment, he said, "My ex is in Little Rock. She stopped by my house to see me and then has been trying to hunt me down. Sarah saw her and now can't get rid of her."

"What does Cora want?" Hattie asked.

CHAPTER FORTY-ONE

Jackson shrugged. "Money, probably. She's called and texted me a few times, and I've ignored it. I don't want to have any contact with her." He cast his eyes toward Harper who had sat back with her face expressionless. "You okay?"

"I don't know what to say. Do you want to go back and handle it?" Harper toyed with the spoon on the table.

Jackson shook his head, annoyed. "How can you ask that? I'm not leaving. I'm annoyed Cora is bothering my sister, that's all. I thought I had put all of this behind me. I'm not going anywhere."

Harper remained quiet as dessert was served. Jackson and Hattie talked about Cora and his best plan of action, which was to ignore it. By the time they were done, Harper wanted some space from it all. She wasn't jealous or even angry. The mere mention of Cora keyed up Jackson so much that Harper wasn't equipped to deal with his mood, especially not right now while they searched for a killer.

Besides, Harper harbored a secret of her own. Her ex-husband, Nick, had been texting her since he had been released early from prison a few months back. A text here and there, which Harper ignored. Nick had even called her once, but Harper didn't even listen to the voicemail message. Nick didn't take the hint that she wanted nothing to do with him. He wouldn't leave her alone. Now, Harper felt like karma was coming back to bite her for not telling Hattie and Jackson.

When they were done with dessert, Jackson paid the check even though Harper insisted she wanted it to be her treat. They left to head back to Dante's. Harper remained quiet on the walk home, thinking about the trip to the cemetery. She wondered if she needed to be there at all. When she suggested it to Hattie, her aunt told her to go.

"Be there to support Dante. I think it's foolish he wants to check Pierre's tomb, but if he thinks it's going to prove something, then so be it."

Harper didn't disagree with her. "Det. Joya said if there was no body, it might lend more credibility to Dante's story. I hope they release Rory Gleeson soon. The poor kid shouldn't have to sit in jail long."

When they got back to Dante's, Lucinda and Iggy were already there and waiting. Jackson pulled Harper into the living room before they left. "You seem upset that Cora is in Little Rock. I hope you know this isn't my doing."

Harper smiled and reached her arms around his neck. "Of course, I know you didn't do this. I'm not angry at all. I think this case is getting to me. I'll be happy to be home and then we can deal with Cora together."

Jackson pulled back and looked at her. "It doesn't change anything between us, does it?"

Harper shook her head. "I have an ex, too. I know how it goes. It doesn't change anything, just like I know it wouldn't change anything if my ex reared his ugly head."

Jackson raised his eyebrows. "Did something happen with Nick?"

Harper patted his arm. She didn't want to lie, but this wasn't the time. "Story for another time." Harper kissed him sweetly and pulled away from him. "Take care of Hattie, and I'll be back soon." Harper left Jackson standing in the living room staring after her with a worried expression on his face.

"You ready to go?" Harper said as she entered the kitchen. Dante, Iggy, and Lucinda nodded and headed for the back door. Iggy and Lucinda both had bags slung over their shoulders. Harper didn't ask the contents and figured she'd know soon enough.

As they walked the several blocks to the cemetery, Harper stayed snug in between Lucinda and Iggy. She didn't like walking the French Quarter streets at night. The sights, smells and people crowding the streets overwhelmed her.

As they reached the cemetery, Harper noted the sign that said the St. Louis Cemetery No. 1 was closed except for scheduled tours. The locked gates and lack of any illumination in the cemetery, except the moon overhead, reinforced that message.

"Are we even supposed to be in here?" she asked, looking around wondering how they were getting in.

Iggy shrugged. "I'm a Catholic priest in a Catholic cemetery. Let them try to stop me." He pulled a key out of his pocket and unlocked the gate. Dante and Lucinda didn't hesitate. They walked right through with Iggy behind them. Each of them pulled out a flashlight no one bothered to tell Harper she'd need. She hadn't thought to bring one. It's not like she broke into cemeteries often.

She hesitated at the entrance, letting the three of them get several feet in front of her. Most of the tombs were taller than Harper, and the maze-like rows ensured she'd be lost if she didn't keep up. Nothing bad happened when Harper stepped onto the hallowed ground, but the vibe that fell over her was akin to being stuck in a corn-maze as a child, wondering if you'd ever find your way out again.

"Do you know the location of Pierre's tomb?" Harper called to their backs.

"Up here," Iggy said, guiding them as they walked through rows, turning left and right in a way that caused Harper's head to spin. "It's not far now."

After it felt like they had walked a mile, Dante and Lucinda reached the tomb first with Iggy and Harper pulling up the rear. The tomb itself was a simple Greek Revival structure. The Lacourt name had been etched on the front. It was less imposing than Harper thought it would be.

Lucinda pulled a crowbar out of her bag and went to work. Without a key to unlock the tomb, they were breaking in. Harper hoped Pierre wasn't in there because she assumed disturbing someone's final resting place might come at a karmic price. Lucinda made quick work of breaking in and within moments had the front door off. Harper had never seen the inside of a tomb so she wasn't sure what she was going to find.

Dante and Iggy stepped in front. They shined their lights around, but there was nothing, not even a casket or urn. Iggy stepped into the small space and pushed on the walls and stomped on the floor. "We might as well see if anything is hidden in here," he said as a way of explaining his strange behavior.

Iggy stepped out of the tomb and shook his head. "If Pierre is dead, he wasn't put in there."

"Could he have been cremated?" Harper asked.

Iggy threw up his hands. "Maybe, but why have the tomb if there is no one in it." He hit the side of it with his hand. "This is one of the oldest here. You can tell by the design. You're telling me in all these hundreds of years no one from the Lacourts needed a final resting place?"

"Only if none of them died." Dante looked up at the moon. "I knew he wasn't dead."

"We had to prove it," Lucinda said then turned to Harper. "You should call that detective and let him know."

Harper pulled out her phone to make the call but stopped short. She raised her head. "What am I supposed to tell him? That we broke into the cemetery and there's no one in the Lacourt tomb?"

Iggy motioned with his hand for her to give him the phone. "Let me make the call. No point you getting in trouble. I don't think he'll say much to me."

Harper scrolled through her phone to find Det. Joya's number, but as she hit the call button and handed the phone to Iggy, she stepped back in fear. Two men stood right behind Dante and Iggy. They were dressed in dark clothing from head to toe. One man had a scar that ran down from his forehead to his chin on the left side of his face. Evil radiated from them. The hairs on the back of Harper's neck stood on end.

Lucinda stepped toward her from her right. "Harper, you need to run.

CHAPTER FORTY-ONE

Now!"

There was no mistaking the warning. Harper tucked herself in between the Lacourts' tomb and another. She didn't know where she'd go or how to get out of the cemetery. Harper ducked down behind a tomb and peeked around the edge of it. Two more men encircled Lucinda. There were four in all. Even Dante had backed up at this point. The look on his face was pure terror.

Iggy threw off his bag, unzipped it, and pulled out a small dagger. He stood ready to defend. Lucinda transformed right before Harper's eyes. Gone was the face of a beautiful woman. In its place, her skin wrinkled and puckered and her teeth filed into sharp fangs. She morphed into a demon, one that would probably haunt Harper's nightmares for months to come. Lucinda's black eyes transfixed on the man in front of her as her hands gripped long silver blades. Harper had no idea where Lucinda had pulled the blades from so quickly. They were just there for her at the ready.

There was no mistaking it – they were ready to do battle.

Chapter Forty-Two

Hattie and Jackson sat around the dining room table and had been talking for the last hour about his ex. Jackson tried several times to write a response in text asking Cora to leave Little Rock and leave his sister alone, but the words hadn't come out right.

"I give up," Jackson said, dropping the phone to the table and shoving it away.

Hattie looked at him sympathetically. "I don't think it's something you need to worry about now. Let it ride and see what happens when you get home. Sarah is a big girl and can handle herself. It might be important for Cora to know she can't manipulate your family anymore to get to you."

Jackson nodded. "How have you been? You haven't seemed yourself since we arrived."

"I'm better now. This has all just been a lot to take on."

"It certainly has..." Jackson started to say but was interrupted by someone knocking on the back door of Dante's house. Hattie and Jackson shared a look of concern. He got up to answer the door, leaving Hattie resting at the table.

A few moments later, Hattie heard Jackson speaking with a woman who spoke in a rushed insistent tone. Jackson wasn't letting her in, and she argued that she needed his help. Hattie stood to see what all

CHAPTER FORTY-TWO

the trouble was about. As she moved through the kitchen to the back door, Hattie couldn't believe her eyes. She recognized the woman from the photos Dante had shared. Celeste stood there disheveled. Her hair looked like it hadn't been combed in a week. She had dark circles around her eyes, and it was obvious she had recently been crying.

"Please, let me in. I need to speak to you," Celeste cried, visibly shaking.

Hattie wanted to open the door and usher in the woman, but Jackson wasn't having it. He turned to Hattie. "How do we know this isn't some kind of trap?"

Hattie hadn't thought of that. She had assumed all along Celeste was being held captive, but she had killed Marie Lacourt and lied to Dante about their child. "Where have you been this whole time?" Hattie asked, eyeing the woman.

"I've been in Vermont hiding out for years," Celeste said. "Please, I mean you no harm, but we have to stop them. They sent me here to bring you to them. They told me they'd kill my daughter if I didn't." She held out her hands. "No tricks, I promise you. I finally talked them into letting me do this alone, but I'm sure they are watching."

Hattie stuck her head out of the door but didn't see anyone else in the darkness of night. She stepped out of the way to let Celeste in against Jackson's better judgment. "Come in, but we will be watching you."

Celeste stepped through the door. "It looks the same in here even after all of these years."

"This isn't a time for memory lane," Jackson barked. "Get to the point. What is going on?"

"Stop being so mean and give her a chance to speak," Hattie said, shoving past Jackson and walking Celeste to the table. "Sit right there and tell me what's going on."

Jackson stood on the threshold of the kitchen and dining room. Hattie waved him in, but he shook his head. Hattie understood and was grateful he was so protective. Hattie reiterated, "Celeste, we can't help you if you don't tell us what's happening."

Celeste nodded. She started slowly, "I don't know where to start."

Hattie told Celeste they knew all about the curse. Hattie surprised her by explaining they even knew she had killed Marie Lacourt and why. "Start with how you got mixed up with the Lacourts and why they put voodoo in my yard. You created it, I assume, but a man buried it. Explain that."

Celeste's face lit up. "You know that was me?"

Hattie cocked her head to the side. "Dante knew it was you, but it still doesn't explain why you tried to cast dark magic against me."

Celeste held up her hand. "Let me explain. Months ago, I was kidnapped off my property in Vermont. I was brought here to New Orleans. At first, I thought they were after me for revenge for killing Marie, and in a way, they were. When we killed Marie, Pierre started to die. He has been slowly dying over the years. He redid the immortality spell but nothing worked. James Lacourt found another immortality spell. The spell worked but only for a while. As Pierre's power diminished so did that of James, Ann, and Alexandria. They all started to die."

"How do you fit into this?"

"After I killed Marie, they assumed some of her power went into me. She told them I was having a child. I don't know how long they searched for me, but they finally found us. I traded my life for my daughter's and said I'd go with them." Celeste exhaled and looked to Hattie and then to Jackson. "They have been making me help them gain their power back. I didn't have anything to do with the murders. I told them that wouldn't work, but they threatened to kill me and my daughter if I can't help them. They are running out of time."

"The spells aren't working?" Hattie asked.

"Nothing is working. Pierre gets weaker and weaker every day. I'm

CHAPTER FORTY-TWO

surprised he's still alive. The rest of them still have immense power but not like they once did."

Jackson stepped forward. "You never said why they put spell work in Hattie's yard."

Celeste nodded. "I'm getting to that. They won't go near Dante. I think it might have been protection spells he's done. They wanted me to spell cast him, but he has protection around his house, too. I can't do any harm here, but they found out he was in Little Rock helping so they followed him up there. They have known about you all this time. When they saw Dante going to Little Rock to your house, they told me to put a spell on him there to try to limit his power. That was the first spell I did. Pierre buried it in your yard. He was weak, but since then he has been rapidly deteriorating. Then they found out Dante was in contact with Matthew Inslee and they went to him. But all Matthew Inslee did was complain that Dante wasn't very good, which the Lacourts took to mean my spell was working. They told Matthew Inslee I'd help him put the spell on you. I didn't put my full power into it, but I made sure to leave my mark. I had hoped someone would find it and when they did, Dante would know it was me. I was trying to send a message."

"That seems convoluted to me," Hattie said. "Surely, there were other ways to get the message to him."

"You don't understand," Celeste said, gesturing with her hands. "They will find my daughter and kill her if I don't help them. The only reason they stopped looking is that I promised to help them. My daughter doesn't know anything about the curse. She doesn't know anything about this world. I have protected her all of these years. Now, they want you to help them, and they aren't going to take no for an answer."

"Me?" Hattie asked, bringing her hand to her heart. "How could I possibly help them? I don't know anything about voodoo. All I've ever practiced was white magic. I rarely even do a negative spell."

Celeste locked eyes with Hattie, pleading, "I told them that. You have to help me, please. I don't know what else to do."

Jackson looked at Hattie and then back to Celeste. "How did you leave it with them? Do they trust you?"

"I don't know. I haven't tried to run from them. They know I don't want them to harm my daughter so I've been playing along until I could plan my escape, but I haven't had a chance. I know they are watching me. They have people – men who protect them. They are evil. I'm pretty sure I was followed here." Celeste went to stand, but Jackson quickly moved towards her until she sat back down. She held up her hands in defeat. "I mean you no harm. I'm looking for a way out."

"Why didn't you come here when Dante was here?" Jackson asked, standing with his hands on his hips as imposing as Hattie had ever seen him.

"I..." Celeste started to speak, but she didn't get out an answer. She looked to Hattie, but she wasn't going to help Celeste out of this. Hattie wanted to know the same thing.

"I think that's a question you're going to have to answer," Hattie said not wavering an inch.

"They made me come here now. They know Dante is with the priest. They have men following them." Celeste looked down at her hands.

"Are they in danger?" Jackson asked keyed up and angry.

Celeste cast her eyes up to him. "I don't know but probably. Dante is getting too close. They have always feared that priest."

"Harper," Hattie said, standing. "Jackson, do you know what cemetery they went to?"

"I don't know." Jackson rubbed his hand over his bald head. "I don't think Harper said. If she did, I don't remember."

"They will kill me if I don't come back with you," Celeste said.

Jackson turned on her and growled, "It's not going to matter because I might kill you myself if anything happens to Harper." To Hattie, he said, "I don't know what to do."

Hattie stood and went to him. She put her hand on his arm. "I'm scared, too. Let's trust Harper is okay with Lucinda and Iggy. I'm sure they will take care of her."

Jackson didn't say a word. He just stared down stone-faced at Celeste. Hattie couldn't blame him. As much as she tried to stay calm on the outside, she bubbled over with rage inside.

Hattie went and stood in front of Celeste. She said angrily, "This has put my family in danger, and it doesn't even have anything to do with us. You want to save yourself and your daughter, great. Now, tell me, how do we stop them?"

For the next thirty minutes, Hattie, Celeste, and Jackson hatched a plan at the dining room table. Hattie knew Jackson still didn't trust Celeste and the plan seemed farfetched at best. Hattie felt like they had no choice but to move forward and hope that the messages they sent to Harper and Dante would reach them in time. Hattie gathered up the supplies and put them in the bag she had brought with her to carry her other magical items. She slipped the strap over her shoulder and they set off into the night with the hope to stop this madness once and for all.

Chapter Forty-Three

As the battle waged on, Harper hid behind a crypt. Every so often she'd peek her head around to see what was happening. Harper ducked her head low and watched the action for longer than she had before.

Lucinda swung her blades expertly like they were extensions of her arms. Fluid, slicing movements. Two men dropped dead to the ground. Dante was nowhere to be seen. Iggy was no longer the tottering old man Harper had initially met. Standing before her was a warrior engaged in a fierce battle. As the demon swung at him, hissed and hollered, Iggy remained steady, dodging blows and jabbing forward with the blade. Iggy wasn't fast enough. The demon reached out and gripped the priest by the neck. Harper forced her eyes shut and balled herself up, hoping not to be seen. If she had any idea how to get out of the cemetery, she'd have already made a run for it.

Harper tentatively opened one eye, praying that Iggy was still alive. He was, but still in the grips of the demon who had him by the throat, lifting him off the ground with one hand. Iggy's limbs flailed as he tried to save himself. He couldn't, the demon was too strong. It was Lucinda who saved Iggy's life. With one hand she fought off the demon to her left as she sliced the demon holding Iggy right through his midsection with her other blade. The demon dropped Iggy to the ground with a thud and then turned on Lucinda.

CHAPTER FORTY-THREE

The demon was injured but not out of the fight. Lucinda's blade would have killed a mortal, but the demon still fought on. Lucinda managed to take on both at once. She stepped back regrouping, swinging both blades around in circles by her side. The demons stood in front of her each slightly off to her sides.

Harper wanted to close her eyes and shrink back and not witness the horror about to unfold in front of her, but she sat mesmerized at Lucinda's power. They attacked at once but Lucinda was too strong. In one fluid movement, Lucinda sliced one across the neck, dropping him dead in seconds flat. She stabbed the already injured demon through the abdomen again. As he fell to the ground, he looked up at Lucinda and with a dying breath asked, "You'd kill your brother?"

Lucinda stood over him and with no trace of emotion drove the blade into him again. "I'd kill a thousand of my brothers to rid this world of evil."

Harper breathed a sigh of relief. She got up from her crouched position. "Where is Dante?" she asked, frantically searching the area.

Iggy held his hand up. "Harper, stand back. You shouldn't even still be here." Iggy got out a bottle of what Harper believed to be holy water and sprinkled the ground where the fight had just taken place. He held his hands in prayer while he chanted words in Latin that Harper didn't understand. Before her eyes, the bodies of the demons vanished, leaving no trace a battle had even taken place.

Harper felt the presence behind her before she heard the hiss in her ear. A shiver went up her spine and her flesh goose-pimpled.

"You're a pretty little thing," a demon hissed right behind her. "I'll take you for my own." It reached out and ran a strand of Harper's hair through its fingers. A breath caught in her throat.

Iggy turned abruptly and threw the holy water in Harper's direction, splashing her in the face. The demon dropped her hair as its skin sizzled and it shrieked a language Harper had never heard before.

"Don't move even an inch," Lucinda said, gaining ground on her with her blade at the ready. She sliced directly over Harper's shoulder. The blade whizzed by Harper so close she felt the metal against her neck as it sliced right into the demon's face, dropping it to the ground behind Harper.

A silent scream escaped Harper's mouth. Her eyes grew as wide as saucers. "Can we get out of here now?" she asked Lucinda, who had transformed back into a beautiful woman.

Lucinda pointed to a spot on the ground across from where Harper stood. "They killed Dante first before the fight even started. He should be awake at any moment. His regeneration only takes a few minutes."

Lucinda left Harper standing there speechless. She couldn't believe Dante had been killed. Harper took a few tentative steps towards Dante, whose feet were sticking out between two tombs.

"I wouldn't get too close to him," Iggy cautioned, waving a finger at Harper. "The last thing he'll remember is the demons attacking."

Harper stepped back immediately, and it was a good thing because a few seconds later, Dante took a huge gasp of breath and got up from the ground ready for a fight. He sprang out from between the tombs confused by the scene in front of him.

"We handled it," Lucinda said. "They are all gone, but I'm sure more will follow. We need to get out of here and get Harper to safety. We nearly lost her to a demon a few minutes ago." She looked around on the ground to make sure they had everything and then pointed. "Let's get out of here. Harper, you walk in front of Iggy and Dante. I'll walk to your side. Don't get ahead and don't fall behind."

Harper did as she was told and expelled a breath as she walked. She knew the entire night would haunt her, but hearing Lucinda admit how close she had been to being captured by a demon wasn't something she wanted to think about right now. She felt around her pants pockets for her phone. Harper had no idea how much time had passed, and she wanted to let Jackson and Hattie know they were on their way back.

Harper looked at the screen and read a text from Hattie as they twisted and wound their way out of the cemetery. As they crossed the threshold back into the street, Hattie's words made Harper's heart race. She stopped dead in her tracks and had to reach out and grab Lucinda by the arm to stop her. "I got a text from Hattie. Celeste showed up at the house and convinced Hattie and Jackson to go with her to try to kill the Lacourts."

Lucinda shook her head dramatically. "That's not good at all. Unless their bodies deteriorate on their own, nothing can kill them except my blades because their souls have been fortified by demons. Only a demon can kill them."

"What's happening?" Iggy asked, looking at Lucinda and then at Harper. Lucinda explained quickly and when she was done, Iggy said, "No, no this is terrible. They should have never gone with her. They can't trust her."

Dante stepped forward, holding up his phone. "I had the same message. Hattie said Celeste was taken against her will. I believe that. Celeste would never help the Lacourts unless her life was at stake. She had Marie killed. There's no way she'd be helping them willingly unless she had to. Hattie can trust her. I'm sure of it."

"But they still can't kill them," Lucinda countered. "If Hattie and Jackson go with Celeste, they are putting their lives in danger. Who knows what the Lacourts will do to them?"

"We have to get to them now." Harper didn't wait. She started walking away, but only got a few steps and had to look down at the text for the address. When Harper read it, she turned around to face Lucinda. "This isn't in the French Quarter. They are at a deserted warehouse the Lacourts own down at the port. Jackson and I went out there earlier this evening. It's abandoned and all fenced off. There's no one for miles around them."

Lucinda cocked her head to the side. "Sounds like the perfect place to be up to no good. You need to go back home, Harper, and let us handle this alone."

"No, absolutely not. I'm going with you. We are safer all together anyway." Harper stood firm. Lucinda, Dante, and Iggy tried to argue with her and plead with her that it was safer to go back to Dante's, but Harper didn't give an inch. Finally, they gave in and the four of them quickly walked back to Iggy's house and piled into Lucinda's SUV.

Harper tried to call Hattie but there was no answer. She sent a follow-up text as well. Dante tried, too. Harper couldn't even gather her thoughts during the drive out to the port, but she managed to send off a quick text to Det. Joya and to Rick, explaining to both where they were and what was happening.

Harper knew earlier when she stood in front of the chain-link fencing staring at the Lacourts' warehouse that she'd be back. She just had no idea at the time that Jackson and Hattie would be in danger like they were now. Harper sighed. Her gift was only developed so far. If she were better, she could have protected them.

As if reading her thoughts, Iggy turned around in the passenger seat. "This isn't your fault, Harper. Hattie didn't have to go with Celeste."

Harper wanted to respond, but her words caught and she couldn't speak. She was so overwhelmed with emotion. Harper couldn't even think about losing Hattie and Jackson. They were both her whole life now.

Lucinda had programmed the address into her navigation so she didn't need to ask for directions. They drove in silence the rest of the way. For Harper, the drive felt like it took longer than before. When they finally pulled up to the chain-link fencing, the feeling of what Harper now realized earlier was dread came over her again. Lights flickered off in the distance on the second floor of the middle building. Harper would do everything she could to make sure Hattie and Jackson

CHAPTER FORTY-THREE

walked out alive, even if it meant sacrificing herself.

"I think you should wait here, Harper," Iggy said. Lucinda and Dante echoed the same. Harper heard them but didn't respond. She had already opened the SUV door and her feet were on the ground heading toward the fence to try to find an opening.

Chapter Forty-Four

Nothing had gone according to plan for Hattie and Jackson. They had planned to follow Celeste back to the warehouse where Hattie would pretend she had a few tricks up her sleeves to be able to help Pierre while they stalled for time. Hattie assumed she could summon spirits to help as she had in situations before. She had the spell Deidre had given her, but it was untested. Hattie wasn't even sure she could pull it off.

If worse came to worse, Jackson would kill Pierre. Celeste claimed she had found a knife that would kill him hidden at the warehouse. Jackson had been to war. He was more than equipped to handle the mission. But for all intents and purposes, the whole thing had been a trap just like Jackson had predicted.

They barely made it three streets from Dante's when two menacing men walked up to them and forced them at gunpoint to follow them. Jackson had tried to get Hattie to make a break for it, but she wasn't leaving him behind. Jackson certainly wasn't going to leave her behind either so they were stuck and forced to go with the men.

Now, they were in an empty, dirty warehouse lit up by candles on the ground all around them. There had to be at least fifty, giving off the only light in the room. Hattie would have preferred darkness to the scene unfolding in front of her. Pierre sat in a chair against the wall. His frail body had been propped up by pillows. The man's face had

CHAPTER FORTY-FOUR

sunk, leaving his eyes to bulge out grotesquely. He had no muscle mass and was nothing but bones and tattered clothing. His eyes stared off into the distance not focusing on anything. At first, Hattie wondered if it was the dead man Harper and Jackson had found, but no, it was Pierre and he was breathing but barely. Ann and Alexandria stood by his side. There was nothing else in the space, just a wide-open room. Hattie saw only one exit, but it was blocked by a man standing guard.

Upon arriving, the two men who had brought them there tied Jackson's hands behind his back and forced him to sit on the floor with both standing guard over him. They had taken Hattie's bag as well. Jackson was up to something; Hattie was sure of it given his expression. She hoped he didn't do anything stupid.

Hattie stood in the middle of the floor wondering what they had in store for her. James Lacourt stepped out of the shadows toward her. While Hattie had seen the man in photos and in her vision, she knew immediately Celeste had been telling her the truth about his diminished power. He had lost weight and moved a bit slower even from her vision. He still oozed an evil that made Hattie shudder.

"You're going to help us. Celeste said you have powers beyond her own." James pinned his eyes on Hattie as if trying to hypnotize her and pointed a gun at her.

Hattie held his gaze but then blinked and looked away. "There are some things I could try. What seems to be the problem?"

"Look at us," James tried to yell, but his voice couldn't quite hit the octave. James turned to his daughter. "Show her."

Alexandria stepped forward and reached her hand up to her head. Slowly, she pulled off a wig to reveal her nearly bald head with just limp strands of hair left. Hattie looked away when Alexandria pulled the skin from under her eye and it folded back on itself. "Look at me," she cried. "I'm falling apart. It's been happening faster and faster as the days go on."

Hattie didn't look at Alexandria's face. It was too disturbing. Instead, she glanced over at Ann. "You, too?"

The woman nodded but made no move to show Hattie, for which she was grateful.

"What do you expect me to do?" Hattie asked James.

"Fix us." James looked down at his hands, which appeared to be the hands of an eighty-year-old man, far older than the rest of his body appeared.

Hattie didn't understand. "I thought you made a pact with demons to help you stay alive. Why aren't they helping you?"

"They won't help anymore," James said, not meeting Hattie's eye. "We keep trying to redo the spell but nothing works. If you don't help us, we will kill you both."

"Did you do something to the demons that made them stop helping you?" Hattie asked, ignoring the threat.

James shook his head. "It's just time to pay up, and we aren't ready."

Hattie looked to the two men guarding Jackson. She knew without asking they were demons. "Why are they guarding you if they won't help you?"

James took a menacing step towards Hattie. "For a woman who I could kill at any moment, you sure ask a lot of questions. We double-crossed the demon who granted us power. These are others. It's not like everyone gets along in the underworld, but these here don't have the power to help us stay alive. Neither do the ones who have probably already killed your niece and that stupid priest. If you think you're going to be rescued, think again. We've already taken care of them. The only way you two are getting out of here alive is if you save us."

Hattie didn't believe him. Even if she could help them, he wasn't going to let her and Jackson go. Hattie remembered the voodoo doll in her pocket. She reached her hand down and squeezed it. When she did, a volt of courage flew through her body like electricity.

"How many have you killed trying to make your spell work?" she asked, her voice strong and clear.

"What does it matter?" James asked dismissively. "Can you help us or not? We are wasting time."

Hattie knew she had to try the spell Deidre had given her. She swallowed hard. "I have my bag over near Jackson. I need it to be able to help you."

James looked across the room at her bag and then back at Hattie. "Don't try anything funny."

With her surge of courage, Hattie moved toward her bag. "Do you want my help or not? I need the materials I brought."

Hattie ignored the two men standing guard and rummaged around in her bag until she found the large container of salt she had taken from Dante's kitchen. She also grabbed some crystals, a black candle, and a mirror. She asked Jackson if he was okay and he assured her that he was. Before Hattie stood upright, she grabbed the pocketknife she had tucked away for safekeeping in the corner of the bag and slid it across the floor around Jackson's back. Hattie had no idea if he'd be able to maneuver his tied hands enough to grab it and do anything with it, but it was worth the shot.

Hattie carried the items to the middle of the room. She lit the black candle from a candle on the floor. She waved James back. "You need to put the gun down and cluster around each other so this spell will work. You're all very weak and it's going to take a lot of forced energy into one space."

James and Alexandria shook their heads. Ann remained where she was with Pierre. "How do we know this isn't a trick?" James demanded.

Hattie sighed as if she was bored with them. "You summoned me here. You've asked me to help. Now, either you trust me to do that or you don't and we will go. Which is it?"

James and Alexandria shared a look but did as Hattie asked them to do. James tucked the gun in the waistband of his pants, and the three of them crowded around Pierre. Hattie tried to keep herself from smirking. She placed the mirror at their feet and made quick work of drawing a half-moon of salt around them. It couldn't be a full circle because they were up against the wall, which was probably better anyway. She made sure the salt line was thick and had no breaks.

Hattie motioned for Celeste to come stand near her and she placed some protection crystals at their feet. Hattie held her arms at her sides and began to speak a language that was not her own. She had practiced the words with Deidre, who said the language was an old Haitian Creole. The language of Deidre's mother's ancestors. The words were awkward for Hattie at first, but she could feel the power starting to build. As it did, the words flowed out of her like they were her own.

The room grew dense with the energy of all the souls the Lacourts had taken over the centuries. Hattie saw them appear one by one. They created a blanket of protection between her and the Lacourts.

"What's happening?" James shouted, not seeing the spirits but probably feeling them. He ripped the gun from his waistband and pointed it at her. He tried to step forward and cross the salt line but was slammed back into the wall. He knew then Hattie wasn't helping him. His face contorted and Alexandria screamed. Ann simply stood there and closed her eyes, accepting her fate.

Hattie didn't take her eyes off them even as the men protecting them grew concerned and started yelling. Out of the corner of Hattie's eye, she saw a flash of movement, and the guard standing at the only exit fell to the ground. Still, Hattie didn't stop. She chanted the words over and over again, causing the energy to build and build until the whole room seemed to be spinning. Hattie couldn't see what was happening, but she sensed movement all around her. She wasn't going to stop until the spell worked. The spirits who had been summoned now all formed a line between Hattie and the salt line and the Lacourts. They chanted the words along with her, building the energy even more, to the point where the whole room felt ready to burst.

All at once, Hattie pulled her arms back as far as they could go and then shoved the energy forward, screaming the chant at the same time. The energy surged forward and blew out all of the candles, leaving them in total darkness. Spent, Hattie dropped to the ground and passed out.

Chapter Forty-Five

Hattie blinked her eyes open and reached to rub a spot on the back of her head. Suddenly, Harper appeared over her on one side and Jackson on the other.

"Aunt Hattie," Harper said quietly and tentatively, "are you okay?"

Hattie had never been so happy to see their faces. At least, they were still alive. Hattie struggled to sit up, not sure what she'd see or if the spell even worked. Jackson and Harper both reached hands out to help her up. As she got to a sitting position, Hattie turned her head slowly around the room. Dante and Celeste were on the ground side by side. Iggy and Lucinda were standing over the bodies of the three men who had been guarding them. The Lacourts were nowhere to be seen.

Hattie tried to stand but couldn't get her footing. She heard male voices echo in the distance and she looked to Harper. "Are we safe?"

"That's probably Rick and Det. Joya finally getting here. I called them before we arrived."

"What's happened?" Hattie asked, not remembering anything after shoving the energy with all her might toward the Lacourts. "Are Dante and Celeste alive?"

Jackson reached his arms down under Hattie's and got her up to her feet. As he did, Jackson explained, "Dante and Celeste passed out when the Lacourts' souls were sucked into the mirror. They are breathing but haven't regained consciousness."

CHAPTER FORTY-FIVE

As Hattie got to her feet, she motioned for Jackson to grab her bag. Someone had relit the candles so at least they could see. Hattie stood there mesmerized as Iggy performed a ritual and the bodies of the three men turned to dust in front of her eyes.

"Are you sending them back to the underworld?" Hattie asked Iggy.

"No, they are dead, no souls, returned as dust to the earth."

Hattie nodded and grabbed a vial from her bag. It contained jasmine, citrus, and peppermint oil. Hattie took a few tentative steps toward Dante and Celeste, not fully steady on her feet yet. Harper took her aunt by the arm and helped her over to them.

Standing over Dante and Celeste, Hattie dropped a liberal amount of the oil on their foreheads, their chests, and their legs. While she did that, Hattie said more words in Haitian Creole that Deidre had given her. The spell she was performing was supposed to wake the soul. It would only work on someone living or in between worlds, still having a tie to life.

As Hattie finished the spell, she reached for Iggy and the two stood there together saying a prayer for Celeste and Dante. A moment later, the far-off voices Hattie had heard were louder, just outside the door. Rick and Det. Joya came through, confused expressions blanketing their faces. Det. Joya had his gun drawn but quickly dropped it to his side.

He rushed to Harper. "You sounded like you were in danger. I rushed right here." He looked around the room, taking in the candles on the floor. "What happened here?"

Harper held her hand up for him to wait. "Dante and Celeste are waking up," she said, pointing to the two of them.

Dante sat up first and then Celeste, both appeared shaken and afraid, but Hattie assured them they were all fine. Dante got to his feet first and helped Celeste up. They embraced awkwardly and then Dante stepped away.

"It's okay, Dante. Celeste helped me," Hattie assured him. "I didn't think so at first, but there was no other way. The Lacourts were hurting too many people. I didn't know if the spell would work, but it seems it has."

Dante reached for Celeste's hand and she smiled up at him. "We have a lot to sort through. I want to meet our daughter."

Celeste assured him it would all get sorted.

"Can someone please tell me what is going on?" Det. Joya asked, clearly frustrated with them all.

Harper explained what happened at the cemetery and the demons that came for them. "We got away though and came straight here. Hattie texted me and told me about Celeste coming to get her."

Det. Joya scratched his head. He looked to Lucinda. "You killed men in the cemetery?"

"Not men, demons," Lucinda corrected. "Don't worry there are no bodies. Iggy sent them back to the earth. The same with the three that were here."

"You killed men here, too?" Det. Joya asked, shaking his head and looking around.

"I only technically killed two. Jackson killed the other." Lucinda smiled over at him. "He's pretty good with a blade. Quicker on his feet than I would have thought."

Jackson smiled shyly and cleared his throat. He explained to Det. Joya how Celeste had come for their help and they went. "We were kidnapped by the Lacourts. They tied me up, but thankfully Hattie had a spell to try and it saved us. When she grabbed the items for the spell she needed out of her bag, she slipped me a pocketknife so I could free my hands. At that point, Harper, Lucinda, Iggy, and Dante arrived. Lucinda killed the demon at the exit and charged the demons near me. She dropped one of her blades in the fight, and I grabbed it stabbing one demon while she took down the other."

CHAPTER FORTY-FIVE

Harper went over to him and kissed him on the lips right in front of everyone. She looped her hands through his and whispered, "You've never been more attractive. Demon fighting is a good look on you."

Jackson laughed nervously. "That's never happening again so enjoy it now."

"Celeste, where is the knife you said you found?" Hattie asked.

Celeste walked to a far corner of the warehouse and dropped to the ground. She pried up a board and came away with a knife that looked similar to Lucinda's. "I found this in the upstairs of Ann and James's house in the French Quarter where they took the victims and performed the spells before killing them."

Lucinda walked over and took the blade by its handle. She held it up and examined it. "This was my brother's. It's not for mortal hands." No one argued with her when she tucked the knife away in her bag.

Rick, who had been quiet until now, stepped forward. "That sounds like a wild tale, but where are the Lacourts?"

Hattie pointed. "Banished into the mirror. A friend of mine gave me a very old Haitian voodoo spell for banishing dark and evil souls. I didn't know if it would work or not. She had never tried it." Hattie shrugged and grinned. "I guess an old lady has still got it."

Det. Joya walked toward the mirror and the gun that was on the floor next to it. He bent down to pick them up.

"No!" Hattie shouted. "You can take the gun. I assume it's the murder weapon, but Iggy and Lucinda need to destroy the mirror or the Lacourts could come back. They aren't dead just trapped."

Det. Joya stepped back and held his hands up. "I won't touch it." He toed the gun away from the mirror and looked down at it. He looked back at all of them. "It's the gun with the DL initials like we thought. What you're telling me is the Lacourts really were immortal and killed all the victims. Now they are banished to a mirror and the demons working with them are dead, but no bodies remain?"

"That's exactly what I'm saying," Hattie said proudly. "Look on the bright side, you have a clean crime scene."

"I know this is overwhelming," Harper started to say while walking over to him. "This is one of those stories that you're going to have to spin. You found the Lacourts here at the warehouse holding Jackson and Hattie captive. You saved them and the Lacourts are dead or vanished. I'm sure when you search the homes you might even find the body of Alexandria's husband. You'll be able to figure it out, I'm sure."

Det. Joya drooped his head and didn't speak for several moments, absorbing it all. When he looked up, his relief was evident. "The murders are over? There won't be another?"

"Not by the Lacourts," Harper said. "You can tell the city the murders are over. You get credit for taking down a serial killer. I'm sure it will be news, but Rick can help you spin the tale."

Rick stood off to the side. "I think we can take it from here, Det. Joya. We can make this work."

"I guess I don't have a choice." Det. Joya reached out a hand to Jackson and then to Harper. When he got to Hattie, he wrapped her in a huge hug. "I don't even know if I can believe all of this, but if the voodoo murders are over, I'm just going to be grateful."

Hattie patted him on the back. "If you ever get to Little Rock, stop in for some tea and treats."

Jackson groaned. "I can't wait to get home."

Harper laughed and patted his stomach. "Soon enough."

Chapter Forty-Six

A few days after the night at the warehouse, Harper sat in the back of her SUV listening to Jackson and Hattie rave about the restaurant they had visited the night before. It was a good dinner. They had left with full bellies and enjoyed their last night in New Orleans.

After Hattie rid the world of the Lacourts, Det. Joya decided there was no one to arrest because there were no bodies or evidence of a crime even if they had fully confessed to killing demons. The next day, Det. Joya received warrants to search all of the Lacourts' known properties. The New Orleans police turned up a trove of evidence going back more than one hundred years of people the Lacourt family had stolen from and murdered. There were stacks of journals with some of the darkest magic known. The police called in local voodoo experts to examine the journals to make sense of them.

The formal statement to the press blamed the Lacourts for the recent voodoo murders, sidestepping a real motive. When pressed by the media, Det. Joya simply stated that the police had found evidence to indicate the Lacourts had built a criminal empire cloaked in a family foundation. While the family certainly did good for the community, it did not outweigh the bad. Of course, some people couldn't believe and probably never would. Others, who had long suspected the Lacourts of nefarious behavior, finally felt justified in their beliefs.

Det. Joya said in the press conference he alone had chased the Lacourts to a warehouse where they were holding several people hostage. By the time he had arrived, the hostages were safe and the Lacourts were long gone. Det. Joya went through the formal process of issuing warrants for their arrests and all the other formalities police go through when they had criminals on the run. It was the only way he could see himself out of the situation and have it make any sense.

Iggy and Lucinda bid Hattie, Harper, and Jackson farewell later that night and left with the mirror they said they'd destroy. Harper wanted no part of anything more to do with demons and demon hunters or even an exorcist priest. She was happy to return to Little Rock and pretend none of it existed.

Harper could tell Jackson felt the same. Later that night after getting back to Dante's from the warehouse, Jackson had struggled with having killed a person. Reminding him that it wasn't a person but a demon didn't seem to have much of an impact. Harper finally realized it wasn't about the demon at all, but the entire situation had brought up some post-traumatic stress from his time in the Army. She accepted that he knew Harper was there for him if he wanted to talk, but she wouldn't force the issue. Two days later, Jackson seemed back to his old self and said it would take time but he was working through it. Harper had no doubt they'd all have lingering effects of their time in New Orleans for months or maybe longer to come.

The trip to New Orleans had reinvigorated Hattie. She had no idea she had that much power. Where once she had refused to use any darker magic at all, Hattie had come to believe that as long as there was bad in the world, it would take knowledgeable people and resources to bring them to justice. If darker spells were required, so be it. Hattie was quite pleased with herself that she had rid the world of the Lacourts and as a result, reversed Dante's and Celeste's curses. At least that's what they hoped.

CHAPTER FORTY-SIX

There was no real way to tell. It's not like they could kill Dante and see if he came back. Dante said after the Lacourts were banished and he and Celeste woke up on the floor, he had felt the heaviness that cloaked him like a blanket leave. Dante said he felt lighter and freer than he could ever remember feeling. Hattie took that as a good sign. Celeste had come back to Dante's house and the two were working to repair their relationship. They were even making a plan for Dante to finally meet his daughter.

Hattie had offered to go to a hotel so Dante and Celeste could have some time alone, but he wouldn't hear of it. Hattie, Harper, and Jackson settled in for a few days and finally had a chance to explore the city as tourists, which they greatly enjoyed.

The time spent in New Orleans weighed heavily on Harper. She did have enough for a good article for *Rock City Life* magazine, which had been the one promise she made to Dan. In some ways, it felt like she was leaving behind one set of problems for another. Only this time, it was personal.

Harper's cellphone buzzed at her side for the seventh time that day. Nick was demanding to see her. She had ignored his messages and even blocked his phone number. All that served to do was have him text and call her from another number. The message she had received this morning was that he had arrived in Little Rock and was waiting for her, which meant both Jackson's ex-wife and her ex-husband had descended on the city at the same time. She had just helped to rid the world of demons and this was her thanks.

As if feeling Harper's mood, Hattie turned around in her seat, "Is there something wrong? You've been quiet."

Harper debated for only a moment. She'd have to tell them before getting back to Little Rock and they saw Nick for themselves. Harper sighed loudly. "Nick is in Little Rock."

Jackson glanced at Harper in the rearview mirror. "Your ex?"

Harper nodded. "He said he's waiting for me."

"What does he want?" Hattie asked.

"I don't know. All Nick said was that he wants to see me."

Hattie offered Harper a sympathetic smile. "Well, it seems both you and Jackson have some reckoning with the past that needs to happen. It's funny the universe has done it at the same time for you both."

Jackson glanced at Hattie. "What do you mean?"

"The universe is making you both go through the same thing at the same time. You can commiserate with each other." Hattie laughed. "And you'll both be so busy dealing with your respective exes you won't have time to get jealous."

Harper wasn't sure why but that made her laugh. Hattie was right though. Harper reached up and squeezed Jackson's arm. "Dealing with our exes has got to be easier than fighting demons."

Jackson chuckled. "You haven't met my ex-wife."

Harper smiled but knew Jackson wasn't kidding. There wasn't anything either of them could do about it right now unless they were going to take a detour and start their lives over someplace else. Harper leaned her head back and closed her eyes. The drama would start soon enough, but for right now, she was just going to enjoy the drive and being once again in Jackson's capable hands.

About the Author

Stacy M. Jones was born and raised in Troy, New York, and currently lives in Little Rock, Arkansas. She is a full-time writer and holds masters' degrees in journalism and in forensic psychology. She currently has three series available for readers: paranormal women's fiction/cozy Harper & Hattie Magical Mystery Series, the hard-boiled PI Riley Sullivan Mystery Series and the FBI Agent Kate Walsh Thriller Series. To access Stacy's Mystery Readers Club with three free novellas, one for each series, visit StacyMJones.com.

You can connect with me on:
- http://www.stacymjones.com
- https://twitter.com/SMJonesWriter
- https://www.facebook.com/StacyMJonesWriter
- https://www.bookbub.com/profile/stacy-m-jones
- https://www.goodreads.com/StacyMJonesWriter

Subscribe to my newsletter:

✉ http://www.stacymjones.com

Also by Stacy M. Jones

Read Harper & Hattie Book #5 - The Witches Code

Access the Free Mystery Readers' Club Starter Library
 PI Riley Sullivan Mystery Series novella "The 1922 Club Murder"
 FBI Agent Kate Walsh Thriller Series novella "The Curators"
 Harper & Hattie Mystery Series novella "Harper's Folly"

Sign up for the starter library along with launch-day pricing, special behind-the-scenes access, and extra content. Hit subscribe at http://www.stacymjones.com

Please leave a review for The Forever Curse. Reviews help more readers find my books. Thank you!

Other books by Stacy M. Jones by series and order to date

FBI Agent Kate Walsh Thriller Series
 The Curators
 The Founders
 Miami Ripper

PI Riley Sullivan Mystery Series
 The 1922 Club Murder
 Deadly Sins
 The Bone Harvest
 Missing Time Murders
 We Last Saw Jane
 Boston Underground

The Night Game

Harper & Hattie Magical Mystery Series
Harper's Folly
Saints & Sinners Ball
Secrets to Tell
Rule of Three
The Forever Curse
The Witches Code
The Sinister Sisters

The Witches Code

A missing emerald necklace thought to be cursed. A few murdered mobsters. The two exes who may hold the key to it all. The timing couldn't be worse for Hattie Beauregard-Ryan and her niece, Harper Ryan, who are just getting back from a harrowing trip to New Orleans. Before they even pull into the driveway, trouble is brewing.

Harper has been accused of stealing an infamous emerald necklace and word has reached far and wide that the Ryan women are hiding it. All sorts of unsavory characters descend on the town to find it and claim the reward. Someone is even willing to kill to get to it first. Harper must use her magical gifts to uncover who is putting her and Hattie in harm's way – all the while searching for the necklace and dealing with her ex-husband who wants her back. It all spells trouble for Harper's new life.

Meanwhile, Hattie must deal with the angry ghost of a dead mobster who refuses to leave until she finds his killer. If that wasn't hard enough, Hattie must protect them all from the witch who cursed the necklace and is bent on revenge. Her powers are far stronger than any Hattie has seen both living and dead. Can the Ryan women use their powers to find the necklace and catch a killer before the curse claims another victim?

Made in the USA
Monee, IL
13 July 2025

21054191R10154